BILLY MAKIN

O'MALLEY – THE WRONG PACKAGE

Published by B and M Publishers UK

ISBN: 978-0-9955533-1-6 (Print)
ISBN: 978-0-9955533-0-9 (Mobi)

Dedicated to

MUSCLES, MAC, and BOB …R.I.P.

Also

JIM, PADDY, and MOLLY …Wherever you are.

CONTENTS

INTRODUCTION

It was a simple enough job.

Deliver a package – a human package.

Why did MI6 need the SAS to deliver it?

Why did the IRA not want it delivered?

Why did the IRA bring in their most lethal killing machine?

Why were the SAS not good enough?

Why did so many people have to die?

The novel is largely based on the real life story told to me by an ex SAS trooper who wished to remain anonymous. He wanted people to know the truth. Only he survived – *Billy Makin*

Sometimes history doesn't always tell the truth.

Governments rarely tell the truth.

There are few accessible records for much of what you are about to read. Those that are available, resonate ominously with the details contained within the novel.

Much of O'MALLEY and THE WRONG PACKAGE may be fictional.

Much is not.

You will have to decide for yourself what is real, and what is simply an over active imagination.

MAYBE IT WAS ALL JUST A DREAM!

A FACTUAL FICTION by *Billy Makin*

CHAPTER 1

A BROKEN MIND

Sometimes I become confused, dreams become reality, but reality doesn't seem real.

Memories are not what they used to be, they keep changing. Memories should always be the same.

They say that I have Post Traumatic Stress Disorder. Paddy used to say that.

Can you remember Paddy? We used to be in the SAS together.

The doctors say that I am delusional. There are no records of me ever having been in the army.

I was, honestly, but I must not tell anyone, it's a secret.

I hope that Julie calls in to see me today. I haven't seen her since we got engaged.

I can't imagine living without Julie. I don't think I would want to.

I keep getting these head-aches. They tell me that I had an accident.

I've got a dressing on my forehead. Paddy has one in exactly the same place.

Paddy says that we were never in the SAS. I'm sure he's wrong.

Paddy has been acting very strange since they put that dressing on.

Why isn't Molly with us; can you remember Molly? Paddy can't.

The Major came to see me today. He's a nice man. He brought us here.

He told me that his son is in the Navy. 'A Nancy boy', he said.

He told me that he phoned his daughter Mary today. He said that I had met her once.

I can't remember her. I will ask Paddy to see if he remembers her.

CHAPTER 2

FLASHBACK

'You never cease to amaze me Jimbo – you really are one over educated – upper class – lucky bastard.'

'Thank you very much Paddy, that's extremely nice of you.' Killeen feigned a hurt look, as Paddy, the six and a half foot Irish giant, sat down on the only chair in the bleak army barrack room. The old and flimsy wooden chair creaked and threatened to collapse under the 17 stone bone and muscle frame.

'Why do all these bleeding lucky things happen to you Jim and not to me? You were born on the good ship *LUCKY BASTARD*; your dad is worth a fortune, and you never had to fight your way through school as I did; nor did you have to fight half the fucking Irish gipsy community just to make a living. I've always been unlucky – if I fell into a vat of tits, I would probably come out sucking my thumb. A quarter of a million quid a year, tax free, and all you have to do is babysit a couple of teenage tarts in a Sheik's palace; what's all that about for God's sake Jim? You lucky – lucky – bastard.'

Paddy suddenly burst out laughing as he continued. 'I don't suppose that you have considered the possibility that the girls could easily be the ugliest couple of tarts in the whole of the Middle East. We never actually saw their faces as they were covered from head to toe in them black Burpers. I'm sure one of them was crossed eyed, and that's the only bit that we could see; they could have had 3 tits and a dick bigger than yours for all we know.'

Captain James Killeen, British Army Intelligence Corps, and Special Air Service (SAS) section leader, smiled, and winked, before settling his gaze on Paddy's bearded, weather beaten, angular face, moving his head from side to side as he did so. 'I think that they may have been wearing Burkas, and not Burpers Paddy, at least that is what my over educated, upper class brain is telling me.'

Sgt Liam Paddy Jackson, like Killeen, himself a product of the Hereford 'Torture Chamber', as many SAS men loved to describe their Hereford depot and training camp, continued, this time in a much more serious tone. 'Why you Jim – there must have been a hundred better qualified men than you are that applied for the job? You've never done close protection work, in fact, you've never done any protection work – it's a specialist's job. What do you know about driving at 30 mile an hour in reverse, then spinning it into forward, and accelerating away in the blink of an eye? I learned the skill in Aldershot when I was personal body guard to the colonel, and it isn't as easy as it looks. Most people never get the hang of it and have to move on.

Most of the people that you have ever *LOOKED AFTER* Jim have died, that's what we do in the SAS, that's our job. Would you really be prepared to take a bullet in order to save some poor little crossed eyed rich girl with 3 tits and a dick? I bloody wouldn't. I hate to say this Jim, but I smell a rat – a bloody great stinking rat – something about it all just doesn't add up. I think that you should have a word with sniffer Wardle before you decide anything Jim, he can smell a rat before it's born.'

Captain Killeen's expression changed from smile to frown, as his brow furrowed, and his voice took on a more serious tone. 'I must admit Paddy, I'm more than a little suspicious myself, I didn't even apply for the job. It seems that Sheik Armani asked for me by name. Maybe his elder daughter wants my body, you saw the way that she looked at me through those adorable crossed eyes when we met outside the Sheik's palace.'

'Now I know for sure that your over educated, upper class brain has gone haywire,' Paddy laughed. 'Too much inter-breeding, that's your problem Jimbo. Rich upper class folks only shag rich upper class folks; your gene pool probable doesn't stretch to more than a couple of hundred women in the whole county.'

'Sounds ok to me kid, I've still got 50 to go then.' Killeen winked and grinned.

'In your dreams Jimbo old boy,' Paddy laughed out loud, and continued in a mocking tone. 'You certainly won't be adding to your score at Sheik Armani's gin palace mate, have you seen his human rights record? Slip a piece into a tart outside of marriage, and your head comes off; either that, or his religious Muslim subjects hurl bloody great rocks at you until they knock it off – besides, can't you remember how we looked when his two daughters saw us? Muscles and Bob were covered from head to toe in blood

– none of us had washed or shaved for days – and we all stunk like a herd of skunks in a box – well, you certainly did, I had to sleep downwind from you.'

It was now Killeen's turn to laugh. 'You didn't exactly smell like a rose garden yourself, some nights you were farting loud enough to wake them up at the palace, your arse could have jeopardized the whole operation, anyway, there's the attraction for the females Paddy old son – rugged good looks – a body like Tarzan – and….'

'A smell like a skunk's arse,' Paddy interrupted, then he paused; there was no point in carrying on – Captain James Killeen had gone quiet, and his eyes had taken on the far – away 1000 yard vacant stare. This was becoming a fairly frequent occurrence of late, ever since Muscles and Mac had been killed. One minute he was talking, then, the next minute his mind and thoughts were somewhere else. Paddy knew to keep quiet, a worried frown appearing on his forehead.

Captain James Killeen's physical presence was still in England, still in the bleak barrack room – his unseeing eyes looking directly at Sergeant Liam Paddy Jackson, but his mind and his whole being had metaphorically moved back in time – back to the time when he was still in control – still in command – still the competent, self-assured leader of D1 SAS troop.

Killeen's mind was now back on active service – back in the Gulf, and soon, someone was going to die. He had no idea of why they should die, nor did he care. He was by now fully anesthetized against death – he had developed a complete indifference when killing people. The whole process of ending a life was no more than a job. The British army had spent millions in order to turn Killeen and his troop into effective killing machines. Some people sat at desks and shuffled paper for the army – Killeen and his troop killed people when asked to. It was just a job. A job that became easier and more enjoyable as time went on. The danger – the magnetic attraction of fear, primed the adrenaline pump – the action, and the killing, pumped in a never ending supply of fuel. Dopamine levels in the brain went stratospheric.

Coming down from an operation could be a problem. It was easy to move on during the daytime, but at nights, during periods of broken sleep, faces appeared – faces that other people could no longer see – faces that only he could see – faces that were now in the graveyard.

Paddy became concerned. Killeen's body suddenly became rigid. His eyes began to flutter uncontrollably, and his mouth began to speak – no words came out – no sound at all.

Killeen was now staring down the barrel of an AK47 assault rifle held by a kid – a bloody kid no more than 15 years old. What the hell was the kid doing there, and why had he crept in from the other direction? It was as if he was making his way *from* Sheik Armani's palace rather than *to* it. This had been why he had been able to sneak up on him.

Why hadn't Paddy spotted him? Paddy was on lookout. If there was one person in the world that he would trust with his life, it was Paddy – so where the fuck was he? Had he fallen asleep?

'Christ,' Killeen had thought to himself. 'What a fucking epitaph – blown away by a kid.'

For four long, hot, boring, stinking days and nights, the 6 man SAS team had been lying in wait for the arrival of what had turned out to be a three man assassination squad. The assassin's target was the Sheik himself – a Sheik who wanted his subjects to love him. Absolute control and obedience was essential in all the Arab kingdoms; there was no way that any form of insurrection could be allowed to foment – this could jeopardize the billions in oil money that found its way into the private Swiss bank accounts of the Sheik and his extended family of Princes and Princesses.

Captain Killeen and his section's job was therefore quite a simple one; they were to eliminate the assassins and any witnesses quietly without the use of guns, and destroy all evidence of their ever having been there. They were also told to dispose of the bodies.

'Stuff that for a game of soldiers,' Paddy had said. 'I'm not a fucking undertaker. What happens if we get compromised? Half of us have to protect the other half as they dig the fucking graves? That's not how it works in our job Jim – you know that. Tell MI6 to send the cleaners over.'

Killeen, and the other 4 men in the section had agreed with Paddy – how were they going to dispose of 3 or 4 bodies without leaving a trace? In any operation there had to be an exit strategy if things turned tits up; being stuck in the middle of hundreds of miles of sand offered little enough protection as it was.

The cleaners were now somewhere in waiting.

THE CLEANERS were a shadowy outfit, neither military nor civilian; no one knew, and no one wanted to know. Their task was to 'Clean the Scene', and if necessary, to dispose of the bodies. Occasionally, evidence was planted and the blame was passed on. This was particularly so in Northern Ireland. A dead Protestant was automatically assumed to have been killed by a Catholic hit squad, and vice versa. No one ever questioned the work of THE CLEANERS: – some things were better left alone.

As far as MI6 and the British government were concerned, Sheik Armani, as Paddy had christened him, was a good Sheik. His Royal Highness was in the middle of protracted negotiations with the British Foreign Ministry, and very soon, he would be placing orders worth millions of pounds for British military equipment. This in fact made him a very good Sheik: it mattered not at all to the British Government that half of his adult life had been spent touring the world's most glamorous locations and flesh spots – drinking the finest wines and champagnes – escorting the most expensive women, and feeding millions of pounds and dollars into the hungry jaws of the uncompromising and avaricious roulette wheel. At home in his small desert kingdom, among the sand, the flies, the goats, the camels, and the poor people, he was a good Sheik – a good Muslim.

MI6 had somehow got wind of the assassination plot, and that was why Captain James Killeen – SAS – was now staring down the business end of an AK47 assault rifle held by a kid – a bloody kid who should never have been there.

He weighed up his options. There *were* no options. The rifle was too far away to grab, yet the kid was too close to possibly miss if he had tried to dive away. Anyway, where would he dive to? He was in a flat piece of desert with no cover whatsoever near him. Why had he positioned Bob on point? Bob could speak Arabic; he had never thought about that, then again, why should he have? This was a simple enough job, almost a training exercise – eliminate – call in the cleaners, and then home.

He closed his eyes, expecting and waiting for the inevitable. His mind flashed a mental picture of Julie – his Julie. As she wasn't his next of kin, how would she know that he was dead? This was the SAS; mention of it wouldn't even make the papers. The authorities would never admit to British military involvement in such a sensitive and volatile part of the world. Paddy would tell her – he could rely on Paddy.

Killeen heard the crack and visibly shuddered. It didn't sound like an AK47; he had certainly heard enough of those these past few years, many of them being fired at him. He felt no pain: surely he would have felt something as a 7-62mm round passed through his body at 3000 feet per second, pushing out skin, flesh, bone, and whatever internal organ got in its way – nothing.

He opened his eyes to confront a grinning Sgt Paddy Jackson. At his feet, that bloody kid – his head twisted at a strange angle – his eyes still wide open, staring at nothing, as the blood from his still slowly beating heart no longer reached his brain, all connections severed by one swift twist – a twist delivered by a man so colossally strong that the action was no more than snapping a twig to him.

'What took you so fucking long Paddy? The little bastard could have killed me.' Killeen almost screamed.

'I wanted to see if you would shit yourself.' Paddy was now laughing openly.

'You fucking stupid Irish moron!' Killeen shouted, loud enough for the rest of the section to hear, his brain now flooding his body with adrenalin. Strangely, there had been no adrenalin as he had stared down the barrel of the AK47. For the first time in his army career he had felt fear. It was a strange feeling, almost like floating high above himself, and looking down on a stage where he was the principle actor; a feeling similar to the fear and nervous anticipation that he had felt when he had first asked Julie out for a date, only this time, he had got a positive result. Were love and death so closely related that their emotions interfaced, he momentarily wondered?

'Well?' Paddy quietly and calmly inquired, his arms open in a questioning gesture.

'Well what?'

'Did you shit yourself?' Paddy was still grinning.

Being an SAS officer was nowhere near as glamorous as Killeen had imagined it would be, the responsibility and safety of the men under their command weighed heavily on all officers when subjected to imminent danger; being Sgt Paddy Jackson was much simpler. That was probably why Paddy seamlessly glided from one joke to another. Nothing fazed Paddy; one-liners spewed forth even in life threatening situations, but of one thing Killeen was sure – it was better to be with him than against him.

It was always reassuring to know that when the chips were down, Paddy was close to hand. Paddy was good. Paddy was very good. He moved easily and silently for such a big man, and his prodigious strength and technique meant that he could break a man's neck as easily as snapping a twig; this was something easily accomplished in Hollywood films, but nowhere near so in reality. Get it wrong, and the man yells out, or instinctively fires his weapon; not something that you want on an undercover operation.

The rest of the section had used a different method on many occasions.

The victim was grabbed from behind, left hand over mouth, and the head yanked up and back. The knife was plunged deep into the throat on the left hand side, and at the same time, the head pulled from right to left. The knife was then ripped from left to right with considerable speed and force. Messy, but effective – breathing gone – vocals gone – job done – almost instant death. The victim was then held firmly in position until the body went limp.

There was another way of course – there always is. Instead of the deep knife thrust and the ripping out procedure, the entry wound is from the outside – more slitting the throat. Unlike in the films however, this leaves the target alive for quite some considerable time, giving him plenty of opportunity to break free and shoot whatever weapon he may be carrying. The operation requires quite a fair degree of force – pretty much like slicing up a tough steak – more of a sawing action, often utilizing a more serrated blade; again very messy, but equally effective. The skill is in avoiding the spurting blood and directing it away from your own body.

Sometimes things didn't go according to plan. On this occasion, Molly and Mac had been silent and deadly in dealing with their own would be assassins, but at the last moment, Muscles' target had turned around. Both Muscles and Bob had been covered from head to toe in blood, as Bob had lent a hand on seeing Muscles wrestling with the struggling man.

'I thought that bearded bastard was never going to die; damn near cut his head off – no matter what I did he just kept on fighting.' Muscles said, with a shake of his head.

'Tried to fuck him, not slot him, with the look of things Muscles.' interrupted Paddy.

'That's right Jim,' said Bob, ignoring Paddy's comment. 'I've never seen anything like it in all my life. The man was dead, but refused to accept it; there wasn't anything left to cut; it was as if his body didn't need his head.

We both had to jump on him and hold him down; the blood was shooting everywhere like a fucking fire hose.'

'Both tried to fuck him then.' said Paddy, with a big grin on his bearded face.

The tension had gone; the mission was accomplished, and Sheik Armani would be able to sleep easily that night with the knowledge that his omnipotence was re-established. It was now time to call in the cleaners and head for home and a well deserved break, as always, leaving no trace of either their, or any British government involvement. The lucrative defense contracts were safe.

'Fancy a few pints of bog oil *Apeman*?' said a grinning Molly, the youngest man in the section, as he gave Paddy a playful dig in the ribs before jumping well away from Paddy's booted response.

'Fuck you *BOY*,' was Paddy's threatening and grinning reply. 'Any more comments like that, and I will punch you to where they brew it. You know this entire shit hole is dry; not one fucking drop of alcohol in the whole country. You would think that Sheik Armani could arrange an odd drink or two, after all, we have just saved his bacon.'

'He doesn't eat bacon Paddy, he is a Muslim.' Molly winked at the rest of the section as he spoke.

Killeen, Muscles, Mac and Bob waited for the final demolition job.

'Well what does he eat for breakfast then smart arse *Boy*?' Paddy said mockingly.

'Probably sheep's eyes and goat's bollocks.'

Paddy fell into Molly's well planned trap. 'The dirty bastard – in the civilized world we eat bacon and eggs.'

'I thought you came from Ireland Paddy, not the civilized world?' Molly delivered the anticipated coup de grâce, and for the second time moved smartly away from Paddy's well aimed boot.

'Fuck you *Boy*.' Came the not unexpected response from Paddy.

No matter how hard he tried, Paddy could never get one over on Molly. Few people ever could, and despite Paddy's well honed boxing skills, landing any kind of punch or kick had always proved equally elusive.

Captain Killeen opened his eyes, blinked rapidly a few times, shook his head, and rejoined the present. Paddy was still there, but there was no kid and no AK47. He and Paddy were still in the same bleak and spartanly furnished barrack room somewhere in the south of England, and had been discussing crossed eyed princesses before his latent memory had transported him back in time.

Killeen could visualize and remember his section like it was yesterday. Paddy, Molly, Bob, Muscles, and Mac; with Ken Wardle doing the coordinating. Bob was now doing undercover work in Northern Ireland, and Muscles and Mac were dead – *HIS* mistake had killed them.

The 3 remaining members of the D1 SAS section, Paddy, Molly and himself, had been shipped out of Northern Ireland shortly after the repatriation of the dead bodies of Muscles and Mac. Accompanying them was Ken Wardle, the section coordinator; his job was to closely observe and monitor the fall out, and to look for signs of any potential mental problems. They had all been granted a long leave, so serious was the trauma often felt after the death of a close knit section member.

'Jim,' Paddy said in a serious and concerned tone of voice. 'You were drifting again. You really do need a break. It could be the early onset of PTSD. It's happening more and more often lately, no one is immune from it, not even you. I've seen it before at both Aldershot and Hereford when the lads have been through something really bad. The Yanks call it the 1000 yard stare; if it isn't treated, it can lead to full blown PTSD: remember, some men *never* recovered from "shell shock" after the first world war, it's the same thing Jim, just a different name.'

Killeen already knew that he had a developing problem. The nightmares, and frighteningly real daytime visions and flashbacks, had started shortly after Muscles and Mac had been killed. He was sure that a long break with Julie would see him right. Post Traumatic Stress Disorder had no place in his line of work – men's lives depended on him getting it right. He had never doubted his ability before, most of his decisions had been made on instinct, he had always had a gut feeling of what was the right decision to make – now, well, he questioned every move that he made. If he got it wrong, who else would die?

'Seriously Jim, you haven't been firing on all cylinders for some time now.' Paddy then broke into a big grin. 'I reckon that a spot of babysitting for a couple of horny, crossed eyed Arab tarts, in Sheik Armani's golden palace, may well be just what the army doctors would recommend – you lucky bastard. What does Julie think, have you told her yet?'

Killeen hadn't even had time to tell Julie that all their plans for the next few weeks may be about to change.

After a much too long tour in Northern Ireland, where the section had been posted for the past few months, their mission – to find and terminate O'Malley and his 'A' team of assassins – he had just started what was to be his extra long leave, and after seeing his parents, the next few weeks belonged to Julie. He had thought about jetting off to America, to New York, then off to Florida. They had often talked about seeing Disney World, Sea World, in fact – *Any World* would do as long as it wasn't the world that he had been living in for the last few months.

Often unwashed – unshaven – and living in the same stinking underwear for days on end; sitting ON, and shitting IN, a real toilet had become almost an obsession with the section. Paddy had claimed that on his return to England, he would not be sleeping in any bed that didn't have at least 2 women in it; instead he was going to spend the first week sat on a bog drinking Guinness.

The unit had been operating in the land of Guinness, but 6 dirty, smelly men, five of them with English accents, plus Paddy, who still retained much of his Belfast brogue, would probably have raised more than a few eyebrows, and would certainly have brought out the young hotshots trying to make a name for themselves.

There were no Special Forces in Northern Ireland… That was the official British line, and much of their time had been either spent under cover, or hiding away from the well informed IRA intelligence network. Capture would have meant certain torture, followed by an even more certain death.

On their return to England, and on their second day of leave for many months, a black MI6 limo had collected both Killeen and Paddy from their respective homes, and brought them to the barracks that they now found themselves in. There had been no prior warning; they were given no explanation, and any questions that they asked remained unanswered.

Why the secrecy? They were in England now. None of the unit had seen leave for months. There were plenty of other SAS Troopers who could do the same job as Killeen and his team. All the other teams were up to scratch, both numerically and in capability. D1 unit were three men short. Two had been killed, and one was working undercover in Ireland.

What was the use of a three man team and one coordinator, and why were they now billeted at an Army camp that they had never even heard of?

What the hell were MI6 up to, and why were they involved? MI6 was supposed to be the Intelligence Service that looked after all things foreign. MI5 looked after the UK and Northern Ireland – not MI6. Something big was going off, and neither Killeen nor Paddy was particularly interested; both men were mentally and physically drained. Even machines have to stop for servicing occasionally, and they were not machines.

Killeen, more than anyone, was feeling the strain. His dreams were becoming too real. He was being transported to different locations and situations; always situations where his life had been in danger whilst on a mission. He was reliving every shot that had been fired, either at him, or by him, and as the mental body count rose, so did the vivid reality of his dreams. He would often wake up after a couple of hours sleep trembling and covered in sweat. In the past he had always dreamed of Julie – his beloved Julie. Now, often all he could see was that bloody kid with the AK47 assault rifle pointing at him, and standing behind him was O'Malley – Michael Patrick O'Malley; grinning, and holding a gun to his head. He would see the flash and hear the bang. It was at this point that he always awoke. Was this to be the final chapter in his life? Was O'Malley to be his nemesis he wondered?

He was now in a relatively obscure army camp in the south of England, wondering why both he, and Paddy, had had their long overdue leave so rudely interrupted. The place didn't seem like a normal military base. There was a complete lack of activity – there was no marching of recruits – there was no screaming and shouting by non coms at some poor unfortunate lower rank. The whole place and pace of things screamed out "Civilian"; none of the personnel around wore Military clothing. There was also a noticeable mix of air force and naval personnel, most of whom spoke with Irish accents. Killeen wondered if the place was simply a training depot for undercover agents, learning the rules of how to stay alive in the hostile, yet beautiful shit hole that was Northern Ireland.

The whole set up confused him: after years of working in military intelligence, surely he should be aware of a secret camp in the south of England – after all, his family home was barely 30 miles away.

Killeen thought about checking on the site by using a few of his ex intelligence colleagues; his own personal clearance was up to and including "TOP SECRET" level. It had needed to be; counter terrorism wasn't just about gathering and analyzing information; often under cover contacts became compromised, and rapid evacuations were necessary. Long before joining the SAS, Killeen had led these evacuations, usually from the troubled counties of Northern Ireland.

He decided against checking. He was tired; his mind was drained dry, and his body was knackered. All the surplus energy and pumping adrenalin of the last few months, in fact virtually all of his life, had disappeared.

He was no longer "James Killeen – the Killing Machine", as the rest of his section had christened him after a particularly brutal contact.

The section, and a small attachment of SBS men, had needed covering fire during a hazardous evacuation from a small African country following a government sponsored assassination. Killeen and Paddy had provided that cover; Killeen had taken out the targets, while Paddy watched his back. Few bullets missed their mark, and he had emptied 3 magazines from his Israeli made assault rifle, only stopping his onslaught when he was sure that the rest of the section were in the clear.

Captain James Killeen was no longer that effective section leader – no longer a killing machine – the batteries were flat – he was an empty shell, riddled with self doubt, and plagued by blood dreams and death nightmares.

He needed sleep; he needed a long, long, rest – a complete break from the army and all leadership responsibility.

What the hell was he doing here then? He was no longer of any use to the army in this condition. He was now having serious doubts about his future within the army. If only Julie would say "yes". That's all it would take, one simple word, and he could move on.

He could leave all these nightmarish walks down the memory lane killing fields behind him.

He could say goodbye to that bloody kid with the AK 47.

Just one simple 3 letter word was all that it would take.

CHAPTER 3

THE CAPTAIN

Captain James Killeen – Jim or Jimbo to his section when not in the presence of superior officers, was due to be 32 years old in 3 days time.

He had only ever been in love once in his entire life. He was still in love.

Success with the opposite sex had always come easily to the teenage James – too easily; being tall, athletically built, and of a wealthy family, his handsome boyish looks ensured a never ending supply of would be girlfriends. He dated only occasionally, never wishing to form any lasting attachment; that was until he met Julie. James Killeen was now hopelessly in love, and had been for a number of years.

The army was not the approved career for young James. Mother had almost fainted when he first broke the news of his intentions; father had gone seemingly mad, and protested long and hard. 'After all the money I've spent on your education, why do you want to go and get yourself shot? What is wrong with running the family business? I have worked my balls off for over 30 years, and for what? So you can run around playing at soldiers. Who the hell is going to run the fucking business when I retire?' James had never heard his father swear before.

Father certainly had a point; private schools and boarding schools since the age of 6, a string of GCE O and A levels as long as his arm, and a guaranteed place at Cambridge awaited him.

What James had tried to, but had never been able to explain to his parents, was the constant build up of energy inside his body – it had to be released, or like an over pressurized vessel, someday it would explode. He had run, swum, boxed, often to the point of exhaustion, but this only provided temporary relief. Soon the pressure would start to build up again.

It always seemed as if his internal adrenalin pump was permanently set to fight or flight mode, and he could not switch it off. It hadn't always been like this; only during puberty did these barely controllable bouts of surplus energy and adrenaline start to surface. He had always been a little hyper active, but as with all children, life was lived at running pace and things were kept under control.

What the pre, and early teenage James could not control, was his anger at the way children at his boarding school had formed themselves into little bullying alliances according to wealth, or the military rank of their parents.

His was a fairly expensive boarding school, his family being quite wealthy; yet to him, all the children were to be judged on merit, not the price of the family car, and most certainly not on the military rank of their fathers. Many of these mid-range, to expensive boarding schools, catered for children from military families in order not to break up the child's education during overseas postings.

Strangely, officer's children only seemed to mix with officer's children, and were often contemptuous of the children whose fathers were of lower military ranks. Bullying was rife, and often, James resolved these problems on behalf of the less fortunate children with his fists.

James's frequent physical resolution of these schoolboy problems of social class bullying often got him into trouble; they also earned him unprecedented respect. He was a natural leader, and most certainly an alpha male at a very early age. This leadership quality was observed, admired, and noted by both teachers and lecturers alike. It was also quite apparent on James's first day at the Army Recruit Selection Centre.

> *This assumed superiority was something that James also noticed throughout his army career, most noticeably at social evenings in the company of other officer's wives. It was often the wife of the officer that appeared to wear the badge of rank, and invariably assumed control of the evening in a manner appropriate to her husband's rank.*

'So you want to join the *Para's* son?' The sergeant at the recruiting office had said, at the same time eying Jame's height and physical presence. 'Hard bunch; not like your private schoolboy chummies – these guys are hard bastards. I got attached to them myself once, couldn't wait to get away – real hard bastards.'

Four weeks later, James found himself at the Recruit Selection Centre at Sutton Coldfield, near Birmingham.

'So you want to be a *Para*?' The major had said. 'Over my dead body, – these test results of yours, together with your boarding school recommendations, and your educational qualifications, are some of the best I have ever come across in over 20 years in the army. You are off to Sandhurst Mr. Killeen; some day you may well become a *Para*, but firstly, you will learn how to conduct yourself correctly, and how to become an officer and a gentleman.'

Sandhurst Officer Training Academy rapidly became James's second home; it really was what he had been searching for throughout his teenage years. He proved more than a match for the rest of his intake, and excelled to the point of excellence in most disciplines, passing out as number one – the best in class.

'*Para's? – PARA's*? – over my dead body Lieutenant Killeen,' came the same words from the same major that had been at Sutton Coldfield. 'With grades like these, number one in class for God's sake, why would anyone want to waste them on that mob? You are off to join my old outfit lieutenant; the Intelligence Corps; that is where the army keeps its brains.'

Accelerated promotion saw Second Lieutenant Killeen rapidly rise to full lieutenant, then to captain, at the time, working closely with MI6 and MI5 on counter terrorism; firstly at the Intelligence Corp headquarters, and then at the ultra secret Old Manor House deep in the heart of the Cumbrian countryside.

Six years flew by, and the gradual build up of latent energy, fueled by his over active adrenalin pump, started to surface again. Being deskbound was not the right outlet or treatment. He only truly came to life during the occasional incursion into Northern Ireland, in order to relieve, and return to the UK, compromised under cover agents.

Everything changed on his first day of training with the SAS at their Hereford headquarters. He soon discovered that being the best of the bunch at Sandhurst had come easily, but was nothing like being the best of the best. This was physical and mental torture – he loved it – this really was home. Sandhurst had been the taster – Hereford was the main course. Even the days and nights spent tramping and camping in and around the bleak and freezing Brecon Beacons, had their own particular charm, and stimulated his desire for ever more action and adventure.

In common with all the men that ever had to take the SAS selection course, he was not too impressed with the final three days of the course. No one ever was. Physical and mental interrogation had to be endured without revealing whatever secrets they had been told to keep secret. Like many of the SAS recruits, he steadfastly retained his sanity, and survived by promising to himself that everyone involved in the "torture", would one day be paid back – with interest – much interest.

It was on his first day at Hereford that Captain James Killeen met Sergeant Liam 'Paddy' Jackson. Paddy had made the same promise as Killeen. As time passed, the two of them, together with the rest of the section, often discussed the various forms of pain and torture that they in turn would love to inflict on everyone connected with the Hereford "Torture Chamber". They also realized that the soldier's who had failed to pass the SAS selection course, could never have survived some of the tasks that THEY had needed to perform. Only one man in a thousand could survive those:-

"*THEY*" were the best of the best – *THEY* were SAS – Special Air Service.

> *The Special Air Service (SAS) is a regiment of the British army, and is universally regarded as the world's most elite body of soldiers. It was originally formed as a long range desert commando force in 1941 by David Stirling, and trained to operate behind enemy lines in the North African campaign of the second World War. The Regiment has become a role model for most of today's military throughout the world. The American equivalent is the Delta Force; most other countries retaining the Special Air Service name, or simply "Special Forces".*

Captain James Killeen served three tours of Northern Ireland, sandwiched between which were short deployments to other world trouble spots in order to fulfill a role thought unsuitable for the average British army soldier. His D1 SAS section was always present, and operated as a self contained unit. Their last tour had gone horribly wrong, and Killeen was no longer the assured and effective leader, nor was he the controlled killing machine of previous campaigns. He was not sleeping well, and was troubled by re-occurring nightmares and flashbacks. The tour had been in the semi-lawless colony of Northern Ireland; deemed part of the British Isles by Britain and the resident Protestant population – and coveted as part of a United Ireland by the Irish Catholics.

Killeen's team had been decimated by the man that they had been sent to eliminate.

Captain James Killeen and his section had proved no match for *Michael Patrick O'Malley*.

The hunters became the hunted.

CHAPTER 4

IN THE BEGINNING

Britain is a medium sized island to the west of mainland Europe.

A little over two centuries ago, the British Monarchy ruled over one third of the world – not the known world – the world.

Part of this empire was a small and very wet island called Ireland, which lies a few miles to the west of mainland Britain.

Over the years, Britain gradually gave back the Empire to the people to whom it belonged, often very reluctantly.

Ireland was different; the Irish people wanted their country back, and the British didn't want them to have it back. Why should they give it back? Most of the country was owned by the English Gentry. Her Majesty, Elizabeth the First, Queen of England, had given much of it to their forebears for services to the crown over 500 years before, and Oliver Cromwell had distributed the rest to his acolytes almost a century later. It may well be called Ireland, but it damned well belonged to the people of mainland Britain – well, to a few very rich people.

Problems first appeared in the 16th century, and were brought to a long term insoluble and serious sectarian divide at the Battle of the Boyne in 1690, when the Protestant, William, Prince of Orange, defeated the Catholic king – James the Second. Major problems resurfaced in the 18th century with a series of country wide rebellions, and catastrophically, came to a serious head in 1845 with the great potato famine. A potato blight devastated the entire country's potato crop, the staple diet for the poor Irish peasantry, who worked the land for their English Lord and Masters.

Over one million people died of starvation, a further one million emigrated, mostly to America and Australia.

The rich English landowners could have saved these people; they had adequate supplies of wheat growing in the country. They didn't want to save them, they could not care less; wheat was bringing a good price back in England; it was much too valuable to feed to the starving millions in Ireland.

The Irish people never forgot nor forgave this callous treachery, and so the seeds of "THE TROUBLES" were sown.

1919 was a particularly bad year for the Irish; the Irish Republican Army (IRA) was reformed, and rebellion was beginning to stir. The Irish War of Independence began.

Britain countered by sending over troops in their thousands. These were not ordinary well disciplined soldiers. These men had lived through the horrors of the Great War (1914–1918). They had watched thousands of men die in a single day, sometimes tens of thousands. They had lived for months, often years, in stinking, freezing, corpse and rat ridden trenches. Throughout all of this carnage, and in a state of constant fear and deprivation, they had somehow survived, and were now expected to be policemen to a bunch of unruly Irish peasants. This did not happen, life was cheap, they had seen too many men die to have feelings. Innocent people were dragged from their homes - beaten, tortured, and often killed, merely as a result of a whisper or a rumor.

These men were the BLACK AND TANS.

Military law was forgotten or ignored - the Black and Tans were the law. The Irish people did not forget.

1949 saw the creation of two separate countries in the island; six counties in the north became Ulster or Northern Ireland, and remained under and subject to the Crown and Parliament of Great Britain; the rest became Eire, or simply Southern Ireland, governed from the capital Dublin.

At this point, things should have remained relatively stable; they didn't. Religion, and near xenophobic sectarianism reared its ugly and uncompromising head.

The LOYALISTS, that is the people loyal to the crown of England, were almost exclusively Protestant, and were by far in the majority in the northern 6 counties. The southern 26 counties were almost exclusively Catholic.

Not everyone in the north however was Protestant. The 6 counties also contained a significant number of Catholics or REPUBLICANS, who did not want to be governed by the British Parliament; they wanted Irish unification, with their governance coming from Dublin, and the Southern Irish Parliament.

To a neutral, the obvious question is 'so what, where is the problem?' Both Catholics and Protestants have the same God.

The problem was that the Protestant majority favored the Protestant majority. Catholics went to different schools, and were excluded from government, councils, the police force, and most other forms of worthwhile employment. Catholics also had more children; contraception was not allowed by the Vatican, and the balance would in future years swing more and more in their favor. This concerned the Protestants; they feared being out-bred, out-numbered, and subsequently – out voted.

1968 was the year when THE TROUBLES can be said to have begun. Catholics were tired of being second class citizens, and began to march in protest at their treatment, and the subservient way that they were forced to live. Full scale riots soon followed, with all the associated violence and damage that inevitably accompanies them.

The Protestants retaliated. Catholic homes were torched. Catholic men, women, and children were abused and beaten; many fleeing for their lives to relatives who lived in the Catholic South.

The police, the Ulster Special Constabulary, (B Specials), stood idly by and watched; after all, the victims were only Catholics – Fenian bastards – and they, the B Specials, were all Protestant.

The Catholic IRA was reformed, and the bombings began in 1969.

The BRITISH ARMY was called in to guard important services and infrastructure, and soon began patrolling the streets in order to protect the Catholic minority from Protestant attacks.

In addition to the regular army regiments, a new regiment called the Ulster Defense Regiment, (UDR) was formed, consisting of mainly volunteers. The original intention was for a nonpartisan regiment with a 50/50 split between Catholic and Protestant. By 1972, only 3% of the entire regiment consisted of Catholics. This 3% were in grave and constant danger from both sides of the religious divide.

Nobody truly knows why things changed – No one knows where it all went wrong.

The protectors became the targets – the Catholic IRA turned on the British Army. Sweet and friendly Catholic ladies willingly gave the heroic soldiers, who had been sent to protect them, cups of tea and slices of homemade cake. The tea was laced with weed killer, the cake with powdered glass.

In July 1970, 15 soldiers were shot and injured by IRA gunfire.

The first British soldier to die was in February 1971, shortly followed by 3 young Highland Fusiliers, who were lured to their deaths by 2 pretty young girls whilst off duty.

The big bang came in January 1972, when British Para's killed 14 and wounded 27 unarmed rioters, in what became known as BLOODY SUNDAY.

The world's media noticed, and Americans in their thousands, many of them distant relatives of the potato famine refugees, began collecting money for these brave IRISH FREEDOM FIGHTERS, in order to free them from British tyranny. After all, hadn't they kicked the British out of their adopted country during the American War of Independence?

Bloody Sunday was the pivotal turning point. Guns and Explosives flooded into the country, not just from America, but from all over Eastern Europe and the Middle East: the Libyan despot Gaddafi could not resist funding and arming any potential revolution, and himself, soon became a target of British Special Forces.

Britain was now embroiled in what was almost a full scale war. Thousands of bombs exploded throughout the province, and soon, inevitably, these atrocities spread to mainland Britain – not even the British Prime Minister and her Cabinet were safe.

Bombs exploded in English pubs, killing and maiming hundreds of young people who were out enjoying themselves. Their crime? – Simply being in the wrong place at the wrong time.

Members of Parliament were blown up and killed. Margaret Thatcher, the British Prime Minister, narrowly escaped death when the Grand hotel in Brighton saw a massive explosion as she worked on her next day speech for the Conservative Party Conference.

The last IRA bomb to explode on the British mainland was at Ealing in 2001.

During the 30 year campaign, almost 4,000 people lost their lives, and over 12,000 were injured – many of them still remembering the days of THE TROUBLES as they fit their prosthetic limbs each morning.

What did all that death and destruction achieve?

Northern Ireland is still Northern Ireland, and the South is still pretty much the same.

O'MALLEY – The Wrong Package, is set somewhere in the1970's and early 80's. Catholics were killing Protestants, and Protestants were killing Catholics. British soldiers were the favorite "*GAME*" of the IRA shooter. Every soldier that was shot and killed earned the shooter a good wedge of money. The higher the soldier's rank, the bigger the pay day.

At the time of the novel, the dynamics had changed. There was a killer on the loose; an ex British Royal Marine and Special Forces expert.

Michael Patrick O'Malley was good – he was very good – he was better than anything that the British Army could come up with. Two specialist teams of highly trained SAS soldiers were drafted in – their mission?

TERMINATE O'MALLEY AND HIS TEAM.

They were not good enough. Casualties mounted. Someone very high in either the Government or the Security Services was leaking important information.

Much of O'MALLEY – The Wrong Package is factual.

The Official Secrets Act can be very restrictive, and has to be signed by all military personnel. It is still enforceable on leaving the services.

CHAPTER 5

RE-UNITED

There was barely a knock on the barrack room door – just the faintest tap. Killeen and Paddy listened, their senses were still heightened. "Coming down" from an overly long tour of active service, where danger often lurked around every street corner and behind every hedgerow took time.

The door crashed open, and in jumped Sgt Major Ken 'Sniffer' Wardle, closely observing the reactions and expressions on the two men's faces.

Wardle had been the D1 team's coordinator for two years, and like Killeen and Paddy, had been recalled from leave on his arrival back in England, shortly after the repatriation of the bodies of Muscles and Mac.

'Relax chaps – no one is going to shoot you in here as long as I'm around.' Wardle said, a big grin creasing his well shaven and weather beaten face.

Sniffer Wardle recognized only too well the look on *their* faces, and the defensive postures that both men had taken; fight – flight – fear – alarm – response. They were all there. They were all symptomatic of men who had been in the field for far too long under intense pressure, with the ever present whiff of death being just around the corner. Death had come to them, and no-one in the unit was taking it well – especially not Killeen. Wardle was particularly concerned with the time it took Killeen to recover. Paddy's recovery had been immediate – Killeen's not so.

Wardle had been there himself on more than one occasion during his time with both the Royal Marines and the Special Boat Squadron – SBS, the naval equivalent of the SAS. Sometimes it took him weeks to "come down", – to return to normality.

A little over 15 years before, whilst still a Royal Marine Commando, he had been tortured for days in Malaya – resumed as if nothing had happened; then, mentally cracked once the unit had been stood down. A mixture of pills, alcohol, and a few weeks leave in Singapore had returned him back to himself, but he never forgot. He was fully aware of the symptoms of PTSD, and was concerned at the response shown by Killeen. Dare he proceed with the operation that had been weeks in the planning? Was Killeen now a liability – a spent force – a man who could possibly put all their lives at risk?

He had been wrestling with the problem for a few days now. Up until the point where Muscles and Mac had been shot, Killeen was the outstanding – in fact – the only candidate for the task ahead, of that he had no doubt; but now, doubts were beginning to surface. A different Captain James Killeen was standing before him. This Killeen no longer carried his own force field around with him. The alpha male presence had disappeared, and had been replaced by an insecure, almost inconsequential shell. Killeen was there in body only – the "special" was no longer there.

Wardle himself had always been a "special", but not in the same way as Killeen. Wardle was probably the most "special" of men in the British military, his fame extending way beyond the shores of England. He had now been put out to pasture: no longer a field operative; he was the coordinator of D1 unit operations. D1 was the designated code allocated to Killeen's SAS unit. Only occasionally did he perform a more operational role. This was when a very "special" skill was called for. Wardle had that very special skill.

Only a handful of men in the world – possibly even less than that, could put a bullet into an orange at 1000 yards – Wardle was one of them. Maybe even the only one.

Only 5 more months to serve of his 22 year stint, and her Majesties' government would begin paying him a not too generous pension. It often annoyed him to think that some *poxy* civil servant, sitting in a nice warm central heated office, would be drawing twice as much as he would without ever having put his life in danger. Wardle had put his life in danger many times. He often wondered why? Nevertheless, he was still dreading the alternative. What would he do? Where would he live? He had never before thought about living in one place and settling down to a quiet domesticity. The military had always been his life – his wife – his family. He knew nothing else, and was fearful of the future.

Becoming a mercenary was not an option; he only squeezed the trigger for his country, either under orders, or when absolutely necessary – never for the money.

'The old man wants to see you Jimbo – pronto,' Wardle said to Killeen. 'And when you've finished, can we all meet up in the sergeant's mess for breakfast; we need to talk, all 3 of us – this could be serious.'

'On my way Sgt Major Sniffer.' Killeen said, as he headed for the door. Taking hold of the door handle, he paused and turned his head, a big grin creasing his boyish face. 'I think I might just let the colonel know what you just called him – it's about time I got a promotion.'

'Arse licking again are we Captain Snitch? – I always wondered how you got promoted so fucking quickly; now I know.'

'Bollocks to you Paddy, if you had ever learned how to handle a couple of pints of Guinness without belting someone, you could have made General by now.'

'Thick, bog oil swilling apes don't make General very often Jim.' Wardle cut in.

The three men laughed, as Killeen exited the room, straightened his back, and marched across the square to the colonel's office.

As soon as Killeen was out of earshot, Wardle turned to face the bearded, and slightly angular face that belonged to the giant of a man stood next to him. 'What are your views on this Arab job Paddy? Personally, I think it stinks; it doesn't smell right. Something is wrong, but I can't quite put my finger on it.' Wardle tightened his lips and shook his head as he spoke. 'There is no reason to approach Jim for the job – no reason at all; there must have been fucking hundreds of people that applied, not just from the British Special Forces, but from all over the world. A job like that is a guaranteed retirement package after a couple of years. I don't like the smell of it.'

'Same here Ken,' replied Paddy, shaking his head even more violently than Wardle. 'Why would Sheik Armani want Jim? He only met him the once, and Jim has never worked protection in his life, and certainly not close protection. Something does not add up.'

Wardle grinned and closed his eyes, his face suddenly changing to display anger. 'Did a job for the Sheik myself once; well, my SBS team did. It was about 7 years ago, and both O'Malley and myself met his Royal Sheikness. There was a bit of an insurrection brewing, and the British Government, for whatever reason, sent us out to 'nip it in the bud', I believe the phrase was. There were about 20 of us altogether, SBS – SAS – and American Navy Seals.'

'Why the Americans Ken?'

'Oil I guess Paddy – that's the usual reason for any interference in that part of the world. Personally, I think it was the Americans that wanted us there in the first place, probably because of our long standing relations with the Sheik's family – anyway, the slightly more educated of his subjects were pretty pissed off with the Sheik, and were marching on the palace. They were all unarmed, and didn't want to kill him or anything, they just wanted to get rid of him.'

'Why's that Ken? He seemed a pretty decent bloke when we met him; he thanked us all personally; he even took us on a tour of his military set up in his gold car.' Paddy had a puzzled and questioning look on his face.

'We had probably just saved his life don't forget Pads, he couldn't afford not to be nice; anyway, for such a small kingdom, it is immensely wealthy, with vast oil and gas reserves, probably running into billions of pounds. However, as in all the Middle East, none of this money filters down to the people. Almost all of it is siphoned off by the Sheik and his extended family, and usually ends up in either Swiss or London bank accounts or property. All any of these people who were marching on the palace wanted, was a share of the country's wealth, instead of having to raise goats to feed their families. The SAS did the initial scouting, and when the 200 or so of these protesting blokes came into view, we were in position.'

A puzzled frown crossed Paddy's face as he spoke. 'What about the Sheik's own army Ken? He buys enough equipment from us; everything I saw out there was British; he's got more bloody hardware than we have, and most of it is more up to date than the crap that we get issued with.'

Wardle's face broke into a big grin, and laughing out loud he went on. 'They wanted him out as much as the people did; so the generals conveniently conducted military exercises some 50 or 60 miles away. That way, if it had all gone tits up, they were in the clear; if it had succeeded however, they would have taken power, and the cycle of corruption would have continued, with all the oil money going into the general's pockets instead of the Sheik's. I suppose that the powers that be, in both Britain and America, worked on the "Devil you know basis", they feel more comfortable that way.'

'O'Malley and I were on opposite corners of the eastern outer wall of the palace, with 7 or 8 shooters on the inner wall below us. We were given very explicit orders – from the military I might add, not the Sheik – we were told not to shoot to kill unless absolutely necessary; in other words, only if the situation became life threatening.

As the protestors approached, and got to about 200 yards from the palace, both O'Malley and I fired a warning shot in front of them. They stopped for a few seconds, then, they kept on coming. Instead of firing another warning shot, O'Malley cut loose – shot after shot – kill after kill. The lot of them turned tail and ran. O'Malley just kept on firing into their backs. We were all screaming at him to stop, but he was like a fucking man possessed – he just kept on firing. 27 shots – 27 dead bodies, the last one close on three quarters of a mile away: flat open desert you see, there was nowhere to hide.'

'Fucking hell!'

'It was for those poor bastards Paddy; most of them just lay face down in the sand. Every single one of them that kept on running…died.'

'What happened to those that lived?'

Wardle let out a sarcastic grunt. 'Your pal the Sheik, who you seem to think is a pretty decent bloke, had them all rounded up, driven out into the desert, and beheaded.'

'Fucking hell!' Paddy shook his head violently, gritting his teeth and closing his eyes as he spat out the expletive.

'This is only the tip of the iceberg Paddy; the whole of the Middle East is the same; Libya – Syria – Iran – Iraq – Saudi – Jordan – the Emirates. They all work on the same principle. The unwritten, yet unquestionable rule, is that the Sheik and his family have a divine right to rule; the same also applies to which ever dictator is in power at the time; his sons will also have the same divine right to rule when he dies.'

'Why doesn't someone do something about it Ken, the Yanks could take them all out in days?'

'Why should they or we even bother Paddy? Things work just fine as they are. We buy their oil, they buy our weapons. If you broke up the status quo, some fucking Muslim religious fanatic would probably take control, and then who knows where that will lead?

The most stable countries in the Middle East are the ones run by the most brutal regimes. The way to run a successful dictatorship hasn't changed since Roman times, probably long before that. You simply make sure that the generals and the police commissioners are some of the best paid people in the country, you then enforce the law by brutality. In other words, you govern by fear. Once you have control of the military and the police, you are pretty much fireproof. No way are the senior military and police ever going to give up their privileged lifestyles unless of course they take power for themselves. That is why Stalin kept executing his senior lieutenants. Whenever he thought that they were becoming too popular, or powerful, he had them tried on some trumped up charge; found guilty without exception, and hanged or shot – he usually had them branded "Enemies of the State" or "Spies". Hitler got to power the same way.

Mark my words Paddy, someday it will all change. It will only take one rebellion to succeed, and the whole of the Middle East will collapse like a line of dominoes, each one pushing over its neighbor. In the meantime, we need the oil, so we either tolerate the regime, or we prop it up. That's why mugs like us are always first in and first out, without the rest of the world even knowing that we were ever there, or that there was ever even a problem.

Anyway, about half a dozen of us spent a couple of nights in the servant's quarters at the palace. The Sheik himself gave O'Malley quite a tidy sum of money – thought he was a fucking hero – the rest of us wanted to kill the bastard, especially the Yanks. They would have done as well; that's why we were in there, and they were kept outside the palace walls – we had to wait till they went home. If it had been up to me, I would have let them string the bastard up.'

Paddy starred at Wardle, a frown creasing his forehead. 'Three quarters of a mile you said, are you sure? That's a fucking long way. I couldn't even see a man at three quarters of a mile?'

'O'Malley and the Sheik paced it out – straight between the shoulder blades. I counted the spent cartridges as he left. Twenty eight – one shot in the sand as a warning – five men killed by shots to the chest, and twenty two in the back. Twenty seven unarmed, innocent men, probably all with families. The thing that sticks in my mind the most though was the look in O'Malley's eyes.'

'Demented – completely mad …fucking bonkers.'

'Fucking hell Ken; why didn't we kill the bastard in Northern Ireland?' Paddy clenched his fists and gritted his teeth until his jaw ached. 'Muscles and Mac would still be alive.'

'Too bloody smart Paddy,' replied Wardle with a shake of his head. 'He always has been. To my knowledge, no-one has ever even taken a shot at O'Malley, and I have worked with him for close on 20 years all over the world, and in enough life threatening situations to write a book about.'

Wardle went quiet for a few seconds, before shaking his head and pursing his lips. His face broke into a big grin as he imagined the title of his book.

O'Malley – The Mad Irish Bastard.

CHAPTER 6

SERGEANT LIAM 'PADDY' JACKSON

Paddy Jackson was tough – he had to be. He was also a very dangerous man to cross. At over six and a half feet, he towered over all of his contemporaries.

Paddy had grown up a Catholic in the Loyalist, Protestant, working class area known as the Shankill, a district of West Belfast – the Northern Ireland capital, and soon discovered that he was different. He went to a different school to most of the kids around him, and the older and bigger kids often bullied him, sometimes quite violently, calling him a ' Fienian or Catholic Bastard '.

Paddy grew quickly, and grew up quickly. He became good with his fists, and rapidly changed from bullied Fenian kid, to the most feared teenager in the area. Tough guys from different districts of Belfast travelled to the Shankill to put the 'Fienian Bastard' in his place. They only came once – no one ever returned to chance their arm. Paddy was simply too big, too strong, and had the power in his fists to consign a man to hospital with a single punch. Standing well over six feet by the age of 15, he just carried on growing until he finally bottomed out at a little over six and a half feet by his 18th birthday. Paddy didn't just grow upwards; he had shoulders to match, and hands like shovels; weighing in at over 17stone without an ounce of fat.

Paddy loved to box, but as his strength and reputation grew, it became increasingly difficult to find anyone who would climb into the ring with him. He had to travel to the outskirts of the city in order to earn a fairly respectable living with his fists against the travelers and gypsies that constantly moved in and out of the city. This was bare knuckle stuff – fierce, bloody, and uncompromising – no referee, and almost no rules.

Soon, even the gypsies got the message, until one dull and freezing overcast day in early winter, whilst still only 17, he took a fearful beating from a gypsy twice his age, and almost as big as he was.

It hadn't been too difficult for Paddy to counter the gypsy's initial attack; for such a big young man, Paddy was quick on his feet, and possessed lightening fast reflexes. A crushing and concussive right hand had battered the gypsy to the ground. One more punch, and he was ready for a long, deep sleep – maybe even a trip to the hospital to have his face re-aligned. The semi conscious man had slowly climbed back to his feet, and just as Paddy was about to deliver the Coup de Gras, the gypsy suddenly brought up his right fist into Paddy's groin. Two of the gypsy's mates grabbed Paddy's arms, and a helpless Paddy was then subjected to the fearful beating that left him recovering in bed for over a week, and with a badly broken nose that had refused all attempts to straighten despite two operations.

Paddy swore revenge, and word spread round the travelling community very quickly indeed. The gypsy realized that he had made one hell of a mistake, and sensibly disappeared to join family members in the south of the country. The gypsy's two companions that had held Paddy down, were not quite so smart, and were soon in adjoining beds in hospital, their voices being their only recognizable feature.

Word was out however that Paddy had killed his gypsy opponent. He became even more of a social outcast. THE TROUBLES hadn't yet started – killing people was still not fashionable in Northern Ireland – things were about to change.

It was an angry, very fierce young man that joined the Parachute Regiment a couple of months after his 18th birthday.

He was no longer a Fienian bastard – he was a paratrooper. No one ever asked him about his religion, everyone simply knew him as Paddy, and everyone was proud of Paddy. He became the best boxer in all the three main parachute battalions, and had wiped the floor with all comers from the rest of the armed forces.

He rapidly made corporal, then sergeant. His descent back to Private Paddy Jackson was even swifter, and so he started again. Firstly to corporal, then to sergeant, and then back to private once again. It wasn't that he was a bad soldier, far from it, he was an excellent soldier; he just could not resist a challenge; often something as completely stupid as drinking 20 pints of Guinness in less than one hour. Paddy could, and Paddy did, and the next morning Paddy found himself in the guard room and a private again, rarely remembering the reason why.

Paddy never officially killed anyone in Northern Ireland, nor anywhere else for that matter, either in civilian life or as a soldier. How could he have? He stayed back in Aldershot when his parachute battalion was posted to Northern Ireland, where they became involved in the "Bloody Sunday" problem. His teenage history in the province would have marked him out as an obvious target, and as an SAS trooper, he was never there – none of them were ever there – where ever '*there*' was.

For Paddy though, army leave was a major and insoluble problem. As a Para, then an SAS trooper, advertising the fact would have placed his whole family in peril – they still lived in Belfast. Good Catholic kids did not join the army. The soldiers were now the enemy of all Northern Ireland's Catholics; without them, there would be nothing to stop full blown Irish unification.

The Catholics did not want to be subjected to British rule – they wanted *one* Ireland. They wanted to be governed by Dublin – not London. The very fact that the vast majority of the population in Northern Ireland was Protestant and wanted to maintain the status quo was unimportant.

If the IRA couldn't win at the ballot box; they would bloody well win by terrorism and intimidation. Their ballot box morphed into an Armalite rifle and a bomb.

Their solution was change by force – not by consent.

CHAPTER 7

THE PACKAGE

Back at the barracks, it was a confused Captain James Killeen that left the colonel's office.

Six years working alongside MI6 and MI5 in Intelligence, had taught him to take nothing at face value; everything had a purpose – this didn't. There was no logic, no reason, and no purpose – why him, and why this way? Why had he and Paddy so urgently and so secretly, been recalled from leave, and what the hell was the MI6 involvement all about?

'Collect a package and drive it to the secret MI6/MI5 intelligence headquarters in the Lake District.' the colonel had told him. He was going to go there anyway; he was going to see Julie, so the journey wouldn't be wasted, but why all the cloak and dagger stuff? There was of course the added bonus of the army footing the bill for the journey, in fact, they would be paying not just the petrol money, but also the cost of a couple of nights in a nice Lake District hotel. He would tell Julie that it was his treat.

His mind threw up a picture of Julie and he smiled; she was pretty, with long black hair, and a smile that lit up a room on a cold and damp Cumbrian night. Julie always made him feel good. There was just something about her that turned him back into a little boy again. They had been together for years, ever since his attachment to the counter terrorism section at the Old Manor House by the lake. He would marry her of course; it was just a question of time. This time she would not say no – he just knew it.

He had first met Julie down at the little Cumbrian village pub during a birthday party for one of the MI6 analysts, and had caught her eye a couple of times. He had felt himself blush; this was a most unusual experience for him; he had always been confident in the company of women and never blushed. There was just something about her that made him feel nervous and strange; nevertheless, he had felt good, and was hooked after the first glance. He couldn't really remember who had spoken first, as it had been a pretty good night. He could however remember eventually plucking up enough courage to ask her out for a date, and being crestfallen when she had turned him down.

'I will be in the pub tomorrow night about 8 if you want to buy me a drink though.' She had laughingly said.

During the next few weeks, they had both become frequent visitors to the village pub, and before long were dating. Occasionally, she mentioned John, her husband, and each time, tears would well up in her eyes. She would blink and try to disguise the hurt, but it always showed through. Killeen wondered what the hell was wrong with the man. Julie obviously adored him, yet he was now shacked up with a 16 year old in the next village. He often thought about popping across for a not too friendly word.

After a couple of years, when her divorce came through, Killeen finally asked Julie to marry him.

'I love you so much Jim,' she had said, sobbing uncontrollably. 'But I could not go through that hurt again; I would die; I can never marry anyone again, not ever, ever!'

The next morning, Killeen had applied to join the SAS.

He had never stopped loving Julie, and whenever the opportunity arose, he would make the drive to the little Cumbrian village to see her. He asked her to marry him whenever they met, but was always met with a smile, and a slight shake of the head.

This time she would say yes, he just knew it. She had sounded so excited over the phone – excitement tinged with fear and concern. He had phoned her about the death of Muscles and Mac the evening that it had happened. He had needed to talk to someone. Julie had felt his pain, his guilt; she had heard the sobs. This was a different Jim Killeen to the one that she had been seeing for all these years – he had sounded like a broken man – a man carrying the weight of the world on his shoulders. Over the next few phone calls she had felt as if she was talking to a complete stranger. Her initial excitement was now countered by a deep feeling of apprehension; she didn't want to lose her precious Jim, the love of her life; but somehow, she felt that maybe she had already done so.

'Collect whatever weapons you need Captain Killeen,' the colonel had said. 'Sergeant Major Wardle will fill you in with all the necessary details, he is fully up to speed – he will be your mission coordinator. I believe you have worked together before?'

'Yes sir, many times.' Killeen had replied, surprised to find that the colonel was so well informed. The SAS working relationships were rarely known outside of the Regiment.

'You will collect the package tomorrow morning, and deliver it the same day; any questions Captain?'

'No sir.'

'Good, that will be all then, and good luck.'

Captain Killeen sprang to attention, thanked the colonel in a military manner, and left the office. There was no salute, as he was dressed in civilian clothing; he walked on with a puzzled frown on his face.

Collect the weapons? – Good luck?

What the hell was going on? All he had to do was be a postman for the day; postmen don't carry guns. His mind was buzzing; this wasn't Oman – Yemen – Libya – Northern Ireland, or any of the other trouble spots and shit holes he had been sent to over the past few years, this was bloody England.

Why did MI6 deem it necessary to involve the SAS? Why couldn't they deliver it themselves, after all, the destination was on their patch anyway? He had spent 6 years working at the delivery destination alongside both MI5 and MI6. What could be so important that it couldn't be sent by military courier? He felt concerned; this didn't stack up. He felt a tingling at the back of his neck. A vision of his impending death flashed before his eyes, as he felt himself floating, and looking down on himself as he walked on. That bloody kid with the AK 47 appeared, grinning at him – ready to pull the trigger.

He walked slowly, almost trancelike, across the square in the direction of the sergeant's mess, forgetting all forms of military posture: his mind was thinking of too many things at the same time. Was this now the time to wave goodbye to the army? If he was ever going to marry Julie, it would simply be unfair to her if he were to go and get himself killed. Death was always on the cards in his line of work, in fact, he had almost been shot three times over the last two years – two of the three times had been bloody kids; both of them too young to shave, and the third time had been a British parachute regiment officer.

He hadn't completely made up his mind. The army had been his whole life for over twelve years. Would he ever be able to settle down into a comfortable domesticity? Would he become, in a parody of the Manfred Mann song, "A Semi Detached Suburban Captain James"? He chuckled to himself quite audibly at the thought, as he walked on to meet Wardle and Paddy at the sergeant's mess.

'O'Malley is in the country!'

Killeen froze, and then felt himself physically shudder from head to toe, his breathing becoming momentarily erratic; he then continued eating his breakfast, hoping that Wardle and Paddy had not seen his brief panic attack.

'He's got the whole fucking 'A' team with him,' Sniffer Wardle continued. 'O'Riley, Fitzpatrick, and Mad Mitch Murphy.'

'How the hell did they all get in Ken?' Killeen said, trying to disguise the concern and slight tremor in his voice, and to hide the tremble in his hands, as his fork skewered a fatty rasher of bacon.

'Seems they tagged along with a bunch of Gypo's and Travelers, and hid in the caravans. The fucking security at Anglesey is none existent. You could bring a platoon of daleks in and no one would be any the wiser.'

'Weapons?' asked Paddy, with an unassuming shrug of his shoulders. 'Explosives? What the hell have they brought in with them?'

'I don't know, but it's pretty certain they have brought their weapons, O'Malley's rifle never leaves his side; he treats it better than he ever treated his wife.' Wardle suddenly burst out laughing as he continued. 'Mind you, if you ever saw his wife, you would understand why – she abuses the right to be ugly. Even Paddy wouldn't go there, and he would fuck a porcupine.'

'Already have done,' Paddy laughed along with the other two men. 'Do we know the target, they won't be over here for a holiday?' This time there was a much more serious edge to Paddy's voice.

'No Paddy, but we can't discount the obvious, that's why we've had our fucking leave cancelled.' Wardle screwed up his face, and shook his head as he spoke.

Paddy Jackson and Ken 'Sniffer' Wardle looked at each other – they were worried, but for a different reason than the presence of O'Malley in the country.

Captain James Killeen had stopped eating – his eyes had again, for the second time that morning, assumed the blank 1000 yard stare. His mind was now far, far away, and he was lying well camouflaged at a border crossing near to Crossmaglen in Northern Ireland.

Crossmaglen was in South Armagh; an area often referred to as bandit country. During THE TROUBLES, 58 police officers, and 124 British soldiers were killed in South Armagh, either by booby trap bombs, or by rifle shot.

This was O'Malley killing country.

Following a tip off from a well paid informant, one who had always previously come up with good information, Killeen had deployed his team in a classic SAS ambush formation – one forward look out, whose job was to move in behind, once the target had passed through, in order to cut off any retreat – one man on either flank; these two men were the main shooters – and two 'wingers', as the team always referred to them. The 'wingers' were positioned slightly behind and wide of the two main shooters, where possible, in an elevated position, each with a 90 degree arc of fire.

Killeen should have been suspicious. This terrain was straight from the training manual at the Sandhurst officer training academy; everything was just too perfect – perfect scenarios do not exist in real life soldiering – a blind mouse would have seen the set up, and O'Malley was no blind mouse. There was simply no way that an SBS man with 20 years under his belt would walk into what was obviously, an ideal ambush situation. There were endless options without exposing himself to the guns of one of the two SAS teams that he knew were somewhere out there trying to kill him. There was no dead or alive option – only dead, and O'Malley was aware of this.

Muscles and Mac, the two designated shooters, took the first two hits – 7-62 mm caliber, high velocity rounds, dead-centre of the chest. The two bangs then arrived, two seconds apart. Both men were dead before they hit the ground or heard the bangs.

Even though it was still fairly light, and visibility was good, it was impossible to locate the shooters. The shots had been too close together for one man to have made them.

'Not so,' Wardle had said. 'O'Malley can do it; I've seen him do two aimed shots within two seconds at 1000 yard range on more than one occasion.'

This was Captain James Killeen's introduction to *MICHAEL PATRICK O'MALLEY.*

Two very good friends and members of his section had paid the ultimate price for the introduction.

Killeen's eyes returned to normal, as the three men continued their breakfast and their conversation, both Paddy and Wardle's concern being barely disguised.

Wardle was now having doubts about the up-coming operation. He needed a fully functioning Killeen – a Killeen at the top of his game; not a Killeen who was having difficulty sitting in on a conversation without drifting off into dreamland. 'Where was he drifting to,' he wondered?

Wardle thought back to the time after his days of torture in the Malayan jungle. O'Malley had rescued him, and saved his life. It was only after they were stood down that the nightmares, the horrific visions, and the paranoia had begun. If asked to function normally, he would have been unable to co-ordinate both body and senses.

Was Killeen heading that way? Was he already there? If so – he was dead man walking, and he, Sniffer Wardle, would be the one who had metaphorically pulled the trigger on a man who was incapable of defending himself.

There was still no other option than to go ahead with the operation. There would never be a golden opportunity such as this one. If Killeen was to be sacrificed, he could live with that. If successful, so many lives would be saved. SAS men were always aware of their expendability.

Killeen would just have to be kept out of the loop, and to rely on his own initiative and self preservation instincts. It was his only hope of survival.

O'Malley never left prisoners alive.

CHAPTER 8

SERGEANT MAJOR KEN 'SNIFFER' WARDLE

At the age of 19, Ken Wardle joined the Royal Marine Commandos.

Shock, horror, and disbelief, had reverberated throughout the entire Wardle family.

'Wardle's join the army, not the bloody navy,' his father, the Major had almost screamed. 'The navy is for Nancy boys, not men. What about the family tradition? Where is your family pride?'

The Wardle military family tree went back as far as records would allow them to; many, many, generations. Wardle's had fought at Waterloo, Balaclava, the first and second World Wars, Suez, Cyprus, and just about every other military campaign since records began.

Major Wardle, the family Patriarch, had himself built a display cabinet that held pride of place in the Wardle country home, proudly displaying virtually every medal that the British army had ever issued; all neatly arranged in chronological order. There were no Victoria Crosses though; the Major secretly hoped that one of his 3 sons would complete the set. Not posthumously of course, but then again, very few men lived to receive their Victoria Crosses, and he so longed to complete his collection. One of them certainly wouldn't be of any use. Clive, his youngest son, was earning more money as a Merchant Banker in the city than the Major had ever dreamed of.

The Major's career had also been something of a disappointment. He had been destined for high places; maybe even General someday. Just one mistake – one bloody mistake had ruined his career. Dashing young cavalry officers did not associate with Irish peasant girls, no matter how pretty they were. The Army could never tolerate such behavior. She was an office cleaner at the Chelsea barracks; how could she possibly fit in with the classy, well educated officer's wives at important military functions? The Army Officer Corps had standards to maintain, and so the Major, at the time a full lieutenant, was shipped out to Hong Kong, followed by Cyprus, and was not allowed to return to the UK for a full 3 years.

This misdemeanor would have been overlooked – forgiven and forgotten about, if matters had been brought to a close. All young men occasionally sow wild oats. On his return to the UK – Wardle resumed his liaison with his Irish lover, and continued to sow them. The top brass became aware of it, and his career came to a dead stop at the rank of Major.

Major Wardle never forgave the army and vowed to get even – he would have the last laugh, of that he was both sure and determined.

His middle son Ken however was now a Nancy boy sailor, and had disgraced the Wardle family name and tradition by not joining the accepted cavalry regiment of his forebears. This was something else that the Major would never forgive, nor forget. He now had little love for two of his three sons, and constantly struggled to disguise this bitterness.

Ken Wardle's imposing size and physique were ideally suited to the Marines, whose initial training course was generally regarded as one of the most difficult in the world – outside of the Special Forces.

He had taken orders well, and as he moved up through the ranks, he gave them well. He wasn't too sure when it was first recommended that he tried for the SBS: he stalled for a considerable time; he was quite content where he was, he enjoyed being a Royal Marine Commando, and being in such an elite and admired military unit meant that he saw much action throughout his time with the Marines.

'Go for it,' his father, the Major had said rather sarcastically. 'Now we will see if you are a real man or a typical navy Nancy boy.'

Ken had been put on the spot. 'The crafty old bastard has me over a barrel now.' he said quietly to himself.

'Did you say something Kenneth dear?' Mother had said.

'No mum, I think dad is right, I will join the SBS.'

'We will see if you can make it first son.' Sarcasm and bitterness laced the Major's voice.

Ken now had no choice – he had to make it. He did.

Wardle's attachment to the SAS section, hence the rank of Sergeant Major, had been due to a specialist skill that had been needed for a certain assignment. There had been only one window of opportunity for the shot, which had to be taken at over 1000 yards range. Wardle took the shot, and the section moved on.

Wardle had a skill that created legends. It could change governments, and it could change the course of history. The history of a small African country changed the moment Wardle squeezed the trigger. His was a God given skill. The Marine sniper school simply honed, nurtured, and refined that skill.

Throughout Wardle's entire military career, only one man had ever challenged his dominance with a rifle. He first recognized the latent insanity of that man at the Marine sniper school. Up to that point, they had been friends.

His name was *Michael Patrick O'Malley.*

CHAPTER 9

THE TRIGGER

Wardle and O'Malley had first met as young Royal Marine Commando trainees. Both men had hit it off from day one, and gradually moved ahead of the pack, each one showing a remarkable aptitude for shooting. Senior ranks soon recognized these qualities, and an attachment to the Marine sniper training school quickly followed.

O'Malley was an exceptionally gifted sniper; his camouflaging ability was remarkable.

'That big Irish bastard could hide behind a single blade of grass,' the training sergeant had said to the captain. 'Damned near invisible; I've never seen anything like it in all my life; he can also shoot as well sir.'

O'Malley couldn't just shoot well, his pass out score was one of the highest scores recorded for many years; in fact, only one man had beaten his score in the last 20 years. That man was on the same course – that man was Ken 'Sniffer' Wardle, and Wardle's score had never been bettered, nor equaled, in the history of sniper school. Wardle never missed with a sniper rifle. This ability to co-ordinate his breathing, nerves, and remarkable eyesight, was not trained into him; it was a gift from God – the Marine sniper training school simply refined it.

They had been friends, but things began to change. O'Malley began to resent Wardle; he hated being second best; he considered himself by far the better Marine in every respect – he was fitter, stronger, and at 6 foot 4 inches, a good 2 inches taller than Wardle. O'Malley should have been the best shot in the entire British military; he had medals, cups, and plaques from the military shooting competitions at Bisley – all of them for second place.

Wardle never missed – Damn Wardle.

'He's a born killer you know.' Wardle had told Killeen and Paddy, as the three men continued their second breakfast in the sergeant's mess; the first one having lasted no more than a couple of minutes. Months of eating sandwiches and ration packs in the Irish Province, now being replaced by an insatiable appetite for an unlimited supply of hot fresh food.

'Aren't we all?'

'NO, we are not Paddy. If we kill, there is a reason for it, and that reason is because we are soldiers; we only do what we are ordered to do or what we have to do in order to stay alive. O'Malley cannot help himself; it is like a disease with him – pretty much like the fox in a hen house – once he starts, he can't stop until everything is dead, and that includes animals as well – dogs, pigs, cattle – if it moves, he kills it. Once he is fired up, nothing, and no-one is safe.'

'Fucking hell,' Paddy said, a look of both surprise and revulsion creasing his bearded face. 'You are joking?'

'No joking Paddy,' Wardle now screwed up his face and pursed his lips as he spoke, at the same time shaking his head from side to side as he continued. 'He is completely insane now; mad as a fucking hatter; has been for years, but somehow, he always managed to keep it under control – just enough to fool everyone – everyone except me that is. He always suspected that I knew, I'm pretty sure of that.'

Killeen and Paddy looked at each other, then back to Wardle whose face had now taken on a serious expression as he spoke. 'I'm not joking lads, he really is insane. I have known him for 20 years, and watched him struggle to keep a lid on it. Sometimes he loses it and people die. It's been getting harder for him to hide it for the last few years, all it needed was for someone to pull the trigger, and he would completely cross over; that trigger was the death of his kid.'

"*THE TRIGGER*" – the words bounced around in Killeen's head. If that had been the trigger, then he had pulled it, not literally, but he might as well have done. His eyes, for the second time in the space of a few minutes, again took on the glazed look of a man who was no longer present. The 1000 yard stare returned, as his mind and thoughts wandered into the twilight zone between fantasy and reality.

Killeen and his section were on a stake out at Portadown in Northern Ireland, following a tip off from one of their many informers. A couple of IRA men were planning to plant bombs along the route that the next days' Protestant Orange March was to follow. They were due to approach along the west bank of the river Bann, and meet up with Patrick Flynn, the number one IRA bomb maker, who hid out and plied his deadly trade in the untouchable south of the country. Preventing this was crucial, as a senior Orange Lodge member from Belfast was to be present at the march. If this man was killed, an awful lot of shit was going to hit an awful lot of fans, and the Army was due to be caught up in the middle of whole stinking mess.

Killeen had deployed his section in classic ambush formation, Muscles Morgan on point, Mac Macintosh and Molly Malone flanking, with Bob Kineer and himself taking the wings.

'Don't need you Paddy old son,' Killeen had said, trying his best to sound serious, and at the same time, fighting to suppress an ever expanding grin. 'Why not pop into town and do a bit of drinking, besides, you couldn't hit a fucking barn door anyway.'

Paddy's rifle work had become something of a joke throughout the entire SAS regiment, having attained the lowest ever score on his last assessment. Paddy had been drunk after an impromptu birthday party, having consumed some 20 pints of Guinness and a bottle of Irish whiskey. Not only could he not hit the target, he couldn't even see it.

'I can shoot the bollocks off a gnat at half a mile Captain Perfect, the sights were crap.'

'I had the same crap sights myself once after a heavy night.' Killeen had replied.

Both men laughed quietly to themselves, as Paddy silently crept away to deploy himself. His was a roving role, constantly shifting position in order to keep an overview of the entire section. He was also the eyes in the back of the section's head: occasionally the unexpected happened, and a potential enemy approached from the 'wrong' direction. Without Paddy's roving deployment outside Sheik Armani's palace, it was unlikely that Killeen would have survived that 'bloody kid' with the AK 47.

It was just before first light, as the section slunk silently away after an uneventful night, that Killeen saw the kid's body. Both of his eyes were wide open, conveying a look of abject terror, and his head was twisted at a funny angle, an American made Armalite rifle lay beside the body.

'I had no choice Jim – he had you in his sights – it was almost pitch black – I honestly didn't know that it was a kid as he was crouching down and stalking you. I should have just belted him.' Paddy sounded genuinely sorry, almost tearful, as both he and Killeen surveyed his handy work – his calling card. Killing the 'bloody kid with the AK47' in the desert had presented Paddy with no such problems; he was a witness, and threatened to jeopardize the whole operation; this however was something completely different; this was an Irish kid on Irish soil, and Paddy himself was Irish. He had just killed a child of one of his own countrymen, when a good belt with his fist would have been a far better option.

Killeen took full responsibility for the kid's death. As section leader, he really had no choice. Paddy's family still lived in Belfast. Paddy Jackson, the "Shankill Fenian Bastard", would not be hated by just the Protestants anymore – the Catholic IRA would be looking for reprisals.

The kid was not quite 15 years old.

His name was Sean O'Malley – son of **Michael Patrick O'Malley.**

The trigger had been pulled, and the consequences for the British Army were dire and far reaching.

'Sorry Ken,' Killeen shook his head, and blinked rapidly half a dozen times, as his thoughts left Ireland, and returned to the sergeant's mess to rejoined Wardle and Paddy in the present. 'I was miles away. I was wondering why O'Malley would bring the whole 'A' team over with him?' He then continued eating his second breakfast as if nothing had happened and no time had elapsed, conscious that he hadn't been completely truthful to his companions.

Ken Wardle and Paddy Jackson glanced quickly at each other, then away, each man hoping that Killeen had not spotted the questioning glance.

'Maybe it is something to do with the package, which you will be delighted to know gentlemen, is in the form of a rather tasty little W.R.A.C. lieutenant.' Wardle replied, at the same time winking at Paddy.

'What, a package wrapped up inside a cardboard box with stamps on her fanny?' Paddy couldn't resist saying.

Wardle raised two fingers at Paddy and went on. 'As far as we are concerned, it is wrapped up in cotton wool, and must be delivered unharmed. This is the biggest breakthrough we have had so far against the IRA; she has been working under cover for two years in Belfast, and knows more about the organization than McGuinness and Adams combined.'

Paddy let out a long drawn out whistle that in itself signified true amazement. 'Why did she choose to leave now Ken, was she compromised?

Surely those pricks at headquarters must have realized that anyone so close to the really big boys is worth their weight in gold.' Paddy shook his head and clasped his giant hands together, his knuckles turning white with the bone crushing force, his face contorting in a look of rage, as he visualized both Adams and McGuinness, followed immediately, almost superimposed, by an image of both Muscles and Mac. 'Why were those bastards still alive?' he raged internally. 'What was the use of paying Ken 'Sniffer' Wardle to sit around in this make believe army camp, when he could solve the fucking problem from over a mile away with one squeeze of his index finger?'

'You know as much as I do Paddy, probably more; you used to live there don't forget. Belfast may be a big city, but much of the IRA is still small town mentality; nevertheless, the jungle drums within the IRA hierarchy are pretty effective, anyway, word is that she is wanted dead, probably more than your section are Jim.'

'I doubt that Ken,' Killeen smiled, and shook his head as he spoke. 'We and Charnock's team thinned out most of their main shooters; only that bastard O'Malley and his crew were seriously active by the time we left.'

'Do not kid yourself Jim,' countered Wardle, almost in the form of a reprimand. 'As fast as you took them down, more appeared, and more rifles and explosives are coming in every day now; that mad wanker Gadaffi in Libya is flooding the place with them, he really needs sorting.'

'You seem to have forgotten how many men the Regiment and the Israelis have had on that job for the past few years Ken, yet hardly anyone has even got a sniff of him.' Killeen was now feeling much better, his adrenaline pump was starting to work again, and the trembling had stopped. 'Muscles whacked him straight in the chest a couple of years ago, then we found out that he was using a double at the time – the poor bastard. It upset Muscles no end when he found out he had just shot an innocent decoy – some poor bastard who had been put there just to be shot at, simply because he was unlucky enough to look a bit like Gadaffi .'

'Tell me about it,' laughed Wardle. 'I remember it well Jim; I ought to, I set it up; what a fucking cock up that was. I was supposed to make the hit, not Muscles. I had the real Gaddafi in my sights when he fired. I never got the chance to shoot as he disappeared pretty sharpish behind his female bodyguards. Someday Jim – someday – he can't stay lucky forever. The problem now is that he's completely paranoid, and has retreated behind his palace walls and hardly ever comes out. If anyone wants to get to him, they will have to bomb the palace. Even then, killing the bastard isn't guaranteed, as half the place is underground, and most of the time he is either in a bomb proof shelter or hiding in disguise behind a couple of doubles. The only good thing to come out of the fuck up was that the Libyans blamed it on the Yanks. Anyway, back to the package and Paddy's fanny stamps. I will pick you up at 0700 in the morning; we'll collect the weapons, then the package, and be off before the traffic builds up.'

'We're off to Willy Wordsworth country,' laughed Paddy. 'I'm going to wander lonely as a thirsty cloud, straight down to the nearest boozer for a quick 20 pints of Guinness. What's the village pub like Jimbo, you and Julie seem to spend most of your time there when you are on leave – whatever fucking leave is supposed to be? I hope they serve Guinness.'

Neither Wardle nor Killeen doubted Paddy's ability to drink 20 pints of Guinness; his prodigious drinking had created a reputation in both the Para's and the SAS that was legendary. One thing everyone was aware of though was that after twenty or so pints, Paddy could be a bit of a hand-full. On one occasion, whilst a sergeant in the Para's, he had knocked out 5 military policemen, all of them armed with truncheons, before marching himself off to the guardroom, where he demanded to be locked up in case he lost his temper and hurt someone. The next day he was back to private again for the second time.

'Not so quickly Paddy old son, you and I are back up, but firstly we've got a bit of work to do tonight.' Wardle said, at the same time winking at Killeen.

' *Back up*? – *Paddy*? – For Christ sake Ken, don't let him loose with a rifle – he couldn't hit a fucking barn door.'

Paddy and Killeen exchanged snarls.

'I've got to shoot off now and make a phone call to my brother so I can let him know when to expect us, and to sort out the security and equipment.' Wardle said in a matter of fact manner.

'Brother?' Paddy enquired, an inquisitive look crossing his face.

'I'll explain later.' Killeen and Wardle exchanged winks.

The three men parted company, with Wardle heading towards the admin block, and Killeen and Paddy towards the sergeant's mess bar. Both men needed a drink. What the hell was O'Malley doing in England, and why had he brought his 'A' team with him?

Was he really as insane as Wardle had said – as mad as a fucking hatter? Surely, no-one so deranged could possibly escape the clutches of two SAS teams, whose sole purpose in life for several months had been to eliminate him? Maybe Wardle was wrong – what if O'Malley was as sane as the next man? What if he had been playing Wardle all along? Was the famous Sniffer Wardle hooter being deceived?

Both Killeen and Paddy sat through long periods of contemplative silence as they drank their beers; the memory of the deaths of Muscles and Mac at the hands of O'Malley fueling a burning anger.

CHAPTER 10

THE MISSING DICK

Back in their barrack room after a few beers, both Killeen and Paddy again sat in silence, each man deep in his own thoughts. Paddy was the first to speak.

'Fuck me Jim; all the time we spent over in that peat bog I used to call home looking for O'Malley, and now the bastard is over here looking for us.'

'We don't know that yet Paddy, he has no way of knowing that we are here, we've only just found out that we're here ourselves, and I haven't the faintest fucking idea where *here* is; and as for the girl, I just can't see it, unless of course it's true about the mole in MI5. Ken thinks that there is a leak somewhere, he has done ever since O'Malley discovered our source in Southern Ireland. That's what cost Muscles and Mac. That's why they are dead. Still, I'm hoping for a quiet journey back to the Old Manor House, it still holds some fantastic memories for me, and was an important part of my life. I fancy spending a lot of time with Julie, I haven't seen her for months; I'm going to propose again. I reckon that this time she *WILL* say yes. How the hell can she resist me?'

Paddy knew all about Julie. Long days and nights spent under cover on surveillance, or information gathering work, often led to each team member talking about their lives both past and present, and their plans for the future once they had left the army. Paddy was going to become a professional Guinness tester, touring the world, and making sure that all the pubs, and the Guinness that they were serving, were up to scratch. Killeen was simply going to marry Julie and go into the family business, but first, she had to say yes. This time he was quietly confident. He had spoken to her only a couple of days ago, and she had sounded so happy at the thought of spending a few weeks together. He was positive that she would say yes. He had talked about Julie quite a lot during the long, boring, surveillance operations.

He vividly remembered his comments of one particular boring evening, as his unit grew tired of waiting for the would-be "assassins", close to Sheik Armani's desert palace. The full moon had lit up the unit, making them visible from a hundred yards away. Bob Kineer was on lookout, having deployed himself a couple of hundred yards away at the top of a small Wadi. Killeen's unit could scarcely believe that he was even considering becoming a civilian again. He had been born for the army – born to lead – to command. What kind of life could possibly replace such an obvious vocation?

Killeen's mind moved on in full color, the moon providing the perfect back drop to the unfolding, slapstick, Keystone cops event; back to Sheik Armani and Paddy's goat, and suddenly he laughed out loud.

This had been a particularly bad stake out; almost four days in that shit hole of a desert. Four long, hot, sweaty days, and freezing cold nights. All Paddy could talk about was ice cold Guinness under the relentless sun, and red hot barmaids during the freezing nights. The information that had been received from MI6 had been spot on – the timing however had not. Nothing but sand. Sand that managed to get everywhere; up your nose, in your ears, and particularly round the bollocks. Worse still were the flies; millions of the bloody things, where did they all come from? What the hell did they all feed on as maggots? Then the funniest thing the section had ever seen happened.

Paddy had been bent over in the half light, his bare rear end illuminated by the full moon as he took a dump, when this territorial goat had taken exception to him soiling its own little patch of desert, and charged at full speed, butting him right up where the moon wasn't shining. Paddy was sent flying through the air, landing face first in the sand. The goat should have packed in while it was still winning. It didn't, and decided to charge again – that was its big mistake. Paddy lost all semblance of being a professional soldier on a stake out, wrestled it to the ground, and pummeled the living daylights out of it; his camouflaged trousers still round his ankles. The section had laughed so loud they must have heard them back at the Palace. The section christened it "Paddy McGinty's Goat".

Everyone at the Hereford SAS headquarters knew about Paddy McGinty's goat. Everyone in the SAS knew about Paddy McGinty's goat. No-one ever mentioned it within earshot of Paddy though – not even the high ranking officers.

'Do you think she will agree to marry you this time Jim?' Paddy asked.

'I hope so kid, I can't really keep on doing this job for much longer, this week will probably be my last. Ever since Muscles and Mac died, my heart has not been in it at all; my mind doesn't react instinctively anymore; I find that I am questioning every decision I make; if I get it wrong, who else is going to die?' Killeen suddenly realized that he had been saying the same thing almost word for word for quite some time now. Did he really mean it, or was he looking for an escape route – a reason to get out of the mob? Maybe he was simply trying to punish himself for the death of his friends – his section – his responsibility. Maybe he was simply scared, and could no longer hack it! He should have spotted the set up. The section's life was in his hands and he had failed them.

'You DID NOT get it wrong Jim,' said Paddy a little too loudly. 'We were set up. We checked it out for ages before moving into position; it was NOT your fault. The intelligence we had been receiving had always been spot on; none of us could ever have expected O' fucking Malley to pick up on a family member. Still, what kind of fucking sick animal does that to his own uncle? When they found his body, they reckoned that he had been tortured for hours, they even cut off his dick and stuffed it in his mouth. That would certainly have been that mad bastard Murphy.'

Killeen screwed up his face, and squeezing his lips tightly together, shut his eyes in revulsion at the thought of anyone cutting off a dick and forcing the owner to eat it.

'It worked though Paddy,' Killeen's eyes were still firmly closed and his face contorted as he spoke. 'Not one *DICKYBIRD* came from the south after that, everyone was too scared, also they didn't *find* his body; it was delivered by some poor shit whose family they were holding hostage. You are right though – both O'Malley and Mad Mitch Murphy are two very fucking sick bastards.'

'What do you reckon about this place Jim?' Paddy asked, at the same time switching on the television. 'Everyone seems to have a Northern Irish accent, it's like being back home again. I'm almost expecting someone to say "Good morning you Fenian Bastard".'

'Not sure kid, it has got to have something to do with Intelligence. I suppose that if you pull in enough Paddies, and stick them all under one roof, you are more likely to build up a clearer picture. I recognized a couple of the plain clothes guys from my days at the Intelligence HQ, yet I must confess,

I never knew anything about this place. Sometimes, the Intelligence services play these things very close to their chests: they can't afford to let the IRA find them; same as the place that we are delivering the package to tomorrow. What a bloody target that would be for them – the cream of British Intelligence all under one roof. The nearest that I can come up with is that it's to do with preparing people for undercover work in Ireland, that's why they are all Paddies.'

'Fucking television, it's fucking useless. It just keeps going round and round.' With that, Paddy brought a giant fist down with considerable force onto the top of the television, resulting in an electrical bang, and a puff of smoke, followed by a completely blank screen. 'That's fucked it. I was looking forward to watching the Man United match tonight.'

'Typical Paddy,' Killeen said, laughing out loud as he did so. 'None of you know fuck all about football. You Catholics support Man United, Liverpool or Glasgow Celtic; and the equally stupid Protestant Paddies support Man City, Everton or Glasgow Rangers.'

'I didn't know that Jim. I only support them because my dad does.'

'Really Paddy, sometimes you amaze me. Have you never seen the dozens of buses and coaches that leave Belfast every Saturday morning? Same thing happens at Dublin. They are all on their way to Glasgow, Manchester, or Liverpool to watch their team play football. You won't find Union Jack flags and Irish flags on the same bus, that's for sure. All you get are a bunch of pissed up Paddies on some kind of a religious crusade masquerading as football.'

'I never really found a problem with the Protestants as I got older Jim; if they called me a Fenian bastard, I just belted them, they never did it again.'

'Yes Paddy, I can well imagine.' Killeen's face now sporting a big knowing grin. 'I would think that they quite enjoyed that.'

Eyes closed, Killeen and Paddy both sat in silence for a few minutes before opening them at virtually the same time; both men had been deep in thought.

'I can't get it out of my mind Jim.' Paddy was shaking his head as he spoke, at the same time looking up at the ceiling.

'What, O'Malley's kid? That was what I was thinking about Pads.'

'No, that poor bastard in Malaya that Ken told us about. I wonder if he lived?' Paddy grimaced, at the same time a look of disgust crossing his face.

'If he did, I bet he has no kids.' replied Killeen with a chuckle.

'Sick bastard.' Paddy shouted out loud.

'Who, me or O'Malley?' Killeen feigned a hurt expression.

Both men burst out laughing.

Wardle had told them the story over breakfast a couple of hours earlier, in order to emphasize the sick and dangerous mind that they were dealing with. O'Malley's section had been deployed in the Malayan jungle, during the insurgency troubles that were going on with the ruling British, when they had been ambushed, and come under fire. One of his men had been killed during the battle, but they had managed to capture two of the wounded insurgents, which they now had tied to a couple of trees. Despite a few verbal threats, followed by violent physical interrogation attempts, both men had refused to talk. Up stepped O'Malley, took out his knife, cut off the older man's dick, and stuck it into his mouth, before making him chew it.

The information received from the by now all too willing younger insurgent, had led the section to a small village in a jungle clearing where the rest of the insurgents were supposed to be hiding.

'O'Malley went fucking berserk,' Wardle had spat out the words. 'He gunned down every man, woman, and child in the village. He even shot their dogs and pigs. He fucking loved it. The insurgents had left hours before we even got there. I should have shot the bastard there and then myself.'

'The fucking blood thirsty bastard. Why didn't you report him?' Paddy's voice was tinged with anger as he spoke at full volume, both of his fists clenched. 'I would have ripped his fucking head off.'

'I couldn't Paddy, he saved my life twice; he may have been bordering on madness even then, but he was fucking good beyond belief. He would completely disappear from view for hours on end, yet he could still cut your throat before you saw him. In the jungle, he could become completely invisible, and still be no more than two or three yards away.'

'What about the other men in the section; they saw what happened, why did none of them speak up?' asked Killeen.

'I suppose in retrospect, none of us wanted to be seen as having had any involvement in the massacre; it was much easier to blame the whole thing on the Commie insurgents, and also, better with us than against us. There was always an all pervading feeling of fear whenever he was around, it never left him whether he was on active service or simply sat in the mess. It was ever present – an unseen, over-riding aura – a smell of death that lingered long after he had left. It was nothing tangible, you could never quite put your finger on what it was, but it was always there. Even if you hadn't noticed him, you could feel him; you could almost smell him. That's where my nickname 'Sniffer' Wardle came from. I always knew he would flip one day; all it needed was for someone to throw the switch, the death of his kid was the switch – the trigger – the none-too gentle nudge that pushed him over the edge.'

With that, he had thrown a glance at Paddy.

Killeen saw the glance. 'How do *you* know Ken? Only Paddy and I saw his kid's body, even the rest of the section still think that I killed him?'

'It's called modus operandi Jim; a head facing near backwards? Not a common sight when you come to think about it, only one man I know operates that way.'

Killeen understood – Paddy's calling card.

Paddy was now looking up at the sergeant's mess ceiling, deep in thought. Wardle and Killeen smiled at each other. It was unusual for Paddy to think before speaking; something serious must be going through his often confused Irish brain. He eventually broke the silence.

'Ken, didn't some stupid yank do something similar a few years ago in Vietnam? I can vaguely remember reading about it.'

'You are talking about Calley and the My Lai massacre I presume Paddy,' Wardle replied. 'That was a different situation to the O'Malley one. Several of Calley's men were really pissed off because they had been taking heavy losses, usually by an enemy that they couldn't even see. The unit eventually cracked, and in frustration, opened up on the villagers – possibly under orders – no one knows. We however had been up the bush for weeks without casualties until that morning. None of us fired a single shot other than O'Malley, and by the time we caught up with him, it was too fucking late – everyone was dead.'

> Lt. William Calley was charged with six specifications of premeditated murder in the death of 109 Vietnamese civilians. Calley, a platoon leader in Charlie Company, 1st Battalion, 20th Infantry, had led his men in a massacre of Vietnamese civilians, including women and children, at the My Lai village on March 16, 1968. The company had been conducting a

> "search and destroy mission" in search of the 48th Viet Cong (VC) Local Force Battalion. Calley's unit entered the village, but found only women, children, and old men. Frustrated by unanswered losses due to snipers and mines, the soldiers took out their anger on the villagers, indiscriminately shooting people as they ran from their huts. They then systematically rounded up the survivors, where they allegedly lead them to a nearby ditch where they were shot. Reportedly, the killing was only stopped when Warrant Officer Hugh Thompson, an aero-scout helicopter pilot, landed his helicopter between the Americans and the fleeing South Vietnamese, confronting the soldiers and blocking them from further action against the villagers. The incident was subsequently covered up, but eventually came to light a year later. Calley was originally sentenced to 20 years, but was released by President Nixon after serving less than 4.

Both Killeen and Paddy were still in silent contemplative mode, when there came a gentle knock on the barrack room door, and for the second time that morning, it crashed open, and in jumped Wardle, at the same time screaming 'HELLO'. Once again, he wanted to check the two men's responses.

Paddy glared. 'Fucking hell Ken, you frightened me shitless – if you do that again, I'm going to punch your fucking lights out.'

'Don't worry little boy; that naughty Mr. O'Malley will not hurt you as long as uncle Ken is here to protect you,' Wardle said with an exaggerated grin. 'Anyway, I thought that I would give you a little time to digest what I told you earlier on; also, I had to make a couple more calls to both MI5 and 6. The incompetent idiots can't decide who is responsible for the operation, and asked me for more info. I told them to bugger off and sort themselves out. It looks like we're on our own from here on in. I really don't trust either outfit; someone is leaking info to the IRA, so they are getting bugger all off me.'

'What happened to that man's dick Ken, you know, the one that O'Malley cut off in Malaya, do you think he sewed it back on?' Paddy grabbed Wardle's groin as he spoke.

'I doubt it Paddy, O'Malley made him chew it and swallow it; he then slit both their throats as we left, and if you don't let go of my balls pretty quickly, I will cut your fucking dick off.'

After a none too gentle squeeze of Wardle's genitals, Paddy released his grip, and almost shouted. 'Fucking hell, I think I would want my throat cut if someone cut my dick off.'

'It wouldn't make a lot of difference to you any way Pads; ever since that goat shagged you in the desert, you've barely been with a woman.'

'Bollocks to you Wardle, where do you think I was when those bastards picked me up yesterday? I barely had time for a drink and a shag before they came round. I should have told them to sod off.'

'Anyway Jim, now we've had the run down on Paddy's sex life – or should I say lack of it; I am of course assuming that he was with that barmaid with the tash and the gigantic tits – can you remember her Jim? She's the one that he usually empties his bollocks into when he's on leave. You now know what you are dealing with regarding a certain madman. I think that now's the time to work out how to deal with it.' Wardle grinned at Paddy, who was holding two fingers in the air.

Killeen had his head tilted at a funny angle, and was pursing his lips whilst at the same time closing his eyes. He was never aware that he was doing it, even though both Julie and Paddy had commented on it many times.

'Here we go again Ken, he's just slipping that inbred, upper class, public schoolboy brain into gear; the rest of us call it thinking.' Paddy quipped.

'My God Paddy,' Wardle grinned as he spoke. 'I'm stuck between a streetwise, bog oil gobbling Irish moron one side, and an educated, upper class idiot, on the other – what chance have I got? Let's get down to the business of the 'A' team; specifically O'Malley. The others play follow my leader and take orders, but occasionally Mad Mitch cuts loose and does his own thing. He is as dangerous as he is unpredictable. He is probably best thought of as an O'Malley clone; obviously not so skilled, but dangerous nevertheless. He's a born killer who loves his work. His major weakness is that he's hot headed, headstrong, and often works to his own agenda. He also takes risks, stupid risks: he wants to be a somebody – *an IRA STAR*.

O'Malley however, is a different animal to anything that you have ever come across. He never takes risks; he is cool, calculating, and lethal; the best marine I have ever seen, and certainly the best shot.'

'After you Ken – he has never beaten you; you seem to be forgetting that. I have seen everything relating to your military record; I even lunched with your father, the Major, before you joined the unit, so don't be so modest; no one has ever beaten you.' Killeen interrupted.

'That's where you're wrong Jimbo. Sure I always beat him on the ranges, but in the field – in a contact, I didn't even come close – no-one did. I carefully chose my targets. O'Malley shot anything that moved, almost by instinct. I once saw him put a bullet straight through a kid, a little girl, in order to kill the man standing behind her.'

'Fucking hell Ken, I would have turned his head round to face his arse.'

'Thought about it Paddy, more than once; guess I just never got round to it. I saw him shoot a pig once at about 100 yards.'

'I can do that.' Paddy spoke with a triumphant note in his voice, and a big grin on his face.

'You couldn't hit a fucking barn door, never mind a pig, and you know it.' Killeen could be merciless regarding Paddy's shooting experience.

'Neither could you after 20 pints of Guinness and a bottle of Jameson's 12 year old finest.'

'He has got a point Jim,' Wardle grinned and continued. 'Anyway, as I was saying, a little pig ran across the road at full speed in this Malay village. Well, it wasn't really a road, more a single lane dirt track. It was obviously scared shitless by all the shooting that was going on, and was really moving. O'Malley swung his rifle to his shoulder – followed through – and fired; all in less than a second. He never even looked down the sights. The pig dropped like a stone, absolutely dead center of the head. No man on earth can make that shot.'

'Lucky shot?' Killeen asked, a whimsical yet slightly worried expression appearing on his face.

'It could have been Jim, but I don't think so. When O'Malley fired, someone, or something, always died; he smelled of death – I noticed it the first time I met him. There are two important points to fix in your mind about him.

Number one – he can make himself almost completely invisible, and can lie perfectly still for hours. I have seen snakes and scorpions crawl all over him, and he never moved so much as a muscle; he is the perfect sniper, a complete killing machine.'

'Pointless searching for him then if he's invisible.' Paddy said sarcastically. 'That's probably why we never found him in Ireland – we couldn't fucking see him.'

'Not true Paddy old son.' Wardle smiled as he shook his head very slowly. 'I, and only I, can always find him; no one else ever could. It took a fair bit of time, but I eventually worked it out. It used to drive him mad, as he could never figure out how I did it, so I never told him. His only weakness in the field, is that he never wraps his weapon to camouflage it. He always prefers to use camouflage paint. Tomorrow morning Jim, you will be in possession of a pair of binoculars that eliminate color; you will see everything in black and white. If you look in the right place, the barrel of his rifle will show up as a straight black line; he always lies prone, with his rifle in front of him ready to fire.'

'Second world war stuff.'

'Exactly Jim; once you take the camouflage coloring away, you will be left with the straight black line of the barrel lying on the ground, nature rarely does straight lines.'

'I can't see how that works.' Paddy scratched his head and shook it.

'Well Pads, photographs taken from planes during world war two, were often viewed by color – blind analyst, who saw a completely different picture to the rest of us. They were not fooled by camouflage or colors blending in with the surroundings; they only saw the different arrangement of the camouflage, and could easily make out the straight lines that were covered by it. O'Malley never wraps his rifle in issue camouflage, so the camouflage paint on the barrel will disappear when viewed through these binoculars. You will see nothing but a straight black line.'

'I knew that,' a big grin creased Paddy's bearded face. 'I just thought that it was something complicated.'

All three men laughed.

'You said that there were two important points.' Killeen spoke in a quiet serious voice, looking deeply into Wardle's eyes for any sign of doubt at what he was telling them.

'Yes Jim; the second is the most important one, and may well save your life. When setting an ambush, O'Malley always positions himself 1000 yards from the target, give or take 20 yards or so; his sense of direction and his perception of distance is phenomenal.'

'Why does he do that?' Killeen looked puzzled, a frown crossing his forehead.

'I don't know for sure Jim, he just does, always has done. I suppose that he feels safe from any returned fire at that range; very few people can make a shot at that distance, especially if you can't see him. Like I told you, he never, ever, takes chances.'

Paddy clenched both fists tightly. 'Christ Ken, that was about the distance to the woods when Muscles and Mac were shot; we couldn't follow it up as it was on the southern side of the border.'

'That's why he chose it Paddy. I told you at the time that there was only one shooter. I know him better than he knows himself – clever, cunning, and ruthless, but not infallible. I'm probably the only person in the world who knows what he is going to do before he knows it himself.'

'What are the chances of him going after the girl Ken? What do MI5 think, or should it be MI6? Just who the hell is in on it? Do they even know themselves? If MI5 are supposed to deal with internal problems, why are 6 involved?' Killeen sounded annoyed.

'It's pretty much to do with the movement of weapons Jim; this trade is international as you know. The weapons and explosives are coming in from America, Libya, and the Eastern bloc; the semtex, which is the most dangerous and difficult to track, comes in from Czechoslovakia via Libya, and is paid for by either American or Gadaffi money. As for him going after the girl; neither 6 nor 5 have a clue. There has been zero feedback from Ireland; everyone is lying low; O'Malley saw to that when he cut his uncle's dick off. That was one disgusting yet brilliantly effective move, everyone in Northern Ireland knew about it within hours. We do have one report of another hit team having entered the country, but as yet it is unconfirmed, the 'A' team though are definitely here. Charnock's D2 team has been recalled from leave, and are covering the Prime Minister. Special Branch has got round the clock on all prominent MP's and their families.'

'Come on now Sniffer Wardle,' laughed Paddy. 'What exactly does that super sensitive, disgustingly miss shaped hooter of yours tell you? Have a good long sniff.'

'It's either the girl or the Prime Minister.' Wardle's reply came immediately.

'Which one is it Ken?' Killeen tried to hide the mixture of fear and excitement in his voice.

Wardle close his eyes for a few seconds before speaking. 'I can smell O'Malley; he is close. He would not need a 4 man team for the Prime Minister, that's a one man job, and where possible he likes to work alone.'

Both Jim Killeen and Paddy Jackson felt a shiver go through their bodies. Paddy's shiver was one of anticipation – of revenge, for the deaths of his friends Muscles and Mac – Killeen wasn't sure of his own reaction – it was a mixture of both excitement and fear. He was suddenly conscious of his heart both racing and pounding – pounding so loudly that surely Paddy and Wardle could hear it.

Sergeant Major Ken 'Sniffer' Wardle never missed – either with his rifle – or with his nose. There was a smell of death in the air, and Wardle was on to it.

'I've got to go now and make a few calls to MI5, 6, and base.' Wardle stood and made to leave the room, before turning round, and almost as an afterthought adding. 'If anything else comes up, I'll let you know later. Both of you be ready at 1900 tonight, and try to look normal; get a shave and a trim. We're going to town for a recce, and any resemblance to a couple of human beings instead of 2 Yetis would be useful if we don't want to be noticed.'

'A couple of Guinness as well Ken?' Paddy asked hopefully.

'Maybe a couple Paddy, but not your usual 20 pints of bog oil that's for sure, we don't know what the situation is.'

'Couple of light weights the pair of you – neither of you can handle a gallon or two of man's drink, so I've got to suffer for being out with a couple of poofs.' Paddy pretended to look hurt.

When Wardle left the room, he was concerned, not just about the 'A' team, but about Killeen. He had looked into his eyes when he had jumped into the room, and he did not like what he had seen. He saw genuine fear. He saw the 1000 yard stare. He had co-ordinated the team for two years, and Captain James Killeen did not know fear. He hoped that he was wrong – if he wasn't – O'Malley would eat him alive.

Killeen was the only man capable of carrying out the plan; he was O'Malley's equal in every respect, but only if his mind was functioning at 100%. There was only so much that could be planned. O'Malley was cunning, meticulous, and devious; he could also improvise as the circumstance demanded.

Killeen could also improvise, and was at his best thinking on his feet; that was why he had to be kept in the dark. Wardle needed him to be both proactive and reactive – he needed him to act on instinct. There was no other way, or O'Malley would smell a rat, and like all rats, if spooked, he would bolt for cover. Once he was back below the radar, he would become ever more dangerous and unpredictable.

Too much planning had gone into this operation, and too much was at stake for it to fail. O'Malley had to follow the trail – he had to fit in with the overall plan without ever being aware that he was being led.

Without him even being aware that there ever was a plan.

The same applied to Killeen. Wardle was concerned that maybe he had just signed Killeen's death warrant.

Two of the world's finest military units had just spent months searching for the rogue Marine, and all they had to show for it were body bags – body bags containing the hunters and not the hunted.

CHAPTER 11

O'MALLEY

Michael Patrick O'Malley was a Royal Marine Commando and SBS (Special Boat Squadron) specialist gone rogue.

Two days after his 14 year old son had been killed just outside of Portadown in Northern Ireland, he had gone AWOL, and disappeared from the face of the earth. The army had tried to pass the blame for the boy's death on to the Protestant Loyalists. The men of the Special Forces knew the truth, as did O'Malley – civilian militia do not break necks – Special Forces are taught that skill, and one man in particular was noted for it.

O'Malley swore revenge, not just on Killeen's D1 unit, but on the whole of the British army, and on any Protestant that got in his way. He returned to Ireland and joined the IRA. His Irish superiors feared him as much as the British did, but his specialist skills were much in demand.

"A ballot box in one hand and an Armalite rifle in the other", was the IRA mantra.

O'Malley did not want an Armalite rifle. His 'baby' was the M14 American sniper rifle. He was very good with it, and he wanted four of them – he got them.

He quickly gathered together a team of young volunteers, and took them south of the border for training; there, he had a completely free rein to do as he pleased. The Southern Irish authorities did not want to upset or antagonize the IRA for fear of further bombings in the south. The last series of bombs that had exploded in the Southern Ireland capital, Dublin, had done immense damage to the tourist trade that they had been actively cultivating for years – any further problems, and all those rich Americans doing their once in a lifetime pilgrimage, may just stay away instead of searching for their ancestral roots.

O'Malley's 'A' Team, as he liked to call them, and everyone else now knew them, consisted of his three best recruits;

Michael O'Riley

A quiet, studious, 24 year old: A bit of a loner, who was quite happy reading books when not 'working'. It was his love of history, Irish history in particular, that had fed his sense of injustice, and first attracted him to the IRA. No one had ever taken Michael to be a violent man – he wasn't. He had informed O'Malley that he would only ever shoot members of the 'occupying' army – never civilians, simply because they went to the wrong church. This was accepted, so he rarely crossed the border into the north, and was of limited use to the team whenever assassinating Protestants was the objective.

He was however extremely skilled at bomb making – not the run of the mill, straight forward, explosive and timer bombs; his specialty was the particularly sophisticated booby trap bomb, as several dead and maimed British soldiers had discovered. He had been taught by Patrick Flynn, a master bomb maker in Southern Ireland. Both O'Riley and Flynn were high on the list of targets for the British military. Knowing this, neither man ventured north of the border without armed IRA back up. As long as they stayed south of the border, they were completely invulnerable.

Sean Fitzpatrick

A happy go lucky 26 year old extrovert, completely opposite in character to O'Riley. He could easily slip across the border without being noticed, and was regarded as the eyes and ears of the team. This outward friendliness was however quite deceptive. Both his younger brother and his father had been tortured and shot whilst out drinking one night by a Protestant hit team. Now he, and his twin sister, both hated all Protestants, and often their planning revolved around their next killing. His twin sister, Mary, was much more fanatical about the cause than Sean had ever been: she was also much more ruthless and deadly. Mary was the brains behind many of the 'A' team's assassinations; she was also very high on the military target list. Little was known about Mary; she was almost a ghost like figure, coming and going as she pleased, and almost certainly operating under several different aliases and identities. Neither her photograph nor her fingerprints were known to the British; even the undercover informants were completely in the dark as to the identity of the mysterious Mary Fitzpatrick.

Mad Mitch Murphy

The name was more than appropriate. 23 year old Mitch had always been a tear away. He had killed his first Protestant whilst still a teenager, and his first British soldier on his 21st birthday.

'My number 1 birthday present to me.' he had called it, and boasted frequently about its significance and method of execution.

So far, he had 11 confirmed kills to his name – 8 Protestants and 3 soldiers; these figures did not include the many deaths and injuries caused by the bombs that he had planted. He was a born killer – no fear – no emotion – no remorse. Without THE TROUBLES, he would have been a serial killer in waiting – a time bomb waiting to go off – with THE TROUBLES, he was in his element, and with every life that he claimed, more and more young Catholic men saw him as a hero, and swelled the ever growing ranks of the IRA.

O'Malley saw the impetuousness of Mitch as a potential weakness in the team. He also saw *himself* as a young man. *HE had been restrained by military rules – for Mitch, there were no rules – nothing to restrain his bloodlust.*

O'Malley's early life in Portadown, Northern Ireland, had been pretty uneventful, until a late night drinking session with a group of semi drunken friends, had lead to a major fight involving what seemed to be half of the town's young men. The TROUBLES hadn't yet begun, but tensions between the town's Catholic and Protestant youths often resulted in fights, particularly when alcohol was involved. He was 17 years old, and, bordering on 6ft 4 inches, towered above all of his contemporaries. Having avoided any form of involvement in the fight, he was knocked unconscious from behind by someone brandishing a broken leg from a bar stool, resulting in several days in hospital before he regained consciousness. A blood clot had developed on his brain, and had to be removed by surgery.

From that point onwards, the previously mild and friendly O'Malley underwent a major personality change. He became completely intolerant of all forms of criticism and measured argument, and began to exhibit bouts of extreme and uncontrollable anger and violence. After a few minor skirmishes with the police, each successive one resulting in ever more violence, it was recommended by the magistrate that he channeled his aggression in a different direction, or the alternative was borstal, followed by the inevitable path to prison.

He joined the Royal Marines, and during the early days, became the best of friends with Ken 'Sniffer' Wardle. The two young recruits both passed the selection process with distinction, but Wardle was always wary: there was something about O'Malley that concerned him. He could never figure out quite what it was. O'Malley was always clean and well groomed, and outwardly seemed to be a perfectly normal recruit: Wardle's nose detected something different about him. It was to be quite a few years before Wardle began to understand the significance of this difference.

It was the smell of death. It followed O'Malley everywhere he went, and as his insanity deepened, so did Wardle's powers of detection.

Wardle always knew that one day he would have to kill O'Malley.

CHAPTER 12

THE FIRST CASUALTIES

Wardle arrived at the barracks spot on 1900, he was never late, anyone below his rank was guaranteed an almighty bollocking if they were even a few seconds behind schedule. Killeen and Paddy were ready, being well aware of how prickly Wardle could be over a few seconds.

'Where are we off to then Ken?' Paddy asked, trying not to sound like an excited teenager going out for his first ever drink of beer. 'I hope they sell Guinness where ever it is, I'm dying for a session.'

'Easy tiger, there will be very little bog oil for you tonight, we are working – there may be unfriendly eyes watching out for us.' Wardle screwed up his eyes as he spoke.

'What do unfriendly eyes look like Ken?'

'Like the two I'm about to poke these two fingers into Paddy if you don't shut up.'

Wardle made a lunge for him, but was much too slow. Paddy's boxing skills and reflexes were far too well honed. Many a hard Para from the Regiment had chanced their arm against him; only once; no one ever wanted a rematch, either in or out of the ring. Despite his 6ft 6 and a 1/2in size, and 17 stone of bone and muscle, Paddy moved every bit as quick as any flyweight, and punched like the kick of a mule.

'What exactly are we looking out for Ken?' asked Killeen.

'Unfriendly eyes.' replied Paddy, once again skillfully avoiding the not unexpected dig in the ribs from Wardle.

It was quite a few minutes before three very large, very fit, and very dangerous men had stopped laughing, and made their way into the Butchers Arms.

'Same again lads.' Paddy downed his second pint of Guinness in as many minutes.

'Do you realize Paddy, you just drunk that pint in less than half the time it took the girl to pour it into the glass?'

'The glass was only half as thirsty as me Jimbo.'

Paddy was really on form tonight; all three men could have drunk and drunk. Wardle raised his glass as the third round of drinks arrived.

'To absent friends.'

'To Muscles and Mac.' They all said in harmony, as visions of many a late night drinking session as a complete section flashed before them.

Throughout the Regiment, bouts of heavy drinking followed most of the men around when "stood down", particularly when periods of danger had been involved. These "sessions" were often the only form of release valve open to them before their next assignment.

'Payback time.' growled Paddy.

Wardle and Killeen weren't so sure. Paddy's confidence was limitless: he had never been shot, or received so much as a scratch on active service, other than the little incident with the goat in the desert. There hadn't been any physical damage, but his pride had been severely dented by the recalcitrant goat. Apart from the gypsy, no-one had ever even come close to inflicting pain on Paddy, either in, or out of the boxing ring. Paddy felt invulnerable – Paddy was invulnerable, and had only felt real fear in his life on one occasion; that was because of the "Fucking Great Shark", that had kept him company for the whole of the enforced quarter of a mile swim during an emergency evacuation from Africa.

Killeen and Paddy both felt it at the same time. The room at the Butchers Arms was warm and friendly, yet their bodies were suddenly chilled, almost icy. It was as if their blood was about to freeze in their veins. Three words were all it took from 'Sniffer' Wardle.

'O'Malley is here.'

Killeen was the first to speak. 'Can you see him Ken?' He asked in hushed tones.

'No – I just know it.'

'How?' A tremor entered Killeen's voice.

'I can smell death; told you, I always could whenever he was around.'

'Do you think he knows that we're here?' Paddy quietly asked.

'I doubt it – the girl is nearby though – she's what he's after for sure.' Wardle paused for a few seconds before continuing. 'He is close – very close – I can almost feel him.'

All three men sat in silence for several minutes, each one deep in his own thoughts; each man trying to figure out a plan of action; each man looking for a recognizable face – O'Malley – O'Riley – Fitzpatrick – Mad Mitch.

Killeen spoke first. 'Has she any protection with her?' His initial shock was rapidly beginning to subside, an unexpected surge of confidence – bravado, surged through his body. He was beginning to feel and act like an SAS officer again – the adrenaline was again pumping. He suddenly exuded his normal persona, his personal force field was beginning to return, and he was beginning to feel like the Captain James Killeen of old.

Wardle immediately felt his own confidence surge; his nose instinctively detecting the reappearance of what had always made Killeen special among his contemporaries. Maybe O'Malley would not have things all his own way after all. A fully functional Killeen was in every respect O'Malley's equal.

'One, maybe two Special Branch. I did ask for more, but they wanted to keep it as low profile as possible. If O'Malley finds her, he will swat them like flies. We have got to move her tonight; if not – you know what will happen. – Why the hell didn't we come tooled up? We're not picking the weapons up until tomorrow.'

Paddy sat upright in his chair and spoke with menace. 'We did come tooled up. I'm here; and if I get my hands on him tonight, his eyes will be looking down at his fucking arse instead of his dick. On second thoughts, I might just pull his fucking head right off.'

'Cheers Paddy, I think Ken and I will stick around here and have a few more pints while you pop out and pull his head off.' Killeen said, trying to disguise the slight tremor in his voice. It was no longer a tremor of fear, nor bravado, more an expectation of things to come; a genuine desire to finish the job that his D1 section had begun several months earlier.

Wardle laughed out loud – not too loud: 'He is nearly as big as you are Paddy – 6 foot 4 and a marine boxing champion.'

'Nobody has ever beat me yet except for that fucking Gippo, and he had to punch me in the balls.'

Now it was Killeen's turn to laugh. 'I've seen you make a few bollocks swell up yourself these last few years Pads. Can you remember that little problem you had with those Aussies in Singapore that time? What was that bar called now? Somewhere in Sembawang; Axe and something or other, or was it the Crown and something – yea that's it, Crown and Anchor. I had to pay for the fucking damage before the Chink behind the bar called the MPs.'

'Yea, I remember it well – too bloody well; the rest of you bastards just sat there drinking and laughing while I had to sort it.'

'It was your fault Paddy!' Killeen said indignantly, winking at Wardle as he spoke.

'How was I to know that she was with that big ugly Abbo bastard, she kept on giving me the eye?'

'Probably couldn't believe what she was seeing.' interrupted Wardle.

'Bollocks; anyway Jim, that wasn't in the ring, and there were 4 of them – bollocks were a legitimate target. If I ever get my hands on that fucking Gippo though, I'm…'

'I know,' laughed Wardle. 'You're going to turn his head round so his eyes will be looking down at his arse instead of his dick – correct?'

'Paddy's calling card.' laughed Killeen.

'I might just pull HIS fucking head off as well as O'Malley's,' Paddy grinned. 'The bastard spoiled my good looks when he broke my nose, I should have been a film star.'

All three men knew that they were simply relieving nervous tension; there was work to be done. Each man pondered as to how O'Malley could possibly have got to know of the girl's location? There had to be a leak, but where could it have come from? The only military personnel involved were the three of them, the base coordinator at Hereford, and MI5/6. Even the colonel at the camp didn't have a clue as to what the operation was. Killeen was sure of that. All Colonel Blackford knew was that Special Forces had to deliver a package, and that it might be dangerous. Once he had mentioned the word 'dangerous', he really didn't want to know anything else.

On seeing the fearful look in the colonel's eyes, and the nervous way that he had kept stroking his chin and rubbing his hands together, Killeen concluded that he had probably sailed all the way from Sandhurst officer training academy to colonel without ever getting his feet wet. The poor man had never experienced the discomfort of lying concealed for days on end; days and nights of endless rain, cold, even snow. He almost certainly had never experienced the fear, even terror, of staring down the barrel of an AK47 held by a terrified kid. He also probable earned twice as much as he did, 'Lucky Bastard', as Paddy would have said.

'Was he really a lucky bastard?' Killeen had pondered. 'What was the point of being in the army if you were never to experience fear; surely that comes with the territory. Why join up in the first place?' Yes, he had needed an outlet for all his pent up energy, and he always looked forward to his next assignment, but there was nothing in this world that came close to the exhilaration – the adrenaline rush that came together with the fear of death. So far he had been fortunate, all three of them had been lucky, none of them had ever taken a bullet. O'Malley had never shot at them though. He had shot at Muscles and Mac. O'Malley never missed when in the field. Sniffer Wardle had told them that.

'Invisible my arse,' Paddy almost shouted out of the blue, as the effects of the drink started to kick in on his empty stomach. 'I'm definitely going to pull his fucking head off for killing Muscles and Mac – let's go and find some food first, I haven't eaten since breakfast, I could eat a scabby goat.'

'Paddy McGinty's Goat?' – the three men laughed in harmony at Wardle's comment.

Killeen made a clicking sound with his mouth, before turning to Paddy. 'Calm down and slow down Pads, we have got to think this one through. If Sniffer's hooter is right, and the 'A' team are here, what is their next move? Got to pass this one over to you Ken, you have spent more of your life with O'Malley than you have with your own mother.'

'That's probably true Jim. Marine Commando training at 19, sniper school, SBS course, Malaya, Aden, Cyprus, Oman, Yemen, Africa, Ireland, and now the fucking Butchers Arms.'

'Is he that close?'

'He is that close Paddy – I told you, I can smell death.'

Ken Wardle closed his eyes for a quite a few seconds as the other two men scanned the almost full public bar for signs of a familiar face. After what seemed like ages, Wardle opened his eyes, and shaking his head, again raised the question of a leak. Both Killeen and Paddy had to agree; it had to have come from either MI5 or MI6, there was simply no one else in the loop – no one, it was water tight.

Wardle continued. 'Well then, we do have a bit of time before they can possibly find her, only base and myself know which safe house she is in.

Even the colonel doesn't know, in fact, he specifically ordered me not to tell him. I asked him for a couple of his men to work the street in plain clothes and he refused point blank – scared shitless if you ask me.'

'What about Special Branch, didn't you say that they were looking after her? – They know.'

Wardle banged his closed fist on the table, 'Oh fuck, why did you have to mention that shower Paddy? I had forgotten about them; she might as well have a tracker up her arse. We already know that there's a leak deep inside Special Branch; they have more Paddy bog dwellers than Englishmen working for them. We've got to make a move now before it is too late – shit, I was banking on O'Malley not knowing where we'd stashed her. If he knows that, she's already dead, and we've got a bit of explaining to do to the high ups.'

The three men left the Butchers Arms at roughly one minute intervals, closely observing anyone that walked by as they went, and made their way independently up the street for a couple of hundred yards to a quite recently built block of flats. They moved carefully and quietly so as not to draw attention to themselves. To an untrained eye, there was nothing suspicious about their movement; one man would pause for a minute or so in a shop door way, watching carefully as the next man moved from parked car to street corner, and then into position.

To a trained military eye, each position taken up gave covering fire for the next man's movement. To that same trained military eye, the assumption would be that they were armed. They were not armed, and felt very vulnerable. Without weapons, they were playing a very deadly game of bluff.

'Third floor, room 308,' Wardle had said. 'We'd better take the lift or we'll be like sitting ducks walking up these stairs without weapons.'

As they entered the lift, the icy cold blood started to flow through their veins once again. Killeen's hands started to tremble – Paddy clenched his giant fists.

'We're too late.' Wardle had said. 'He's been and gone. I can feel him. I can smell death.'

Sniffer Wardle's famed nose was right. The door to room 308 was slightly ajar, and inside lay two dead men and a young woman, each one with a bullet hole pretty much in the centre of their forehead.

'Oh shit.' Wardle said out loud, as he banged his fist against the door. 'Poor girl. I picked her myself – so young – so pretty – and so brave. She volunteered you know. No matter how dangerous we told her the job was, she never flinched or hesitated for a second.'

'You mean she was a decoy Ken?'

'Yes Jim, a very pretty, very brave decoy, now do you believe what I told you about O'Malley? No morals and no conscience. At least we know that the Prime Minister can sleep easy tonight – we now know his target.'

As the three men left the room; each one taking one final look at the three dead bodies, and the three expanding pools of blood, which were now meeting in the center of the room in a random death like embrace, Wardle remarked in a completely unemotional way. 'Close the door Paddy, we don't want the local plod involved, the papers will have a field day. I'll call in the cleaners when we get back to camp.'

Paddy was confused and shocked. 'How is all this going to be explained to their relatives?' After all, this was England and not Ireland. Three live people didn't just disappear or accidentally shoot themselves – especially in the middle of their foreheads?

'Don't concern yourself Pads, the cleaners will see to all that; probably a car accident and a fire, or something like that; something to obscure or hide the hole in their heads. I reckon there would be a few questions asked if their relatives were to notice those.'

Wardle also knew that it is not a good idea to think about this sort of thing too much. In fact, it wasn't a good idea to dwell on it at all. He still had flashbacks of O'Malley's killing spree in the Malayan Jungle. All those kids, some of them too young to even walk. There had been no blame apportioned to the military; there were no witnesses other than O'Malley and his section, and the British were employing the principle of winning over hearts and minds. The insurgents were blamed for the atrocity.

FUCKING MADMAN – he should have done something about it then.

He should have killed the bastard himself long ago. He knew that the killing time was rapidly approaching. He had known of its inevitability for almost twenty years. He had delayed it for far too long, and as a result, too many people had died, including his friends Muscles and Mac. In many ways he had felt responsible for their deaths, and it was his responsibility to put it right.

O'Malley had never considered Wardle a threat. Wardle was a range shooter, not a killer. Wardle was a liability in the field. Wardle only took out people who he considered to be a threat. To O'Malley, in an engagement, everyone, and anything that moved was a threat and had to be eliminated.

O'Malley underestimated the real Ken Wardle at his peril. When Wardle pulled the trigger, the bullet always arrived on target. There were no exceptions, and there never had been. The difference was that Wardle chose his targets; whereas, the slightest movement activated the O'Malley trigger finger – be it man, woman, or child.

O'Malley was an assassin without morals or scruples.

A rifle without a conscience.

A dispenser of death.

CHAPTER 13

THE COLLECTION

The three men had agreed to make an early morning stake out before collecting the package, and had been closely observing all comings and goings from concealed positions for over one hour, before going to the safe house and collecting what turned out to be not one, but three women. Two were rather pretty young lieutenants in their early 20's, and one was a 30 something, rather masculine, almost certainly lesbian, slightly overweight captain – all Women's Royal Army Corps – W.R.A.C. All 3 women were dressed in civilian clothes.

Paddy simply could not resist his usual wind up of calling them 'racks', and sure enough, the lesbian captain took the bait, and he gleefully received the expected response. For many years, W.R.A.C., both officer, and enlisted women, had resisted, and resented the use of the word rack.

'We are W.R.A.C. – not racks – a rack is something that you screw against a wall.' The W.R.A.C. Captain, Allison Warburton had told him firmly.

Paddy was delighted that she had swallowed the bait, hook, line, and sinker, and responded with a grin. 'Don't you like screwing against a wall then Ma'am, most of the racks I know love it?'

The red faced captain, who had obviously never been screwed anywhere, at any time, and most certainly not up against any wall, threatened to have him locked up on their return. 'And if it was up to me, I would throw away the fucking key.' she added in annoyance.

'Can you arrange a couple of racks and a barrel of Guinness for company Ma'am? Oh, and you had better make it a pretty strong wall.' Paddy was now in his element, but before he could continue, Wardle cut in. Killeen was too busy trying to suppress a laugh that was threatening to run out of control, and was facing in the opposite direction in order to avoid Captain Warburton seeing the wide grin on his face. He had heard Paddy's wind up so often, he could virtually anticipate the next line. Usually the women accepted the sexual banter in good humor, however, a lesbian officer was a different proposition. Wardle's intervention had been timely; even so, Killeen was mentally finishing Paddy's sentence for him.

'Paddy, go and check that the car park and exit are still clear.' Wardle said firmly, himself trying to avoid bursting out laughing. The whole scenario just seemed so much funnier when a senior ranking lesbian officer took the bait.

As Paddy left, still grinning from ear to ear, Wardle had a few moments to himself – moments to think. 'If O'Malley has got wind of the deception; he will *not* be on the next ferry to Dublin; he will be somewhere pretty damn close.' It was a cast iron guarantee that he was aware that he had killed the wrong girl; he always had a 6th sense for any kind of set up or deception. He moved his head slowly from side to side, and licked his lips, before rubbing his chin as he thought.

This was why Killeen was unaware of the overall plan, and why no other SAS team was employed as back up. He had to be kept reactive; he had to respond on instinct or O'Malley would see the set up and bolt. O'Malley was gifted with an animal cunning, and self preservation was always his most basic instinct.

Wardle still harbored doubts as to Killeen's ability to function at his full capacity. He had felt a surge of confidence in the Butchers arms the previous evening as Killeen's aura had returned; that however had been countered by an obvious fear when in the lift. It was now too late to change the plans. Killeen had to come good or many more people would die, maybe even the rest of the D1 team. Maybe that was the reason for O'Malley being in England. Maybe the girl was simply a decoy for his overall plan. Maybe they were all dancing to O'Malley's tune.

The three women climbed into Killeen's estate car; the still smarting, red faced lesbian Captain Warburton in the front passenger seat, and the two pretty young lieutenants in the rear.

'Which one was the Package?' Killeen wondered, then he smiled to himself thinking of Paddy's comment. 'Which one of them had the postage stamps stuck to her fanny?' If it was the lesbian captain, he wouldn't want to be the postman who had to stick them there. He glanced over to Wardle who was also chuckling away to himself. 'Fucking hell,' he thought, and whispered to himself under his breath. 'He can read minds as well as sniffing out O'Malley.'

Still smiling, Wardle winked at Killeen. 'You've got the '*check in*' places and times Jim; top left hand corner of the car park – just pull alongside and I'll give you any info as it comes up. Don't get out of the car unless it's absolutely necessary.'

Killeen had heard Wardle's words as he drove away, but they hadn't really registered. He was deep in thought; deeply intrigued, and more than a little troubled. His thoughts were still in apartment 308. All three shots had been pretty much dead centre of the forehead, perfectly executed, and almost straight between the eyes. No one could possibly be so accurate, not even if the victims had been perfectly still, even then it just wasn't possible. Was O'Malley really so good? He couldn't be – no way – nobody was.

Ken Wardle hated him with a vengeance, yet when he spoke about him, and you looked through the underlying hatred, there was definitely a form of grudging respect – almost hero worship at the man's abilities. Was there something that Wardle wasn't telling him, not just about O'Malley, but about the whole operation? Why was it that an operation that was supposedly so important that the SAS had to be involved, limited to just three men? Why hadn't he been told about the decoy girl? Where was the Regiment? Why wasn't the package being moved by air? – Why – Why – Why? Something didn't smell right and Ken Wardle was the key. Wardle also knew more than he was letting on, of that he was sure.

Killeen trusted Wardle with his life; indeed, on more than one occasion, he had been the difference between life and death. His mind flashed back to the Gulf, to Oman. The whole section were in a fix, caught in cross fire between two rival factions who had decided to temporarily join forces in order to eliminate the British Infidels. Even though the section had dug in, and were well covered from rifle fire, one of the two sides had brought in a mortar. Two rounds had been fired, and it was only a matter of time before they acquired the range; then, every one of Killeen's men would have been blown to smithereens. There was nowhere to hide, and nowhere to escape to.

One by one, the gunmen started to die, without even being aware of where the shots were coming from. Wardle was half a mile away, and the sound of the rifle shots was barely audible because of the wind direction. Both opposing forces had panicked, and run straight into Killeen's section's guns. There had been no survivors and no SAS casualties. Killeen himself had counted eleven dead from their original two attacking positions; each man with a hole in what was left of his head. He also counted eleven empty bullet cases. Ken Wardle never missed.

His thoughts flew back to apartment 308. Both Special Branch men had drawn their pistols, which meant that they had to have been moving; even the girl had drawn her pistol half way out of her handbag, her hand still firmly clasped around the hand grip, even in death. All 3 shots were dead centre of the forehead in an almost perfect alignment, straight between the eyes. Was Wardle right? Did O'Malley never miss when he was in the field?

Killeen was pretty good himself with a pistol, and had taken more than his fair share of kills in both Belfast and Londonderry. Not in the manner of Mad Mitch Murphy, who was happy to kill anyone as long as they were Protestant; even if it meant killing them in front of their children – in fact, especially if it meant killing them in front of their children. Who the hell cared about Proddys? That sick reasoning would always be at the back of Murphy's sick mind. The more they suffered – the better he felt. For Mad Mitch Murphy, killing Proddys was a labor of love.

Killeen's Irish victims had been the bombers – the ones they could not catch in the act, the ones who nevertheless, killed innocent people indiscriminately. They sometimes made the bombs, and sometimes they planted them, although these two operations were usually carried out by separate people. Killeen always consoled himself with the thought that the assassination of an unarmed man, a bomber, or a bomb maker, would save possibly hundreds of innocent people, no matter how hard his moral conscience wrestled with it. It was therefore justified. A man who planted bombs was a legitimate target in *all* the unwritten rules of warfare.

If the IRA wanted to call themselves a liberation *ARMY*, then the SAS would treat them as soldiers; they would therefore be subject to the rules of warfare, both written and unwritten, and would not be treated as civilians with guns. That was a job for the police – not Special Forces!

Killeen headed due north, and let out a sigh of relief as he left the slow build up of traffic in town, and hit the open dual carriageway. From now on it should be pretty much plain sailing. Pick up the M1 motorway and head north for the Watford Gap services, there, he would link up with Wardle and Paddy. He smiled at the thought of 'Watford Gap'. Even though it was probably situated in the south of the Midlands, to a southerner like himself, it was definitely in the uncivilized, uncultured north of the country. Molly lived even farther north, not too far from his final destination –

Cumbria, the Lake District, and Wordsworth country. Molly however was very civilized, very cultured, and very smart.

Killeen wondered if Molly had been recalled from leave. Molly had travelled back from Ireland with Paddy, Wardle, and himself, but had stayed pretty much alone on the ferry journey. This was very strange indeed; Molly was usually the most gregarious man in the whole section, but his eyes had taken on kind of glaze; they seemed to be looking without seeing. There seemed to no one at home. Molly was present only in body and not in soul. Of the four of them that had returned to England, Molly seemed to be taking the death of Muscles and Mac the hardest. Wardle had told both Paddy and himself to leave Molly alone to his thoughts. Killeen wondered why?

From Watford Gap services, he would proceed past the dreaded Birmingham loop on the M6 motorway, and on to Keele services for the next link up; then onwards past Manchester, Preston, and Lancaster, before turning off for the Lake District. Once there, he only had to travel another 40 or so miles through open countryside that he knew like the back of his hand to deliver the package, whichever one of the three it was, and then round to see Julie. This time she was definitely going to say "yes – yes – yes – I will marry you Jim". He just knew it.

He wondered what would happen to the two 'surplus to requirement' W.R.A.C. women in the car; where did they fit into all of this? No one had mentioned it. Was he to bring them back? No way – no bloody way on earth; stuff that – the bloody army could lump it; he was staying put in Cumbria with Julie, and if the army didn't like it, they could bloody well shove it. He had already given the army over twelve of his best years, and in return, he had been paid considerably less than half of what his father had offered him to run the family business.

He was seriously thinking of resigning his commission anyway, all that it would take was a 'yes' from Julie, and he was on his way; all the way to domestic bliss; all the way to Semi Detached Suburban Captain James. He would no longer have to worry about both those bloody kids trying to blow his head off in that stinking, God forsaken, fly ridden desert – or that self destructive shit hole across the Irish channel. All the way to 'Semi Detached Suburban Captain James' sounded just about right. Maybe both the little bastards would disappear from his dreams –

simply fuck off and leave him alone, instead of appearing whenever he felt stress, or entered the twilight zone between sleep and consciousness.

Another thought suddenly entered his head, as he hummed the Manfred Mann tune. 'Why were there three women? – Were two of them decoys? – Could this even be an elaborate plan to take him alive and deliver him to O'Malley? It was pretty common knowledge that there was a fairly hefty bounty on his head – dead *or* alive. Stupid thought really; was he becoming paranoid? Ken's famed hooter would have smelled a rat there, but on the other hand, there definitely was something that he was being kept in the dark about. He couldn't figure it out at the moment, but he would. All those years working in intelligence had not been for nothing.

'The package is in the shape of a pretty lieutenant.' Killeen suddenly remembered Wardle's words. If so, which one, and why was an overweight, lesbian captain sitting beside him in the car?

He had now turned onto the M1 motorway, and dismissed all stupid and paranoid thoughts from his head. He was smart enough to realize that Paddy's concern over his mental health was well founded. It wasn't PTSD as Paddy had suggested – he was simply over tired, and still grieving over the death of Muscles and Mac. It hadn't really been his fault. O'Malley had simply been too good for them. He physically shuddered as an image of O'Malley appeared in front of him, and planted itself firmly across the windscreen. He blinked hard and shook his head several times before it disappeared. Was he hallucinating? Was he going fucking bonkers like O'Malley himself?

Glancing in the rear view mirror, he noticed that the prettier of the two lieutenants was smiling at him. He smiled back. She did look remarkably like Julie – his Julie. She had the same smiling eyes, the same long black hair, and amazingly enough, the same name. Good body as well, quite beautiful legs and a pretty substantial bust. Paddy had spotted the bust naturally enough, and had given him a knowing wink and nod.

He was now making good time up the M1 motorway for his rendezvous with Wardle and Paddy, and his thoughts again flashed to the similarities between the two Julies and their respective busts. This Julie definitely had better boobs than his Julie, well, they were certainly bigger, and the tightly fitting blouse did little to disguise the fact.

His look in the rear view mirror was longer than normal. Julie was again smiling, and seemed to be pushing her busts ever closer to him.

He did not notice the big silver Mercedes pull along side.

There was a thud, no more than that, and the W.R.A.C. lieutenant sitting next to Julie slumped forward, her head crashing into the back of Killeen's seat. The bullet had entered close to her ear, and she was dead. Killeen was slow to react – what the hell was up with her, and why was the car to his right staying level with him instead of passing him?

'**Drive – Drive**,' screamed the W.R.A.C. captain, as she reached for the pistol in her handbag. 'Get the fuck out of here, she's been shot.'

It was then that he realized what had happened, and as he slammed his foot down hard on the accelerator, the car lurched forward, gathering speed until the Mercedes was left a little way behind.

'Didn't you see him pull alongside you? Didn't you see him wind the window down? Didn't you see the fucking gun? Are you fucking blind or asleep?' Yelled Captain Warburton, her voice bordering on hysterical.

'No, did I hell, I wasn't looking out for anything. Who the hell shoots at you on a British motorway – is everyone ok?' Killeen asked hopefully, already knowing the answer.

'No, Chris is not ok, she's got a fucking bullet in her head. Do you think you would be ok?' Came the high pitched, almost screamed reply from Warburton.

The estate car was now doing 110 mph, and the Mercedes started to gain on them. Killeen tried to move from the middle to the outside lane, but was blocked by the Mercedes as it pulled alongside. The window of the Mercedes slid down, and for the first ever time, Captain James Killeen, SAS, found himself face to face with the grinning Michael Patrick O'Malley. His blood froze in his veins and his hands started to tremble.

Four long months, Killeen and his team had spent searching for O'Malley, the invisible man. During that time, he had lost Muscles and Mac, and the army had lost another 15 men; all killed by a single 7-62 mm sniper bullet: the killing spree hadn't stopped there. Protestants were disappearing from border areas, and live, innocent people, were being turned into corpses in front of their wives and children – their only crime? 'Going to a different church to worship the same God that their killers did.'

The North / South border was too big – too porous, the 'A' team could slip in and out at will. Prominent Protestant Loyalists were the priority targets on their list, closely followed by the police and the military. To Mad Mitch Murphy, any Protestant was a legitimate target: Mitch glorified and boasted of the number of kills to his name. To the many younger Catholic hotheads, Mitch was a hero; to the more senior members of the IRA hierarchy, Mitch was a loose cannon, and posed a threat to what little shred of morality they still clung to. It was only the fear of O'Malley that was felt by the IRA Godfathers' that prevented his elimination.

Not all the IRA gunmen made the border crossing safely. Both Killeen's and Charnock's team had made sure of that. They were assisted by a number of well paid informants that had been bought and planted by MI5; this gave them the edge that they needed. Targets were eliminated and disposed of – the Cleaners were kept busy. Occasionally, blame was passed onto the Protestant paramilitaries, this in turn brought reprisals, with more IRA terrorists crossing the border and coming into the range of the two SAS team's guns.

O'Malley was not fooled, and was rarely drawn from his lair south of the border. He didn't need to move; he had Mad Mitch Murphy to do his dirty work in the north, and Sean Fitzpatrick and his sister Mary to do the necessary scouting and planning.

He was however smart and cunning, and realized that information about the IRA movement south of the border was being passed on and acted on. He sought out the informant: the deaths of Muscles and Mac were the result of him finding him. The informant had been a family relative – O'Malley's own uncle. He had confessed on the understanding that his family would be safe – they weren't. Mad Mitch had firstly tortured, and then slit his wife and 10 year old son's throats in front of the man, and then tortured him for hours before cutting off his dick and stuffing it into his mouth. Mitch enjoyed that. It was becoming something of a trademark of his.

At a stroke, all information coming from the south stopped the moment that the dead man's body was dumped.

Four long, fruitless, months searching for him, and now – O'Malley had done the finding. He was here, in England, on Killeen's territory, and no more than a few feet away, grinning manically at him.

Killeen looked mesmerically into O'Malley's eyes. Wardle had been right; he had got the glazed look of a madman. It was a faraway look – a thousand yard stare that nevertheless bore deep into his brain – it took control and immobilized all thought.

Killeen was now the proverbial petrified rabbit caught up in O'Malley's headlights. He was frozen; completely unable to respond to the danger; he was about to die. He wanted to tell him that it was Paddy who had killed his son. O'Malley already knew that. Killeen knew that he would have worked it out for himself.

He saw that bloody kid in the desert with the AK47 pointing at him, and O'Malley`s grinning face behind the kid. This was just as he saw it most nights in his dreams. He heard the bang as the kid pulled the trigger. Where the hell was Paddy? Paddy was never there when he needed him. Never there in his dreams.

His ears were ringing, and the wind was rushing in through the shattered window next to him.

'Up the verge; get up the fucking verge – NOW.'

This was an order that could not be ignored. No one would dare to disobey – it was screamed with a blood chilling ferocity.

Killeen's mind cleared. O'Malley's hypnotic hold over him disappeared. There was no frightened kid with an AK47. He swung the estate car hard left, narrowly avoiding a white transit van in the inside lane, and shot up the 30 degree grass verge, crashing through a three barred wooden fence at the top of the verge, before taking to the air, and landing with the sickening crunch of bending metal and broken glass in a field of wheat.

'What the fucking hell do you think you were playing at?'

Screamed the lesbian Captain Warburton, as she placed the pistol back into her handbag. 'You nearly got us all fucking killed. Why the fuck did you freeze? Who ever told me you were good was a fucking liar. You are finished; you are going back to a fucking office job, that's for sure.'

Killeen knew that she was right. He was finished. He could not handle it anymore. He was a spent force and had nothing left to give. Paddy was probably right, he did have PTSD. He should have countered the Mercedes; speed was not the answer, his car didn't have the power. Speed of thought was the answer. Maneuver and evade – evade and maneuver. He had forgotten even his most basic army training. He had been hypnotized by the power of O'Malley's manic stare – completely immobilized – he had become physically and mentally impotent.

Where did that bloody kid with the AK47 keep coming from? How could he possibly be personal bodyguard to the Sheik's precious daughters? Paddy was right; he had no experience of evasive driving, and now he had no bottle. He had never been trained as a bodyguard, so why did the Sheik ask for him? Why was there no back up for this job – where were the helicopters – where was the Regiment – where were Paddy and Ken – how could this possibly be an SAS job – how the hell did O'Malley know that he would be driving up the M6 motorway at exactly this time – had he been set up – was he the patsy in this operation – the sacrificial lamb?

Even though Killeen had often been required to operate independent of military orders when the situation had demanded it, it was normal for tactical operations to be rehearsed over and over again, often to the point of tedium. Nothing was left to chance. Detailed maps were drawn up, together with any contingency plan in case things changed during the operation itself. Every feature of a landscape, building, or road detail was itemized and memorized. There was always a well rehearsed exit plan. Right now, he wanted an exit plan. He wanted out; out of the army; out of the country: somewhere where O'Malley would never find him.

On one occasion, the African assassination job that had lead to Sniffer Wardle joining the team, the withdrawal hadn't gone according to plan, and the entire team had to be evacuated by a US submarine. They had conducted the evacuation in what were still the most frightening circumstances any of them had ever encountered. For all their quarter of a mile swim out to the submarine, they had been accompanied by a bloody great shark that would not go away. That was the only time Killeen had ever seen any sign of fear in Paddy's eyes.

'Did you shit yourself Jim?' Paddy had asked as they climbed aboard the sub. 'I fucking did. I reckon the taste of it put it off its meal; that's why it didn't attack us.'

Where was the planning for this operation then? They had had one day's notice – they hadn't even been given a route to follow, and seemingly, no one was remotely bothered. This was England for God's sake. Hereford and the rest of the regiment were only 100 miles away. This was always the problem with 'Need to Know' operations. When assistance was urgently needed – no one knew – no one wanted to know – you were on your own.

Little did he know that this had been the plan all along.

Little did *the planners* know that this was not the Captain James Killeen of old? There was something wrong with *this* Captain Killeen, and O'Malley had spotted it.

The three of them climbed stiffly out off the car, and checked each other for any signs of blood. The dead lieutenant's body was now slumped over Killeen's driving seat due to the force of the landing, blood still pouring from the hole in her head.

'It looks like the car's a gonner Jim,' said the now somewhat calmer Captain Alison Warburton, using his Christian name for the first time since they had met, at the same time focusing her eyes on Lieutenant Julie Bromley, as she rolled her head round and round. 'How are you Julie, neck a little sore?'

'I think I'm ok Ma'am, just got a little whiplash. Did you see the look in O'Malley's eyes? He looked like a complete madman. I've seen him quite a few times in Belfast when he came back to our house with Sean, but he never looked like that, in fact, he could be a bit of a charmer.'

'Well, that's sorted the Package out,' Killeen thought. '*SEAN*?' He said out loud. 'Not Sean Fitzpatrick I hope – surely not?'

'Didn't you see him Jim? Sean was the driver. He was my boyfriend for two years. How else was I ever going to get close to the IRA? It was because of Sean and his connections that I got to meet the really big boys. Who do you think has been supplying MI5 with all their information for the past two years?'

'Why Julie? Why did you risk your life by going undercover in the first place?' Killeen had a puzzled look on his face.

'It's personal Jim, anyway, is your job any safer? Why do you do it?'

'Let's move on.' Captain Warburton sounded irritable as she interrupted, 'Fuck the history, has anyone any idea where we are?'

Killeen couldn't help but smile. He just knew that Paddy's response would have been something like – 'Looks like a field of wheat to me – seems like a good place for screwing a rack.' Slowly, his senses were beginning to return. He really didn't have a clue as to where they were – neither had Paddy or Ken. One thing was sure though; O'Malley certainly knew, and had probably turned off the motorway by now, and would probably be heading in their direction. It was only a matter of time before he found them. It was also pretty certain that he had them outgunned. Three pistols were no match for the sniper rifles that the 'A' team undoubtedly carried.

'We'd better move now – and move *quickly* – before we find ourselves with company. We'll head for that little spinney and have a think.' Killeen said, as his vision started to clear. He was still feeling a little light headed because of the jolt as the car had come to rest, however his experience and leadership training were starting to kick in.

All three of them moved on, barely glancing at the dead girl slumped over the driver's seat in the car – still warm – still bleeding.

There was no time to call in the cleaners, and for sure, she would not be carrying any ID with her. Ordinarily, on operations like this, a cover story was always provided, which would be of little use if she had been captured alive and found to be in possession of military ID.

Killeen had no cover story and wondered why not.

He smiled inwardly as he made up his own cover story. 'I'm a fucking postman,' he would tell his interrogators – 'Check out the fanny stamps.'

CHAPTER 14

BACK UP

'Lost it Ken!'

'Lost what Paddy?'

'Lost the signal.'

'Well find the fucking thing! Without it we're blind.' Wardle shouted a little too loudly in frustration.

'It's not there, it just disappeared for no reason.' Paddy replied, at the same time sticking one finger in his ear and pretending to be deaf.

'Sorry Pads, switch to back up then.'

'Done that Ken, seems funny though, they're not moving. Looks more like a ghost image and we're almost on top of it. Slow down a bit there's a police car parked ahead on the hard shoulder.'

Unknown to Killeen, Wardle had placed the two trackers under his car the previous evening. He had become quite proficient in placing and following tracking devices during his time in Northern Ireland. Many of the top IRA brass and shooters had been travelling around with them for months, their every movement monitored. This was one of the reasons why both Killeen's, and Charnock's teams, had been so successful in intercepting and eliminating the shooters as they crossed the border, on or after one of their bombing or killing missions.

It was Paddy who suggested pulling in behind the police car and taking a look. The tyre marks running up the grass verge were quite prominent, and stood at the top of the verge were two uniformed motorway policemen.

'We've got to go and take a look Pads, it could be Jim's car. That would explain why the trackers have gone haywire. Why the fuck would he have driven off the motorway and up the grass verge though?'

'He probably let one of the racks drive, you know what women drivers are like.'

Wardle laughed. 'For God's sake don't go upsetting that captain again Paddy, we need her on our side, she is one of the best bodyguards in the army, she's a fucking instructor of all things. I requested her specially to cover Jim's back.'

Paddy also burst out laughing at the thought of a rack acting as bodyguard to Captain James Killeen – the Killing Machine.

Both Paddy and Wardle left the car and made their way up the grass verge to the two motorway policemen, who were observing their progress very carefully and with some suspicion.

'Do you know anything about this?' asked the larger of the two police officers with a questioning grimace on his face, and a suggestion of a threat in his voice, as he looked Wardle in the eye. 'It's got me fucking baffled; where the hell is the driver? It looks to me like this girl has been shot and no more than a couple of minutes ago, she's still bleeding like a stuck pig.'

Cursing inwardly, at the same time suppressing a shudder at the gruesome simile, Wardle asked. 'Have you radioed in yet?'

'No, just about to.'

'Well don't, ok – this is a matter of national security. We are both military intelligence.'

'I suppose that you got some ID with you sir, we've got to check?' The man was still a little suspicious, but had changed his original authoritarian demeanor for a more conciliatory attitude.

'We don't carry ID in our job.' growled Paddy menacingly.

The man took a step backwards as he suddenly noticed the size of the imposing and threatening giant in front of him.

'I'm ex-military myself,' volunteered the smaller of the two officers. 'If this is undercover work, and I'm presuming that the IRA are involved, what do you want us to do?'

'Wardle handed him a piece of paper and said, 'Ring this number. Tell the voice at the other end that this is D1 Special Forces on assignment and you need the cleaners immediately. Then give them your location and stay put. Someone will arrive and give you further instructions. Have you got that? In the meantime, sit in your car, and under *NO* circumstances must you come back up here, you will be in danger, real danger – *OK*.'

'Sorted *SIR* – exactly as you have instructed sir.' The police officer sprang to attention and saluted Wardle, the other officer followed suit. Wardle returned the salute.

'They both thought you was an officer Ken, why didn't you tell em?' Paddy remarked as the two men drove away, leaving the two police officers sat in their car and on the car radio.

'Better this way kid. An ex military man prefers to take orders from an officer; they have that air of finality about them and must be obeyed. Old habits die hard, and the respect that they retain never goes away.'

'Why did you never become an officer Ken? Jim told me that you were offered the chance more than once; didn't you fancy all that extra money?'

'I never really fancied it Paddy. All my family have been army officers going back at least seven generations; my older brother is a Brigadier, you will meet him later today.'

'Fucking hell Ken, I've never met a Brigadier before. Do you still call him *SIR*, or our kid?'

Wardle burst out laughing and threw his head back. 'That depends on where we are and what company we are in Paddy; my dad was a Major, and still works in intelligence for the government; sort of a conduit between MI5, MI6, and the politicians, but I still call him *DAD*. Bob Kineer is a lieutenant, but we all call him Bob unless he's in dress uniform, something none of us have ever seen.'

'Fucking hell, I didn't know that Bob was an officer. I threatened to punch his lights out once when he called me an ape – only Molly's allowed to call me that.'

Wardle burst out laughing again. 'You might have got a shock if you had done Pads. Remember that Gippo who punched you in the nuts? Well, Bob would have done the same, only twice as hard and three times as fast, I saw his report before he joined the section. He's a black belt in karate, or kung fu, or something like that. He used to take part in international competitions; he even appeared on the telly a couple of times. Before he joined us, he worked in 'black ops' for the Americans. There have been rumors around for some time now that both Maggi and Reagan have set up a secret unit that work together, maybe that's why he is only on attachment – who knows?'

'Where is Bob now Ken,' Paddy couldn't disguise the obvious concern in his voice, brought about by what the section had suffered with the shooting of Muscles and Mac by O'Malley. 'He disappeared a few days ago and didn't join us on leave, he just disappeared one night without so much as a goodbye. It all seemed pretty strange to me after all we'd been through together.'

'He was doing some very dangerous undercover work north of the border in Ireland. Word was that O'Malley was on his way to a meeting with some of the IRA top Brass in Belfast, and Bob was to be a supposed 'arms dealer' from the States; you must have noticed his American accent, he spent most of his life in New York. The idea was to get close enough to O'Malley to finish him off, something that we couldn't do in over 4 months.

No one has heard from him for over a week now; it doesn't sound good. Not a word about it to Jim though, he must be kept in the dark.' Wardle glanced at Paddy. 'Not a single word Pads, Jim has enough on his plate these next couple of days, we need him to be right on top of his game; O'Malley is like something he has never had to deal with before. If Jim makes the slightest mistake, O'Malley will skin him alive.'

Paddy shook his head and responded almost contemptuously. 'Jim will be ok, he just needs a little time; you've seen how Jim operates Ken, there's no one better in the Regiment.'

'I know that Pads, but what worries me is that he hasn't got a little time. He hasn't got *any* time, this is happening now. Don't underestimate O'Malley. Take it from me, he is the only man I know that is Jim's equal. He may be fucking bonkers, but he is also fucking good.'

The two men drove on up the motorway in silence, each man thinking of their next move until Paddy broke the silence.

'What a fuck up Ken. What a fucking fuck up.'

'Paddy's law Paddy.'

'Don't you mean Murphy's law?'

'Same thing – same bog oil gobblers – just different spelling.'

'Don't you think that we should turn off at the next junction and track back?'

'No point Pads, Jim will have gone to ground by now, you know the score – escape and evade. That dead girl was O'Malley's work, that's for sure. What puzzles me though is why didn't O'Malley just shoot Jim? The car would have crashed and the lot of them would have died; neither Jim nor the package would have ever troubled him again. He could now be heading for the next ferry to Dublin. His intelligence is so good, that he must know that he shot the wrong girl. Where the hell are they now? That is the question. Without the trackers we might as well be blind.'

Paddy changed the subject. 'Why do you always call Guinness "Bog Oil Ken" – it's lovely stuff – I prefer it to shagging sometimes?'

'Having seen your choice in women Pads, I can understand why. I saw a program about it a couple of years back, the water comes from the Liffey in Dublin.'

'So what, everybody knows that?'

'Well, they reckon that by the time it reaches Dublin, half a million Paddy's and Murphy's have already pissed in it.'

'That's what gives it the flavor.'

'You bog oil gobbling, uncouth, fucking caveman.'

Both men burst out laughing; for once, Wardle had almost got the last word in. The banter, or craic, as the Irish call it, continued up until the car pulled into the Watford Gap service station. They both knew that it was pointless. As they pulled up at the top left hand corner of the car park and stopped the vehicle, they considered their options.

'What will Jim do now Pads?'

'Hire car.'

'Sure?'

'Sure, I know Jim better than he knows himself.'

'What about his route, do you think that he will stick to the plan?'

'No way. If O'Malley has worked out his route so far, Jim will certainly be onto that. I would guess back roads only – little unmarked country roads, the way we used to operate around the border country in South Armagh. There will be no motorways; he'll probably change clothes as well, and get one of the girls to drive.'

'I agree completely Paddy, the only problem is that O'Malley will have figured all that out.'

'Is there anything that Mr. O fucking Malley doesn't know?' Paddy shouted angrily.

'So far kid, the answer is *NO*. He has been one step ahead of us ever since he left Ireland – where the hell is he getting all his information from?'

'He won't be one step *AHEAD* when I get hold of him,' Paddy growled. 'He won't have a fucking head; come to think of it Ken, he was always one step ahead of us in Ireland as well.'

Wardle's face turned part grimace and part smile, as he slowly shook his head and spoke. 'Clever bastard; clever and cunning; anyway, let's move on, there's no point hanging around here, Jim isn't going to make it. It's also pretty safe to assume that he won't make the next check point either. I reckon that the best thing for us to do is to go and pick some daffodils upt' north by the lake, and see what Molly has got planned for us.'

'Too bloody smart for his own good that *Boy*.' Paddy shook his head slowly, a big grin crossing his face.

'Oh he's smart all right Pads; he should be earning a fortune in the City, and not poncing about playing at soldiers. That's for thick bastards like you.'

'And you Wardle, you tart.'

'I'm a sailor dear boy, not a soldier – remember? A Royal Marine Commando.' Wardle chuckled.

AGAIN, Wardle had got the last word in. Twice now in two years! Paddy must be troubled.

'I'm still not happy with this operation Ken, too many things don't add up.'

Wardle went silent for a few seconds before looking Paddy in the eye and speaking as he drove. 'I can't tell you too much at this point Paddy; suffice to say that this is the culmination of many weeks of planning. We simply couldn't allow O'Malley to keep potting British soldiers as and when he wanted to. Every soldier that dies draws more and more young radicals into the IRA fold. The Southern Irish government would not allow us across the border to take him out, so we had to devise a way of luring him to England in case Bob doesn't succeed in eliminating him. I have it on pretty good authority that the Prime Minister herself had our two teams posted there, and has given her full authorization for this operation, despite the risks to British intelligence.'

'So who's the bait then Ken, the young rack or Jim?'

'Both of them Paddy, plus I reckon that you are pretty high up the menu list, probably at the top of the starters. O'Malley is no fool, and you left your calling card when you snapped his son's neck. I would guess that he won't be satisfied until he has taken out the entire section. So far, he has killed Muscles and Mac, and now with Bob Kineer going missing, I wouldn't put it past him to go for the full set. I know how his mind works; he's fucking bonkers, and can bear a grudge for years.'

'I WILL rip his fucking head off Ken.' Paddy's anger was not exaggerated.

'He knows that Pads, and so does everyone else; that's why you will never get close enough to do it. O'Malley doesn't take chances. If he considers you a threat, you will go the same way as Muscles and Mac, and he will be near half a mile away.'

'Is he really that good Ken?'

'No Paddy – he's better than anything that you can ever imagine.'

'How much of this is Jim aware of; don't you think that he should be in the loop?'

'Can't allow Jim in the loop Pads, it's critical that he reacts to every situation as it comes along. O'Malley doesn't think in straight lines; remember, he is fucking bonkers, and it's impossible to work out what will be his next move; that is why we need to utilize a brain like Molly possesses. If anyone can get into the mind of O'Malley – Molly can.

Sniffer Wardle had seen the signs on the ferry on their return to the UK.

He knew what to look for in a madman. He had been studying these signs close up for almost twenty years, and he had seen the similarities between Molly and the O'Malley of his early days as a Royal Marine Commando.

CHAPTER 15

ESCAPE AND EVADE

Concealed in the little spinney, Killeen and the two girls discussed their options, at the same time keeping a watchful eye on the little country lane that ran alongside. Killeen was well aware that at a glance, O'Malley would work out their position to within a few feet; sniper school taught ambush and concealment positions – not just accuracy with a rifle.

'At least we know the car that they are travelling in,' offered the W.R.A.C. Captain Warburton. 'That should be pretty easy to spot.'

'Not too sure about that Ma'am,' lieutenant Julie replied. 'O'Malley has got more contacts than yellow pages. It's odds on that he has a back up vehicle; don't forget that another team are in the country. They came in a couple of days after I did; I was the target. When they failed to find me, that's when they called in the 'A' team. I'm pretty sure that they will have linked up by now.'

'Do you know any of them?' Killeen was still intrigued, and a little suspicious at the thought of such a pretty girl putting her life on the line for so long just to obtain intelligence for the British Army.

'Only Poirick O'Riordan and his brother Max. You don't have to worry about Max though, I managed to recognize him at the docks, and he was picked up without a struggle; the rest of the crew disappeared among the passengers. I have no idea who the others are though. It could be any one of a hundred from either Belfast or Derry. I heard that it was a four man crew, so now it will be down to three with Max locked up.'

'It sounds like a funny combination of names for two Irish brothers, Poirick and Max?' Killeen looked puzzled. 'I've never heard of a Paddy called Max before.'

Julie laughed. 'You never know what goes on behind closed doors Jim.'

They all joined in the quiet laughter.

Lieutenant Julie went on, still smiling as she spoke. 'Poirick's father buggered off with an English girl that he met down the pub one night when she was on holiday. His mother got even by shacking up with an English man, and little Maxi was the result. They both had to move to England once THE TROUBLES started, the locals no longer approved of mixed marriages, not just between Irish girls and English men, but if you throw in a Protestant marrying a Catholic for good measure, you can see very little future for them in Northern Ireland. Both Poirick and Max went with them but couldn't settle, so they returned to Belfast after a couple of years and joined the IRA.'

'How come you know so much about them Julie?' Killeen asked, with a glint in one eye, and the other one magnetically drawn to her breast.

Julie followed the progress of Killeen's roving eyes, and taking a deeper than normal breath, strained the buttons on her tightly fitting blouse to the limit.

Killeen was suddenly conscious of what his eyes had been unconsciously doing, and looked away, his cheeks turning a slight pink color.

'Everyone in Belfast knows about the O'Riordan family Jim.' Julie was now laughing out loud. 'There are more jokes about them than the English have about the Irish. How do you stop an O'Riordan from getting into a tight spot? – Fill it with an Englishman. How many more do you want? There are hundreds of them, most of them referring to English dicks and Irish fannies.'

Both Killeen and Warburton laughed; the mood turned a little more serious.

'How do you get *us* out of a tight spot is the current dilemma Jim.' asked Warburton?

Killeen closed his eyes and pursed his lips, as his face went into its usual thinking mode.

'Firstly, we have got to get ourselves a hire car.'

'Too easily traced Jim. We will buy one, and you can both stop looking at me like that.' Captain Warburton said smugly. 'When I am in the field, I am issued with an unlimited credit card; let's go and do some shopping – I can feel a nice Ferrari coming on.'

As the three of them made their way to the nearest town, the conversation turned more and more onto Julie's time spent undercover in Ireland. Killeen was intrigued that anyone could be in a relationship with a killer like Fitzpatrick, simply to obtain information for the British. Did she enjoy screwing him, or was it all faked? How on earth could she fake it for almost two years? He concluded that she must have enjoyed it. The thought excited him; she *did* look so much like his Julie, and he hadn't touched a woman for months. He suddenly realized how much he missed it; and those breasts, they really were something. He had only touched the one woman for many, many years; still, he felt excited. Trying to dismiss carnal thoughts from his mind, he turned his attention to O'Malley as Julie spoke.

'I know O'Malley pretty well; as I told you, he can be a bit of a charmer when he wants to be. Sean was quite jealous, but of course he never said anything in front of him. Scared to death of him, everybody was. Even the top brass of the IRA were careful what they said in front of him. He never got angry, but whenever he said something, no one ever challenged it – except me that is.'

'You are joking.' Killeen said, almost mockingly, and in a state of semi disbelief.

'No, not at all. I think he loved the fact that all these big tough men, most of them with several kills to their credit, wouldn't say a word out of place, and this feeble little woman would. Sean used to be shaking sometimes, he was so scared. Even that creep Murphy kept his stupid mouth shut in front of O'Malley: gobbin off, and boasting about how many squaddies and Proddys he had killed was more his usual style – the mouthy, cross-eyed, deformed, little bastard. I fucking hated him, but was unable to pin him down for your lot Jim. He never worked to any sort of plan. He just killed whatever was in front of him whenever he had the opportunity.'

'How come you got compromised then?' Killeen asked. 'What could possibly have gone wrong after being under cover for two years; did you spit up with Sean?'

'It was probably my own fault really, although I'm not too sure if I could have handled it any differently under the circumstances. Some of the information I passed over was just too good and too up to date. It could only have come from a very small group of people. O'Malley narrowed it down to one, "me", and sent that mad bastard Murphy to deal with it. Sean tipped me off, and I had to leave in a hurry before Murphy found me. I hated the ugly, cross eyed, little bastard, and he knew it. He hated the world and everyone in it, probably because he had been born so ugly. He is also a sadistic, obnoxious bastard; tortures people just for the thrill it gives him; in a way I suppose it's the only substitute he has for sex, a girl would have to be blind to sleep with him, even then the smell would put her off. He really did stink, sitting with him in a car would be like having a skunk next to you.'

Killeen smiled, as visions of Paddy's 'herd' of skunks in a box flashed by.

Killeen had only ever come within striking distance of Mad Mitch Murphy on one occasion.

Murphy had been in the north for a couple of days planting bombs, pretty much at random. It was the IRA policy to ring an accepted contact in the British security forces, or the police, always using a code word in order to ensure that the call was taken seriously and was not treated as a hoax. The location of the bomb was then given, which meant that the authorities had usually just about enough time to clear the area. Sometimes there wasn't enough time and people died. Rarely was the warning given for bombs planted on the English mainland. The bomb survivors were often the unlucky ones. Many had arms and legs blown off, and were often so badly scarred, that they rarely ever ventured, or even now, venture into the open, where people can see them – their facial wounds being so horrific.

Mad Mitch never gave telephone warnings. He also liked to view the carnage from a safe distance; it excited his warped sense of accomplishment. On this occasion he had gone too far; women and children had died, including a heavily pregnant woman, and as public opinion was starting to swing away from the IRA and their policy of random bombings, it was decided by the IRA top brass to decommission him permanently without informing O'Malley. A telephone call was made to a MI5 contact giving details of his vehicle and escape route into the south.

Killeen received the info, and had his men in position, strategically placed along a narrow country road that crossed the Armagh border into the south. His men were well concealed some 30 yards apart, all along the same side of the road in order to avoid shooting each other in the dark. They patiently awaited the arrival of the red Cortina, each man in the section excited at the prospect of finally nailing one of the 'A' team – Killeen had frozen – a voice from behind him had said.

'Drop the fucking weapon *NOW* or I shoot.'

Killeen complied. Meanwhile, a red Cortina shot out from a dirt track between Muscles and himself, and blasted past at breakneck speed across the border and out of reach.

'What a fucking fuck up.' Paddy had said. The paratrooper captain with a 9 mm pistol, now standing behind Killeen, had been given exactly the same information, and was waiting with half a dozen of his own men on the other side of the road behind a hedge.

Both the Para Captain and Killeen were furious beyond belief. No shots were fired, as both Killeen's team, and the Para's, were waiting for the order. Why couldn't those idiots in their comfortable London offices get such simple information right? One shot, and a fire fight between both sections would have certainly been the result. How many lives would have been lost?

It was almost as if someone at Intelligence headquarters had deliberately mislead them in order to ensure Murphy's escape, and to create maximum casualties among the army.

This was the only time that anyone on either Killeen's or Charnock's team had even got close to Murphy; meanwhile, he continued his killing spree unabated.

'Did Sean never suspect anything about your dual role Julie, surely he must have been a little suspicious?'

'No. Not a thing Jim. We went to school together, and were really childhood sweethearts. It broke his heart when dad sent me off to boarding school in England. My dad was the only one in Ireland who knew that I had got an army scholarship to university. Once I had got my degree, I returned home and took up with Sean again. In Sean's eyes I could do no wrong, he was in love, and he wanted to marry me. I know that you are going to ask me why I wanted to work for the army, so I will save you the trouble – Allison already knows the story.

My dad hated THE TROUBLES, which was why he sent me away from Ireland in the first place. The problem was that he refused to be silent about it. He was a man of peace, extremely religious, and was never afraid to condemn the killings and the bombings. The IRA thugs kneecapped him first. The bastards made him sit down in front of my mum, and then they shot him in both knees. When he came out of hospital, they shot him in the head while he was still in his wheelchair.'

'Jesus Christ,' said Captain Warburton in disgust. 'What kind of fucking animals are we dealing with? Every time I think about it I want to throw up. Let's go and get that Ferrari before I'm sick.'

The three of them made their way towards a little village a couple of miles in the distance. They mostly walked behind hedgerows that afforded them protection from passing vehicles, each time taking cover as the occasional car passed by.

Killeen's mind was working overtime. Something about Lieutenant Julie's story didn't ring true. She was obviously extremely smart, and having remained under cover, deep in the lion's den for two years, how could she suddenly find herself compromised by stupidly passing information that could only have come from a very small group of people? He himself had worked with under cover informants in Northern Ireland during his time with both the Intelligence Corps and the SAS, and without exception, they never passed over information that could be directly linked to themselves. Their lives depended on their considered judgement. If compromised, they were either instantly evacuated, or they died.

'What info did O'Malley pick up on then Julie?' he finally asked. 'Surely nothing was important enough to blow your cover, you were far too valuable to the army to do that.'

'That is a 'need to know' question Jim, and you of all people should be aware of that; however, if it puts your mind at ease, I will answer it for you.' Captain Warburton interrupted. 'The British Royal Family was more important. Need I say more?'

'Whaow' – Killeen let out a sharp gasp.

'I was Julie's only contact in Intelligence whilst she was working undercover, to let anyone else into the loop would have been too dangerous for her,' Warburton continued. 'We had to act, even if it meant compromising her. Now put your mind at rest Jim – Julie is one of us, of that I am sure. If it hadn't been for the information that she had been passing over, you, and your blood thirsty band of merry men wouldn't have been kept so busy.'

'This isn't the only time that I've been in deep shit you know Jim,' Julie's voice suddenly became very serious. 'Captain Warburton, and her own band of blood thirsty merry men almost got my head blown off over a year ago.'

'For God's sake, not the Galway bay episode again Julie,' Warburton feigned hurt, and sobbed a couple of times. 'I've told you before, it wasn't my doing; the whole operation was taken out of my hands by someone very high up the chain of command – someone at the top of the food chain.'

Julie grinned. 'Despite your best efforts to have me killed Allison, it was O'Malley that saved both Sean and myself, so in one way, as much as I hate him, I actually owe him my life.'

Killeen was intrigued, and looking directly at Julie with a grin on his face, went on. 'Go on then Jules, tell me about yet another military cock up.'

'Don't tell him Julie, it makes my department look like complete idiots.' Warburton knew that Julie just had to go on.

Julie continued. 'Sean and I had travelled down from Mayo to collect a consignment of "Goodies" for O'Malley, and were waiting on a quiet beach about 3 miles north west of Galway for the delivery. A small rowing boat came ashore from an American cargo ship bound for Cork, and two men unloaded a box. From the shape and size of it, it obviously contained rifles; 4 American M14's to be exact, all bound for the 'A' team. Even though it was around 2 in the morning, it was still pretty light with a near full moon, and we were fairly exposed, so we grabbed the box, and scarpered as quickly as we could to our car and loaded it into the boot.

That's when two MI6 officers appeared pointing their guns at us. The younger of the two men said. "Sorry about this love, but orders are orders, we've been told to take no prisoners". He lifted his pistol to my head, and within less than a second, both of them were dead, each with a bullet through the head.

O'Malley had been there for hours no more than a few yards away from the two MI6 officers, plus Sean and myself, and none of us had seen him; it was as if he was invisible. He just appeared from nowhere, and disappeared just as quickly.'

Killeen had a curious look on his face as he turned his attention to Warburton.

'It wasn't my fault Jim. Julie had passed on the information about the drop to me, and I had passed it on to MI 6, thinking that they would in turn pass it on to their Irish counterparts and intercept the bloody cargo ship. Pretty fucking stupid of me really, the Irish Government are shit scared of upsetting the IRA in case they set off a couple of bombs in the tourist areas, and destroy their precious tourist industry. That's why 6 decided to intercept the cargo themselves, thinking that it was much bigger than it actually turned out to be. If they had known that it was only 4 poxy rifles, none of us would have bothered; the IRA already have hundreds of the damned things.'

'Not just 4 poxy rifles Allison; 4 poxy M14's, one of which almost certainly killed Muscles and Mac,' Killeen was visibly angry as he continued. 'Why kill Julie then, surely it was in every one's interest to keep her alive if she was still providing useful intel?'

'I can't answer that one Jim,' Warburton was shaking her head as she spoke. 'It had to come from someone pretty high up the food chain, as any connection between the British security forces and the death of Julie and Sean would have created a massive diplomatic incident. Southern Ireland is not Britain don't forget, they are completely neutral; two faced bastards the lot of them. The thing that still has my department baffled though, is who the hell tipped off O'Malley, and why did he wait for so long to kill the two men from 6? It was as if he was testing Julie and Sean's loyalty.'

'Clever bastard,' Killeen smiled and shook his head as he spoke. 'Ken Wardle reckons that O'Malley never takes chances; I guess that he was just reassuring himself about Julie and Sean. Still, it's worrying where he is getting his information from. For something like that to happen, he had to have been tipped off, and that could only have come from someone that you passed the information onto Alison.'

'It always struck me as an inside job from within either MI5 or 6 Jim,' Julie pursed her lips. 'My big worry was that if whoever was responsible for this particular leak found out my identity, my life expectancy would have been somewhere between nought and zero once O'Malley got wind of it.'

Warburton looked sternly at Julie as she spoke, 'There was never any question of that happening Julie, not as long as I was your contact; not a cat in hell's chance. I was the only one in my department that was aware of your identity. The big worry now though is, how the hell has O'Malley been able to get so close to us on this operation, when not even my own department has the faintest idea of where I am or what I'm up to?'

The three of them continued their journey to the village in silence, the two women deep in thought, Killeen deep in a trance like state, his body in Middle England, his eyes betraying the 1000 yard stare. His mind flitted between contacts and firefights that he had been involved in over the last few years, and as always, no matter how hard he tried to eliminate him from the picture, that bloody kid in the desert would appear, pointing his AK47 at him. Standing behind him would be the manic face of O'Malley – grinning, and pointing a pistol at his head.

Killeen knew that there was something seriously wrong. He doubted that he was up to the task ahead, but he was now too deeply involved. There was to be no going back; he had to see it through.

He had failed his first test; fallen at the first hurdle when confronted by O'Malley on the motorway, and he was now deeply troubled, not just by his own inability to react, but also as to why O'Malley hadn't killed him when he had the chance.

What was his game?

What the hell was he up to?

Was he toying with him?

Was he the mouse to O'Malley's cat?

O'Malley had looked deeply into Killeen's eyes, and what he had seen was no more than an empty shell.

The soul and the spirit had been left behind, and were now trapped in the killing fields of South Armagh.

Killeen knew that somehow, he had to revive and reunite both his soul and his spirit, and to return them to the empty shell that was now his body. If not, the hypnotic spell that O'Malley had cast from the silver merc would have only one outcome – not just for him, but for his entire section.

CHAPTER 16

STEVEN 'MOLLY' MALONE

Molly had been with Killeen's section for 18 months, and had loved every minute of it. This was his first section attachment after surviving the Hereford torture chamber, and the fulfillment of a boyhood dream.

Unlike most SAS troopers, this life was exactly as he had expected it to be; it was also everything that he wanted it to be. At 5 foot 11 inches, he was the smallest man in the section, and at 23, also the youngest. Everyone at Hereford called him Molly – in fact, as far back as he could remember, he had always been called Molly. There was however one notable exception; that exception was Sergeant Paddy Jackson – Paddy always called him *BOY*.

Molly called Paddy, *APEMAN*, or simply, *THE APE*. Molly was the only man in the world who dared call Paddy anything other than – Paddy – Sgt Jackson – or simply, Mr. Jackson.

The first time Molly had called Paddy "*THE APE*", the world had stopped turning. Everyone froze – waiting for, and fearing Paddy's response. Tension didn't just immobilize the section, all of Hereford shuddered, awaiting the volcanic explosion that was sure to follow.

Paddy's face had broken into a big grin; he had put a giant arm round Molly and said, 'Stick close to me *BOY*, and you might just see your next birthday – unless of course you upset me that is.'

Everyone in Hereford breathed out, and the world once again started to spin.

Molly had a remarkable brain and qualifications to match, and like Killeen, he had turned down offers from several universities. It never ceased to amaze him just how many clever individuals, possibly bordering on brilliant, there were in the SAS. What was the attraction? If they had stayed with their own regiment or corps, promotion would certainly have been accelerated, whereas in the SAS it was notoriously slow. Just what drew these men to this kind of life? Was it the sense of danger, or simply the need to prove themselves to themselves?

Coupled with Molly's brain, was an almost photographic memory. His mastery at reading and reacting to a situation was enhanced by his ability to take a mental picture of a given terrain. This quality was invaluable on a stake out, where the slightest noise registered an exact position in his mind. Killeen always kept Molly close to him; his brain and memory were assets that were much too valuable to be wasted. If Molly was close to Killeen, Paddy was never far away.

For such an intelligent, bordering genius individual, one whose hobby was reading and studying psychology, it came as a surprise to discover that Molly was also a very efficient and effective killing machine. He could afford to be good at his job; he always knew that Paddy was close by – waiting, and watching, like an over protective father.

The first time that he had used his knife to conduct business, had been in the gulf by Sheik Armani's palace. Previously, he had used a silenced pistol, or his rifle, but on this occasion it had to be the knife. The would-be assassin's head had come back and up surprisingly easily. The knife had entered the neck from the left hand side about an inch below the chin, and a viscous ripping motion had removed the vocal chords and the windpipe. All he needed to do then was to hold his hand in place over the victim's mouth until the body went limp. The result had been a nice, clean, textbook job; if indeed any textbook had ever been written covering the subject.

Muscles hadn't been so lucky, his target had been dead but refused to accept it, and had continued fighting for several seconds.

Molly could not help wishing that his victim had put up more of a fight. Certainly he had wanted him to live longer – to struggle more. He had wanted the man to experience the terror of knowing that he was going to die – in fact, the terror of knowing that he was already on the verge of dying and could do nothing about it. He had felt exhilaration and intense pleasure as the knife had sunk in. It didn't last for long enough. It was however much more enjoyable than a silenced pistol.

He had felt envious of Muscles, and wondered if he had felt the same exhilaration that he most certainly felt?

He did not tell anyone how he had felt, but for that brief moment in time, he suddenly knew why he had really joined the SAS.

It had been quite a few hours before his eyes regained their normal cheerful luster.

Back at Sheik Armani's palace, Wardle had noticed the eyes.

CHAPTER 17

A MADMAN TO CATCH A MADMAN

Trooper Molly Malone had a fitful night's sleep. The deaths of Muscles and Mac had been flashing before his eyes for quite a few nights, and sleeping in his own bed in his parent's Cumbrian house, no more than ten miles away from the Old Manor, seemed to give rise to an even greater feeling of guilt than normal. Why hadn't it been him that had taken the bullet? He didn't have much to look forward to now in life; just a slow, inexorable descent into madness – nothing else.

Having spoken at length the previous day to Ken Sniffer Wardle, he had been told things about O'Malley that he could barely believe – his marksmanship – his seeming invisibility – his ruthlessness, and his cunning. One thing that had always bothered him was the death of Muscles and Mac at O'Malley's hand. The rest of the section had always assumed that there had been two shooters; now he was not so sure. Both men had died before they had heard the first bang. Muscles had taken the first chest shot, and a couple of seconds later, Mac had been hit. Instinctively, Mac would have hit the ground on hearing the first bang, but he never moved.

Molly did some calculations in his head. His conclusions were feasible, but surely not humanly possible. If what Wardle had said was true, and O'Malley had fired from 1000 yards; the bullet would have hit Muscles roughly one second after being fired. The bang would have taken some two seconds longer. For the second shot to hit Mac before the first bang arrived, had meant that O'Malley would have had to aim, and then fire his second shot in slightly less than two seconds.

'He can do that. I've seen him do it.' Wardle had said.

Molly mentally pictured his time at sniper training school. Five seconds between long range sniper shots was good; less than two seconds to re-load, aim, and fire with any degree of accuracy was impossible. This was as good as an excellent *pistol* shot could achieve at a range of 20 yards using an automatic pistol. At 1000 yards, the target would be tiny; plus, both men were camouflaged, and near impossible to see at such extreme range.

'He is insane,' Wardle had said. 'Mad as a hatter – totally fucking bonkers; that is what makes him so dangerous. Even though he never takes chances, he is completely unpredictable. Expect the unexpected because that is the only way you will be able to counter him. Remember that there are four of them. O'Malley will deploy them himself. He doesn't just want the girl, he wants the rest of us, and he will be fully prepared to sacrifice the other three of them just to get at us. One thing he will not do however is offer himself. He has a survival instinct that is so strong, barely anyone has ever taken a shot at him in 20 years, much of it on active service.'

'What about equipment Ken?' Molly had asked.

'I've spoken to the Brigadier; work out exactly what you need once you have walked around the grounds a few times, and give him the list. Don't forget the correct scopes. I bet you a fiver that he offers to zero them himself; if he does – *let him*.'

'What; a Brigadier is going to zero the scopes for me? You're on. Make that fiver a tenner.'

'Done; *ten* quid it is then Molly; you will lose, I can promise you that.'

Molly was awake at five o clock the next morning. Sleep had not come easily to him. Ten minutes snatched here, half an hour there. Each brief spell had been punctuated by visions of Muscles and Mac – of the Old Manor House – the 'A' team – the lake and the surrounding terrain – ambush points, plus dozens of other variables. One overriding thought however – one reoccurring vision, was always O'Malley.

"Insane – mad as a hatter – totally fucking bonkers". Ken Wardle had said and stressed. The question was. 'How do you plan for and deal with a madman?'

Molly's photographic memory came in to play. He mentally scanned the psychology books that he had read. Nowhere did he come up with an answer. The people who had written the books had spent months, and in many cases, years, studying their patients. He had just a few hours.

Molly closed his eyes, and again hovered between the conscious and the unconscious, his mind jumping from imaginary scenarios to reality.

Where was the answer to this problem? He had been tasked with fathoming out the mind of someone so mentally unstable, so unpredictable, that he probably didn't even know himself what his next move would be.

Suddenly the penny dropped as he mentally scanned a section by Freud, the father of psychology. He clearly saw the road to Damascus open up in front of him. It was closer than he could ever have imagined. The answer was staring him right in the face.

The way to figure out the mind of a madman – was to become mad.

Forget what a sane, rational man would do. *Do* what a madman would do.

That was why the section had never got anywhere near to O'Malley in Ireland. It wasn't that he was, "so fucking smart", as Wardle had always said: It was because he was insane – mad as a hatter – totally fucking bonkers. He did not follow normal rational rules and thought processes like everyone else. His twisted, mad, and perverted mind worked in a different dimension.

Molly knew that to understand and beat him, he had to move into that same dimension. He was concerned that once he was in there, he might never be able to get out. He had been there once before, briefly, in the desert, at the point where the knife had sunk into the man's throat. He had fought long and hard with his inner demons. He was ok now, but… could he allow himself to cross that very fine dividing line between genius and insanity, in order to enter O'Malley's own unique world?

Molly knew that he didn't really have a choice. It was only a question of time. Every second generation male on his father's side had gone insane. He was second generation. Up until his last birthday, he was beginning to think that maybe he was the lucky one – the one that got away. As he plunged his knife into the man's throat in the desert, *he knew*. He hadn't escaped the family curse. The curse of the Malones'. An insane, incurable affliction that went back as far as records could be traced, stopping only at the Bedlam asylum, where his ancestors had been viewed by countless rich and morbidly curious aristocracy – viewed as if they were zoo or circus animals – viewed simply for amusement. He was beginning his spiraling descent into full blown madness. It was only a question of time: not if, but when!

Of one thing he was sure; there would be no nut house for him – no modern day Bedlam. He would go in his own time – a time of his own choosing, no-one else – there would be no doctors involved.

Wardle had been noticing the signs for many months. The secret was in the eyes – eyes that he had been seeing for close on 20 years in O'Malley.

Molly didn't smell of death as O'Malley did. It was still latent, and hadn't yet fully surfaced.

Wardle was counting on Molly releasing his tenuous hold on reality, and moving into the realms of madness.

Molly's sanity had to be sacrificed to defeat O'Malley – there was no other way – Molly knew that.

Molly now realized that Wardle also knew that.

He also knew that Wardle was counting on it.

CHAPTER 18

PREPARATION AND PLAN

SAS Trooper Molly Malone walked thoughtfully around the lake in the grounds of the Old Manor House. He was careful to count the steps that he took, memorizing both detail and distance. The lake itself was quite pretty at this time of year, spring, and the daffodils had sprung. How poetic he thought to himself; only fleetingly; his mind was now prepared, and ready to enter the twilight world and dimension of his ancestors.

The landscape itself was a military planners dream. A four man team would be deployed in pretty much textbook fashion. The whole area looked as if it had been designed for such a purpose. The main shooter would be positioned on the far side of the lake, which was 100 yards wide – giving a distance of 200 yards to the front of the Old Manor. The back-up shooter would be at the beginning of the drive behind a dry stone wall, his task being to take out any other targets, almost certainly with the rifle set on automatic fire. The other two men would be placed on either flank, in what were a few perfectly positioned shrubberies. Their job would be to cover the two shooter's retreat, and to provide backup fire in the event of a fire fight.

No matter how inexperienced the team leader; there was no other way to deploy a four man team. A team leader would have to be completely insane to even consider any other form of deployment, as the team members would then become completely exposed in any form of a firefight with no chance of escape, and no covering fire to conduct an exit plan. There always had to be an exit plan.

Molly didn't have just the one card up his sleeve though, he had two. The first one was the element of surprise, which would allow the team to take up position, and the second one? For the first time in his life, O'Malley – the madman, was up against someone like Molly – a man operating in the same insane dimension as himself.

There is a very fine, often imperceptible dividing line between genius and madness. Molly had allowed himself to cross that dividing line.

Unlike O'Malley however, he had taken his genius with him – this genius now supplemented his madness.

After one final sweeping look, he walked down the tree lined drive to the Manor House. '70 yards,' he said out loud, 'plus 30 from the beginning of the drive to the edge of the lake.' If Wardle was correct, O'Malley will be in position exactly 800 yards back from the lake, giving himself a shooting range of 1000 yards, and looking straight down the drive. That position was pretty much cast in stone. It was the other three positions that worried him. Where would a madman place his back up shooters in order to gain maximum protection for himself, and to ensure a trouble free getaway if things went wrong? Molly had no doubt at all in his mind. O'Malley would sacrifice the lot of them in order to guarantee his own survival.

As he approached the Old Manor House, he looked up at the façade of the old stone structure, his eyes following the contours. A solid, no nonsense grey Cumbrian stone building, probably built well over a century earlier by a rich Lancashire cotton Baron. It was not designed to impress, nor was it particularly pretty or grand. The owner had obviously wanted people to know that he was wealthy without having to boast about it. As a young man, his parents had taken him to see many old country homes and mansions; this was something that he had always enjoyed. In every case, the building had screamed out to the visitor – "look how rich and powerful I am". Somehow, the Old Manor House was different; it was as if it had been built to live in, and not to visually boast about. None of the others ever gave off that message.

As he approached the century old oak door that hung on enormous slightly rusting hinges, it was creakingly opened for him by a smart well dressed lady, probably in her early fifties. He had half expected this to happen, as the building was dotted with dark grey colored security cameras, shaded to blend in discreetly with the old stone.

'Can I help you sir?' she asked, in a well spoken and educated Cumbrian voice.

'I am here to see the Brigadier, Ma'am, I'm Mr. Malone.'

'Do you have an appointment Mr. Malone?'

'It's personal Ma'am, the Brigadier is expecting me.'

They both walked inside, and picking up the phone, she dialed a two digit number and spoke to the adjutant.

'There is a Mr. Malone to see the Brigadier sir; he does not have an appointment, however he says the Brigadier is expecting him.'

There was a slight pause before she continued. 'No sir, he does not look to be military.'

'If you would like to go up the stairs sir, you will need to report to the adjutant, it is the second door on the right.'

After thanking her, Molly made his way slowly up the stone stairway, taking in the multi circular pillars of the interior. Just like the outside facade had been, the inside was again of a no nonsense lay out. Probably the only changes made in over a hundred years, maybe even 200 years, had been the completely incongruous white radiators, in place of the wonderful stone and firebrick inglenook fireplaces that were now boarded over. There was also strip neon lighting in place of what had almost certainly been something much more grandiose and pleasing to the eye.

Molly's mind pictured a couple of crystal chandeliers, and the grand inglenook fireplace, crackling and glowing with burning logs. He wondered if occasionally the human race had moved in the wrong direction. They no longer built feature fire places, or chocolate box pretty thatched cottages; beauty was now often sacrificed for functionality. Visions of ugly, multi storey tenement blocks entered his mind briefly.

He knocked on the second door on the right, as the pleasant and efficient lady at the reception had said; and as there was no answer, he walked in, closing the substantial heavy solid old oak door behind him. He smiled, as the almost musical creaking sound of the large hinges was identical to the creaking of the main entrance door.

'Who the devil are you? I did not say come in,' came the aggressive response from the slightly balding man sat behind an old fashioned oak desk.

Molly noticed that the adjutant had partially opened the drawer to the desk where he was seated, and had one hand inside the drawer.

'I wonder if I could kill him before he could take out the pistol and shoot me.' Molly thought. He loved setting himself these mental challenges; only today, he really felt like doing it. It would be only too simple. He would rush forward and push the desk into the man's stomach, thereby trapping his hand in the drawer, then he would introduce him to Paddy's calling card.

'Well, what do you want with Brigadier Wardle then? He is a very busy man.' The adjutant appeared to have taken an instant dislike to Molly, and spoke in a clip and unfriendly tone of voice, almost spitting the words out.

'It's rather personal sir, I really must speak with him urgently.' Molly did not want to reveal too much about the operation, and had also taken an instant dislike to the arrogance of the man. His neck was long and slender, almost feminine, and his physique bore little resemblance to that of a soldier. A lifetime of sitting behind desks and shuffling paper had taken its toll.

'And I said that the Brigadier is busy, so speak to me or get out.' The adjutant said in a threatening manner, pushing his hand deeper into the drawer, and viewing Molly's long hair and relatively scruffy appearance with some disdain.

Molly hadn't even been home for one full day before Ken Wardle had called him, and had barely had enough time to clean himself up properly, after months of undercover work and active service in Northern Ireland.

He had also become quite used to being scruffy, and had seen little need to change his appearance. The army could go and stuff itself as far as he was concerned. He had just sacrificed several months of his life living rough in Northern Ireland, and was now about to miss his plane to America for a well deserved fishing holiday – a holiday that he had consistently dreamed about during those long and boring stake out's and seemingly never ending surveillance operations of the last few months.

Molly loved to fish, and had decided to exchange his normal Cumbrian trout fishing tackle for something much more substantial. He was now ready to tangle with the battle hardened, 100 pound tarpon down at Key West in Florida, instead of his more usual brown trout; an elusive prize that barely constituted a decent mouthful when prepared for the table.

The Adjutant reached deeper into his drawer, his hand searching for his pistol – a pistol that he had only ever used on the practice ranges.

'Would you please tell the Brigadier that trooper Malone of D1 section is here – *NOW* – sir; and if you reach any further into your drawer, I will respectfully shove your pistol up your arse and pull the trigger – SIR.'

The adjutant looked into Molly's eyes. He did not like what he saw. It was as if a wild animal was staring at him, ready to pounce at any moment – the scruffy young man looked completely insane.

'Good morning Trooper Malone,' said the Brigadier in a friendly voice, as both the Adjutant and Molly entered the room. 'Or would you prefer that I call you Molly? Please take a seat and address me as sir, unless I say otherwise.'

The Adjutant exited the room on unsteady legs.

'Yes sir, thank you sir. Unless I have been wearing dress uniform sir, I cannot remember the last time anyone called me anything other than Molly, except Paddy of course sir, he has always called me *BOY*.'

'Ah yes, Paddy – the giant Irish *APEMAN*. Our Ken has told me all about Paddy on many occasions. Don't look so worried *BOY*, he can't hear me in here, the walls are over one foot thick. I can't say the same about the roof though – I can't help feeling that one day the whole damned thing will drop onto our heads, bits of plaster and masonry are constantly dropping down.'

'Don't be so sure about Paddy sir; you could paint him bright orange and cover him in bells, and you still wouldn't know that he was there – not until it was too late that is.' There was a pause before Molly, with a slightly puzzled look on his face, spoke again. 'You said *our* Ken sir?'

'Yes, that's right, *our* Ken; the boy who almost broke our father's heart by joining the Marines. "Bunch of Pansies and Nancy boys", he always said. Secretly, I reckon that he was as proud as punch of him, especially when he made the SBS, but he never let on. Ken broke the family army tradition by not joining the usual cavalry regiment you see. "Still a bunch of Pansies and Nancy boys, but bloody tough ones", he said one Christmas after a few too many brandies. That was the nearest that he ever got to offering him any praise.'

Both men laughed out loud. This irritated the still trembling adjutant in the next room. He remembered and could still visualize the look in Molly's eyes. What he had seen had terrified him. It was as if he had genuinely wanted him to go for the pistol – and like a coiled spring, was ready to explode into action and attack at any moment. He had recognized that any sudden movement on his part would have elicited that attack. The man had looked quite mad. A vision of a mad, rabid dog foaming at the mouth flashed before his eyes, as he now fingered his pistol nervously. Was the Brigadier safe?

Should he walk into the other room, pistol ready, and take charge of the situation? Still trembling, he placed the pistol back into the drawer and closed it, before taking a few deep breaths. He hadn't joined the army to put his life in danger – he was admin, and not too far away from his army pension.

'He was right about the tough bit sir,' Molly said. 'Certainly if Ken is anything to go by.' Molly somehow couldn't believe that he, a lowly trooper, was discussing a Sergeant Major on first name terms with a Brigadier. He had never even seen a Brigadier before, let alone sat chatting to one; it was almost as if he was talking over a few pints with a mate down the pub.

A grim look crossed the Brigadier's face. 'Tough barely describes him Molly,' he said. 'They tortured him terribly for days in Malaya. He never told them a damn thing, only his number, rank, and name. O'Malley saved his life, and then went on to wipe out the whole village, and I do mean everyone. It still disturbs him sometimes – not the torture though, he soon got over that; he could never let go of seeing all of those dead children.'

'He's never spoken a word about it sir – not a word – not one single word.'

'I bet you've never seen his back Molly. He never shows his back to anyone. That's our Ken for you. Hard little bastard as a kid; he would never back down, no matter how big the opposition. I had to rescue him from many a scrape and scrap. By the time he was 14, the tables had turned; he was bigger than me and twice as tough. It could be quite embarrassing having a fourteen year old kid as a minder.'

'Yes, I can well imagine sir.' laughed Molly, his respect for Sniffer Wardle growing by the minute.

'Anyway Molly, I am fully up to speed with the operation. I have been since day one. In fact, long before day one. Don't look so puzzled, all will eventually be revealed. The Captain, whose pistol you threatened to shove up his arse, and dad, originally came up with the idea a few weeks ago. Both Ken and dad were involved from the off. Dad has a hot line to most government ministers, and usually gets his way. That is why your team is involved. It was originally planned to be a six man operation, then Muscles and Mac got killed, and now Bob Kineer has gone missing on a one man under-cover operation somewhere in the north. He was hoping to get close enough to O'Malley to finish him off; I fear that it could well have gone tits up.'

'Christ sir, I hope Bob is ok, and as for the problem with the captain sir, I didn't –

'What do you need?' The Brigadier interrupted.

'Some of it may be a little difficult at such short notice sir.'

'Molly – I am the highest ranking officer in the North of England. I have more power than God himself; there is nothing that a Brigadier in the British army cannot acquire, and very soon, with your help, I am hoping to add the 'A' team to my collection.'

With a wink, and a very smug yet reassuring smile, he then took the list from Molly and commented 'Do they have to be M14s?'

'That's what Ken said sir, one with variable sights, and one sight zero'd at exactly 1000 yards.'

'Trust dear Kenneth to choose one of the most treasured, and difficult to obtain marksman's weapons,' the Brigadier laughed as he spoke. 'I should have anticipated it though, he always used one at Bisley. I've never seen him miss you know Molly. I don't think anyone ever has. If O'Malley ever comes within a mile of his sights, I can guarantee you that the internal components of his head will be very rapidly separated from his body.'

'A mile sir?' Molly spoke the words, chuckling at the same time. His head tilted to one side, and a frown creased his forehead, his face now adopting a look of disbelief at the serious expression on the Brigadier's face

'Oh yes Molly – a mile – and I can guarantee you that it will be a head shot as well. Ken Wardle never misses; like I said, no one has ever seen our Ken miss a target in over 20 years. Strangest thing is though Molly, he couldn't hit a barn door with a shotgun on the family estate. I swear the pheasants used to laugh at him.'

'A bit like Paddy with his rifle then sir.'

The Brigadier laughed out loud, before picking up his phone and speaking abruptly to his Adjutant in the next room. 'Ron, get me two of the army's newest M14's within the next two hours. Have them flown in by jet or helicopter, whatever is necessary, and collect them yourself from the base. Make sure that there are 50 rounds of competition grade ammunition with them.'

To Molly's amazement, the Brigadier promised to zero both rifles himself. 'That way there will be no bloody cock ups – we have worked too hard on this plan.'

'And you have just cost me ten quid sir.'

'Yes, I know. Ken promised me a fiver out of it when we spoke last night. There are many things that you don't know about our Kenneth Molly; he can also be a cunning bastard when it suits him, he always was a damned sight smarter than anyone I ever met. It was me that originally recommended his transfer to Killeen's section for the African job. Rest assured, the rifles and the scopes will meet even Ken's specifications. I know exactly what he wants. I went through sniper school myself – shot at Bisley more than once – bloody waste of time that was though, what with Ken and O'Malley there. If they had stayed away, I could have been quite famous; instead, Ken has that honor, and O'Malley carries the scars of defeat – badly, I might add. The hatred used to burn in his eyes – sometimes he looked quite insane.'

"Insane". The word bounced around in Molly's head. He was well aware of what the future held. He had voluntarily released his hold on both sanity and reality; he simply had to conceal it until the time was right to end the pretence – to end everything. He had felt his hold on reality fading as he had confronted the adjutant. It wasn't just an outburst of temper, or petulance, at his disdainful demeanor; it was a genuine desire to literally break the man's neck.

Although excited and exhilarated at the prospect, he realized that such desires had to be suppressed and controlled; there was a far more serious task ahead of him, and that task needed 100% of both his genius and his insane commitment.

As Molly walked around the lake for the sixth time, his thoughts kept flashing back to the Wardle brothers; one a Cavalry Brigadier, and the other one a Marine and SBS Sergeant Major.

'Ken could have *walked* into Sandhurst with our Military connections, the Wardle cavalry tradition goes back to before Adam was a lad. He would probably have even made it to General by now – he was always much smarter, braver, and more streetwise than I ever was,' the Brigadier had said. 'Too bloody stubborn for his own good – always was; he has been put forward for a commission on several occasions, and has always turned it down, family reasons I suppose, a little too personal to discuss.'

There was more to the Wardle family than Molly had ever imagined.

'I tried to join the SAS myself when I was about your age.' The Brigadier had told him. 'I would have made it as well. Broke my bloody ankle with one week to go, and missed all that lovely interrogation on the last few days.'

'I'm sorry about that sir – you really would have enjoyed both the pain and the experience. Why didn't you reapply sir?' Molly had asked.

'I would have done if they had let me take just the last week. Instead I had to take the whole bloody selection course again. Would you go through it twice? I have always thought that people who do either don't feel pain – or they enjoy pain. You would have to be a bloody masochist to go through that torture twice.'

There was a third reason – Molly could not tell the Brigadier what it was. His thoughts turned back to O'Malley. Ken Wardle had told him that he was always very protective towards his men. Not unlike "The Ape and the Boy" really. Paddy was always very protective toward him. If any of his section had received so much as a scratch, O'Malley had gone completely off the rails. Having to rescue Wardle from 3 days of torture by the Malayan communist insurgents, and then losing another man from his section, would explain his killing spree in the village.

By complete contrast, there were occasions when his killings had been meticulously planned, and carried out for legitimate military reasons. The death of Molly and Mac had been an example of such planning; that was definitely not the action of a man whose insanity was running out of control. How could he switch from sanity, to complete insanity, and then back again? Was he actually insane, or was he a schizophrenic?

Molly had made the switch in the desert, and had managed to reverse it. He doubted that he could make the return journey again. He didn't mind – he was now comfortably enveloped by a feeling of relief at finally entering the realm of madness. The self imposed barrier that had kept him barely on the side of sanity was now well and truly dismantled, and he had passed through the open door into a new, exciting dimension. The line had been crossed, and he felt good at the release that it afforded. The door had now been firmly closed – locked and bolted behind him – there was to be no going back. This was to be Molly's new world – a world from which there could be only one means of escape. He, and he alone, would decide when and how. There would be no doctors.

The plan now forming in Molly's head needed O'Malley to be insane and not schizophrenic. He had to be as mad as a hatter – totally fucking bonkers, or it would not work.

Poacher turned Gamekeeper: *A MADMAN TO CATCH A MADMAN.*

If Wardle was correct, and O'Malley was completely insane, Molly was quite certain that he would no longer be protective towards his own men; on the contrary, he would almost certainly willingly sacrifice the lot of them in order to save his own skin. This was what he was counting on; if not, and he had got it wrong – what was left of section D1 SAS would be eliminated.

CHAPTER 19

PLAIN SAILING

'Pretty good expense account you've got there Allison.' Killeen and Captain Allison Warburton, W.R.A.C., were now comfortably on first name terms. 'Just how far will the credit card stretch then?'

'I've never really tested it to its limit Jim, though I reckon I've raised a few eyebrows some months. So far, no one has ever questioned my expenses. So far though, I've never bought a car on my expenses. I did manage a nice little shopping trip to New York last year on it. One of our Irish informants considered that the IRA hierarchy were getting a little suspicious, so he did a bunk to the States.'

'Where did you meet up with him then, in Macys or on 5th Avenue?' Killeen enquired, grinning as he did so.

'Neither of those Jim – I met up with him at the morgue. Someone very high up in that colander masquerading as our intelligence service, had revealed his hideout to the Republicans in New York, and they decided to turn him into a colander. They put over 50 bullet holes in him as a warning. I didn't want to waste the opportunity, so I spent a few days shopping at the army's expense.'

The three of them laughed; from now on, it would be plain sailing all the way to Cumbria, and the pretty young package would be delivered.

Still laughing, Killeen went on. 'Why didn't you test it to destruction then and buy the Jag? You could have always said that somebody nicked it once this job is over with. I don't have a car, in case you haven't noticed, I appear to have mislaid mine somewhere in a wheat field off the M1 – and before you even think about asking; yes, it was my own car, I wanted to claim the mileage – just a different form of shopping trip to yours really Allison.'

The car that Killeen was now driving wasn't really to his liking; it wasn't to any one's liking, it had simply been the cheapest car on the forecourt. The one litre ford was a horrible shade of brown, red, and rust.

'Dog shit brown.' Killeen had said, quoting Blaster Bates, his favorite stand-up comedian.

'Sick and Tan,' had been Julie's description. 'I'll take it if you don't want it then Jim, it will be a nice little run around, I fancy a bit of sight-seeing around the Lake District once this job is finished.'

'And how on earth am I going to explain 11 hundred quid on my exes then Julie?' Warburton interrupted. 'Three portions of diamond encrusted fish and chips at the Cumbrian Ritz?'

Killeen stopped at a driveway to an old farmhouse for a couple of minutes in order to study the map given to them by the car salesman; a man who had looked mightily relieved when someone had finally bought the pile of junk that he had been stuck with for the past few months. He would have willingly sold the car for eight hundred pounds if they had pushed him. For some reason, the three of them had been so eager to make a quick purchase, that he had chanced his arm, and they fell for it. Tonight would be celebration time down the local pub.

Killeen took out a pen from the pocket of his shirt, and began marking out a route. 'We'll cross the M1 and head east, and then skirt the motorway until we are somewhere around Nottingham, taking these smaller 'B' roads. There, we can pick up the M1 again all the way to Sheffield, and then slip across the Pennines to Manchester. From Manchester, the M6 should be busy enough to take us up past Lancaster without being compromised. You can follow our progress with the map Allison. I take it that you do map reading in the W.R.A.C.?'

'You are starting to sound like that oaf Paddy, Jim.'

'Sorry Allison. When you spend 24 hours a day for months on end with someone, you can easily pick up a few of their less attractive mannerisms.'

'You will be forgiven as soon as I get something to eat.' Warburton said, at the same time rubbing her rather substantial stomach.

The dog shit monster, as Killeen had christened it, soldiered on for a couple of hours; past Northampton, and into Leicestershire, before finally pulling into a little roadside café.

As the three of them climbed out of the car, Julie gave him a little wink, making sure that Warburton was facing in the other direction. He returned the wink, both eyes straying to her breasts, and immediately he felt guilty.

It had been months since he had last slept with Julie – his Julie. It had been years since he had last slept with any other woman.

'Is all this fucking army crap worth it?' Paddy had often said. 'I should be in a nice warm bed now, shagging half a dozen barmaids, and supping a few pints of Guinness after each one.'

More than at any time before in his life, James Killeen suddenly knew exactly what Paddy had meant. All it had taken was one little wink from a young woman – a real live woman. He now felt exactly the same way.

What kind of a life had he been living for the last few years? He would be 32 in two days time, and his best years would soon be behind him. He had no home other than the army. He didn't even own a bed. He slept wherever the army told him to – in barracks – in the desert – in a deserted barn – behind a hedge – rarely in a nice warm bed with Julie beside him, the army never told him to sleep there, he had to sort that out for himself, only the army never gave him enough time. There was always something going on somewhere in the world that required his services – services that the rest of the world were not to know about.

It had been so different when he had been in the Intelligence Corps working at the Old Manor House by the lake. He had seen Julie every day. He had slept in the little cottage that her father had bought for her when she had married John. Ah yes, JOHN. He had forgotten all about John with all the things that had been going on; that was something that he intended to sort. In her recent letters, Julie had told him that John was once again becoming troublesome. He would make that little task a priority. Priority meant tomorrow – maybe even tonight if he could find the time.

As the three of them left the cafe, it was Julie who passed the first comment regarding the quality of the food. 'Just like the car Jim – absolute dog shit.'

Killeen was thinking of other things and not the shit cooking. Julie had been looking at him in a peculiar fashion, always careful to avoid Warburton's attention. He seemed to have lost his focus on the matter in hand. His mind flitted between the two Julies. They weren't really that much different. About the same height, same build, and with very similar mannerisms. His Julie was a few years older, yet still very young looking for her age. Lieutenant Julie had great legs and tits. He couldn't remember his Julie's legs and tits. It seemed like a lifetime ago that he had last seen them.

How much longer did she expect him to wait? He would be 32 in a couple of days. Will he have to wait until he is 42 before she finally makes up her mind? Exactly what did she expect of him? He certainly wasn't poor; his family was in fact extremely well off, with a very profitable business, a factory, and several shops to their name. He also had a few bob in the bank: the job didn't allow him enough time to spend even half his earnings, they just disappeared into his bank account and sat there. They had done so for years.

Just as he was about to climb into the driver's seat of the dog shit monster, he noticed the flat tyre. He did not notice the silver Mercedes as it disappeared around a bend no more than 100 yards north of them; his thoughts had been inside lieutenant Julie's tight fitting blouse.

Some 15 minutes later, the flat tyre replaced by a near bald and certainly illegal spare, they continued their journey northwards, following the same route as the unseen silver Mercedes.

Killeen constantly glanced into his rear view mirror, each time his eyes being met by a smiling Julie. After travelling along the quiet country lane for around 2 or 3 miles, the car began to shudder as it entered a sharp bend, swerving slightly in order to avoid a substantial tree branch lying across the road.

'Oh fuck Jim, what is it now?' Warburton said in exasperation. 'On the way back, I think I'm going to call into that garage, and shove whatever is left of this car right up that salesman's arse, and get the army's money back. It can't possibly be another puncture; if it is, we are really stuffed. I am beginning to think that the best idea would be to hand Julie over to O'Malley, and ask him for a lift to the nearest railway station.'

'OK by me.' Killeen winked at Warburton.

'This has to be a unanimous decision – not a majority one.' interrupted Julie, as the three of them climbed out of the car to check the tyres.

'DOWN.' Killeen yelled. '*DOWN* – into the ditch.' He gave each girl an almighty shove, sending them both head first into the ditch, as he himself dived forward, narrowly missing the two of them.

They were just in time. As the three of them were still on their dive downwards, two shots rang out – one from the left of the car, and one from the right. The first bullet shattered the car's windscreen, and the second one ricocheted off the bonnet, and embedded itself into an old oak tree in the field behind them.

'Just my bloody luck,' said Killeen. 'I've landed in the biggest pile of mud and shit in all Leicestershire.' Right beside him was a field drain that was steadily oozing water, turning the ditch into liquid mud. 'Two shooters, both AK47s,' he continued. 'Slightly less than 100 yards range either side of the car, and almost certainly, a third man with a silenced pistol down the road. What the hell are the IRA doing with AK 47s, they always use M16s, apart from the 'A' team.'

'How on earth do you know all that Jim?' Asked Julie, with an inquisitive smile on her face, followed by a chuckle.

It was now clearly obvious to Killeen that any woman who could smile after having just been shot at, was pretty much used to living with danger on a regular basis.

'I saw the bullet hole in the tyre, but I didn't hear the shot; someone had used a silencer at the point where I slowed down to avoid that branch in the road. I should have smelt a rat there and then, there hasn't been so much as a breeze for the last few days, so someone must have stuck the branch there.'

Killeen knew why he hadn't smelt a rat; his mind had been driving on auto pilot, his thoughts' being too preoccupied with both the smile and the enticingly concealed breasts of his passenger.

'And the AK47s?'

'Rather a distinctive sound. I've heard enough of them. Usually, they're aimed at me. It was easy to tell the distance from the car with the time difference between the bang and the bullet impacting. This is not O'Malley and the 'A' team thank God, he doesn't use AK47s, and according to Ken, he never misses.'

'It could be O'Riordan's crew then Jim, he has a three man team now that we have hold of Max, and from what I've heard, none of them are very good.' Julie dusted dirt from her arm as she spoke. 'I don't think anyone else has come over, plus, they like to keep their UK sleepers very low profile, and only use them for the bigger jobs or the bombings.'

'They would also have difficulty getting hold of AK47s if they were UK based.' Warburton added.

'They have shit loads of them in Ireland. I should know, Sean and I collected them on more than one occasion down in Galway, until you and yours tried to have me shot Allison.'

Warburton grinned ruefully.

'Ten out of bloody ten for O'Riordan trying this time then ladies. How the hell could he have known that we were travelling along this road? Christ – how stupid of us; that's how we got the first puncture at the dog shit café, that would have given them time to get into position. They can't possibly have a tracker on the car, so one of us must be carrying one. Check your handbags – you know what you are looking for.'

The two women carefully emptied the contents of their handbags onto the grass at the side of the ditch, after firstly taking out their pistols, which they duly cocked, and simultaneously took off the safety catch; they then sifted through the various creams and containers. Julie self consciously tried to hide a small blue box of Durex condoms, and blushed profusely when she saw both Killeen and Warburton smiling. 'I'm just looking after them for a friend.' she said, her face now turning bright red.

'I do it all the time for my friends.' Chuckled Killeen.

'I can't think of one single reason why I would ever need one.' said a smiling Allison Warburton, with a wink and a sideways flick of her head aimed at the other two.

'The sneaky bastard; it had to be Sean,' hissed Julie. 'Why did he tip me off that Mitch Murphy was coming for me, and then plant this fucking tracker on me. It was completely buried at the bottom of this face cream. I would never have found it for months if I hadn't been poking around in it.

OH SHIT, I was round Cath's apartment yesterday afternoon when we all arrived. That's probably how O'Malley found her. That bullet in her head was meant for me – poor Cath, it's like I killed her. He wouldn't have been able to pick up the signal in our apartment as I put my handbag in the safe; we were told not to go outside of the apartment, so I only took out my pistol. Why would he kill poor Cath though? He knows me. He has seen me with Sean often enough.'

'He likes to kill Julie, you know that, both MI5 and 6 have been after him for months,' said Warburton. 'That's why Maggi agreed to our request for two teams from the SAS to search him out and kill him. Now it looks like he might have turned the tables. Apparently, he was once a very good Marine – now he is a very good psychopath.'

'Maggi?' Killeen lifted his head in surprise, before remembering the two gunmen, and immediately ducking down. You mean that the Prime Minister was involved in our deployment?'

"Need to Know", again Jim. The Government has always resisted any form of Special Force involvement in Northern Ireland in order to keep up the pretense that they have things under control. She has recently appointed a new Defense Minister who appears to have balls – the only one in her cabinet other than herself I might add. As long as you lot remained under the radar, the party line has always been that neither the SAS nor the SBS were in Ireland. Other than Maggi and her Defense Minister, none of the rest of those wankers in parliament are even aware of your deployment, let alone what your remit was.'

Killeen smiled inwardly at the thought of Prime Minister Margaret Thatcher with a pair of balls, his mind now switched into overdrive; somehow, he had to work out how to escape from the ditch, and at the same time eliminate the two snipers, who had them all pretty well pinned down and unable to move in any direction. The snipers had positioned themselves well, and were more than a rag tag bunch of thick Paddies. Somewhere down the line, they had been given training in ambush techniques.

For the moment, Killeen and the two women were well hidden, but to raise so much as a finger above the upper rim of the ditch, would easily be spotted through a telescopic sight.

Killeen's mind flashed back to a similar situation in the north of Ireland some three months previous. Word had come down that a lone gunman, completely unknown, and not on the army's radar, was taking pot shots at army patrols. So far no one had been hurt, as apparently, the would be sniper wasn't a very good shot, nevertheless, it was only a matter of time before he got lucky.

Killeen's section were withdrawn from the bandit country of South Armagh, and their search for O'Malley, and had been instructed to stake out the area with orders to eliminate the gunman. They had been on staggered surveillance for four days and nights, observing military vehicles moving through the area, when a convoy came under fire. The section was radioed in and took up position. They could easily locate the general area where the shots were coming from, but there was no way of getting close to the gunman without being spotted, nor could they in turn spot him.

Paddy, already dressed in army camouflaged clothing, had rolled in a big pile of stinking mud, then covered himself in leaves, twigs, and grass, and having worked himself to the end of the ditch past where the rest of the section were lying, proceeded to crawl on his belly, all the way to the little clump of bushes and scrub where Killeen was convinced that the gunman was hiding. The rest of the section lay down a volley of shots into the bushes to ensure that the gunman kept his head down, rather than pay attention to whatever else was going on around him. Two shots rang out, and an evil smelling Paddy emerged from the undergrowth in triumph, carrying a Remington hunting rifle, and resembling a badly constructed scarecrow. The section returned to the border to resume their fruitless search for the 'A' team.

This was the only chance that he had of getting close enough to the first gunman, without the sniper on the other side of the road spotting him. Unlike Paddy however, he was dressed in civilian clothes, and not army camouflage; this really had to be a complete mud bath. He then proceeded to emulate Paddy's trick until he was baked in mud from head to toe. The two women then began the process of sticking leaves, twigs, and grass on to him, in fact, anything that they could lay their hands on. Julie came up with an empty coke can and pushed it against his groin.

Killeen smiled. 'I will drink it later with a shot of vodka and a slice of lemon.' He said, gently pushing her hand away. She was really making her intensions pretty obvious now.

Before moving off, he repositioned the two women some 10 yards apart, making sure that both of them were well hidden, to await the arrival of the third man, the man with the silenced pistol. He would have to break cover sooner rather than later. Slowly, Killeen edged along the ditch, and, emulating Paddy, crawled and slithered on his stomach along a slight hollow in the field past the solitary oak tree until he could spot the first gunman. He was slightly out of range for a rapid pistol shot, and to make the telling shot with his pistol, would have meant crouching and aiming carefully. This would have exposed his upper body to the second gunman, and at a range of no more than 150 yards, he was a sitting duck. He had to crawl closer, but he was too exposed. He inched himself forward to around 30 yards from the gunman when he was spotted.

He now had only one option. That was to charge, screaming at the top of his voice. This always had the effect of disorientating the defenders. He prayed that the gunman did not have his rifle set on automatic fire, if so, he was dead.

Killeen charged towards the man, screaming as he did so, zigzagging as he ran, and firing his pistol. The man panicked, and fired two un-aimed shots roughly in the right direction, not having the time to look through his telescopic sights. Had he been a trained soldier, he would have slipped the rifle onto automatic fire, and cut Killeen in half.

The first shot to hit him was in the pit of his stomach. He dropped his weapon, and held up his hands in surrender, screaming in pain as he did so. The second shot was in the head.

Killeen was now directly in the line of fire of the second gunman some 200 yards away. He dived over the dead man, just as the bullet whistled over him, missing him by no more than inches.

Killeen slowly raised his head to look for the second gunman, using the dead body as cover. He could just make out the shape of the second man's head, but there was no way that he could move from his present position; not without being shot.

'You prick,' he said out loud. 'What a prick!' He had completely forgotten about the dead man's rifle lying beside him.

He picked up the rifle – adjusted the sights to 200 yards – took careful aim, and pulled the trigger.

200 yards away, a man's head exploded, as the 7-62mm bullet passed through it at more than 3000ft per second. The face was still recognizable. The brains, and the rest of the head, were scattered over an area almost the size of a tennis court. For a brief moment, Killeen saw his own head explode. There was that kid again. That bloody kid with the AK47. Will he never go away? Paddy broke his neck. Why won't the little bastard stay dead and leave him alone?

As he walked slowly back towards the dog shit monster, using whatever cover that was available, two pistol shots rang out, two seconds apart. He hoped that the girls had fired them. It was with some relief that they both appeared. He quickened his stride.

'Nice bit of shooting there.' Captain Warburton said.

'Thank you Allison.'

'I didn't mean you Jim, that's what you are paid for, I meant Julie. A text book double tap – one in the chest – one in the head – absolute perfection. I could do with someone like Julie on my training team.'

'Better get him off the road and behind that hedge. O'Malley could be nearby if he has been following the tracker. I'll call in the cleaners when we get to the next village.' Killeen spoke with a sense of urgency, as both he, and Warburton, grabbed an arm each, and proceeded to drag the body towards the hedgerow.

'This one is O'Riordan Jim, and behind that hedge you will find our chariot.' Julie sported a triumphant grin.

Behind the hedge was the silver Mercedes, the keys still in the ignition. One of the girls had been right, O'Malley had switched cars. Now which girl had it been? Probably Julie; he wasn't thinking straight at the moment. Why did that bloody kid keep appearing whenever he was stressed or felt threatened, and what type and color of car was O'Malley now driving?

Julie seemed elated at what had happened and quipped. 'I reckon finders keepers Jim – tough shit. I've always fancied a Mercedes. If you fix the windscreen, you can have the dog shit monster.'

'And I've still got to explain the little question of eleven hundred quid on my expense account yet Julie, so don't you go giving anything away, especially to Jim. He has a habit of forgetting where he leaves his cars.' laughed Warburton.

The Mercedes was a big improvement on the little Ford, except for the annoying problem of the wind whistling in through the bullet hole in the passenger rear side window, put there by Warburton on the M1 motorway. They drove on in comfort, sticking to the minor roads in a zigzag fashion until they pulled into a petrol station close to Loughborough to fill up. As Warburton filled the car, Killeen threw the tracker, found in Julie's bag, into a trailer filled with straw, that was being towed by a battered and mud coated old Land Rover.

'I hope that trailer is off to a pig farm, it sure smells like it. It's going to be fun to watch if O'Malley is still following the tracker.'

'Speaking of pig farms Jim, don't you think that you had better have a quick splash yourself`?' Lieutenant Julie held her nose, and pulled a face, screwing it up as if sucking a lemon.

He had completely forgotten that he had been rolling in the mud. This was easily done, as he had both looked and smelled like this almost continuously for the last few months in Northern Ireland. Washing and grooming was never very high on the agenda, and without their weapons, they could easily have been mistaken for a party of very fit young tramps. Very rarely were they seen; too many alarm bells would have been ringing.

As they again set off in the direction of Loughborough, Killeen decided to change their route. They had been travelling due north for far too long, and it would have been pretty obvious where they were heading. O'Malley could have tracked them to Loughborough, and assumed that they were going to go north along the M1. Instead, they decided to go due west, through the Leicestershire villages, and head for Stoke on Trent via Uttoxeter. By the time he found the tracker at the pig farm, they would be well past Stoke and sailing up the M6 motorway on their way to Manchester, and then on to Cumbria.

The drive to Stoke was pretty uneventful; a few Leicestershire villages along the country roads, before the high speed run bypassing Uttoxeter, and then connecting with the M6 a couple of miles to the west of Stoke on Trent. This was exactly as planned, and all three of them were now fully relaxed and talking freely.

The silver Mercedes was pure class.

Killeen shook his head as he spoke. 'How the hell did O'Malley get his hands on a machine like this? It must have cost a bloody fortune.'

Julie was the first to answer. 'You have no idea how much money the IRA have access to Jim. It isn't just coming in from the States, much of it is now extortion money raised in both the north and the south of Ireland. They have the guns, so they have all the power that they need to raise whatever they want, and, from whomever they want. Anyone who doesn't comply is threatened, intimidated, and sometimes even killed. What would you do if your whole family was threatened? The police are as scared of the IRA as the rest of the population. The rule of law is of little use when your kids are dead. I'm not joking when I tell you this; I have been present when their lackeys have tipped literally thousands of pounds and punts on to the table, and the hierarchy have simply helped themselves to whatever they wanted. Had a bit of it myself once or twice. Sean and I had a pretty good lifestyle, and we didn't need to work.'

'Didn't you feel guilty?'

'Are you kidding Jim? What planet are you from? Did I hell as feel guilty. You can easily forget all forms of morality when there's free money, especially in a country where the main priority can be simply staying alive from day to day.'

Killeen could not help but smile. It was the vision of Julie helping herself to the lion's share of the cash, and stuffing it into her handbag, leaving just a tiny bit to be shared amongst the hard men with the guns.

The two women must have read his thoughts, and spontaneously all three of them burst out laughing.

'I've been in a luxury Mercedes before,' said Killeen. 'It belonged to an Arab Sheik. Paddy used to call him Sheik Armani. It was probably worth a few bob more than this one though. The whole thing was decked out inside with gold. Gold gear stick – gold switches – gold bloody everything. Even the wheels had gold inlays. It must have weighed as much as a tank as it was bomb and bullet proof. Probably run on gold petrol.'

'You didn't by any chance get his phone number did you?' Julie rubbed both hands together.

'You might have to share him with about twenty other wives,' laughed Killeen. 'That packet of condoms in your bag would probably last you for a couple of years.'

'I believe that Paddy's response to a comment like that Jim, would be "bollocks".'

'Steady on Julie, Sean will be getting jealous,' Warburton grinned. 'He might just send your other boyfriend, that charming Mr. Murphy, to punish you and smack your botty.'

'That ugly, cross-eyed bastard. I fucking hate him.' Suddenly her expression changed, and a big grin replaced the obvious hatred on her face as she went on. 'I can just imagine him now, chasing a pig across a field looking for the tracker.'

Everyone burst out laughing, as the same vision appeared simultaneously to them.

As the Mercedes wound its way down the 270 degree slip road on the outskirts of Stoke and onto the M6 motorway, Julie's mood became more serious. 'I think that we should get a trouble free run from here in,' she said. 'O'Riordan and his crew certainly won't be bothering us, and it seems to me like O'Malley doesn't want us dead.'

'What,' Killeen almost shouted. 'How can you say that? We already have two very dead W.R.A.C officers, and two equally dead Special Branch men. Why would he stop there when you are still alive? You are the package that I am supposed to deliver, and you are most definitely the target.'

'Jim: – He could have killed me any time that he wanted to in the car on the motorway. He looked straight at me first, he couldn't have helped but recognize me. All he did then was smile at you. He didn't even raise his gun. He just smiled. What the hell is he up to? He knows that I have more information on the IRA than anyone else does. Why didn't he kill me?'

'She's right Jim.' Captain Warburton said in a serious voice. 'He just grinned like an asylum inmate. Those eyes – they looked like the eyes of a rabid dog. It was as if he was toying with us and enjoying it. Playing with us as a cat does with a mouse; always knowing that death for us will be on his terms – in his time, and not ours. He wanted us to know that.'

Killeen pulled a face and shook his head. 'I really don't know what is going off here,' he said. 'Nothing about this entire operation makes any sense at all to me. Nothing has made sense since I was first briefed about it yesterday. Tell me Allison, if Julie is such a high value informant, why am I alone with the two of you in the car? Why is she travelling by car in the first place? Why not by Jet or helicopter? Where is the military back up? All I've got seems to be Paddy and Ken, and I have no idea where they are. Where are Molly and Bob? We always operate as a team. Another thing that puzzles me is why we haven't been issued with radios, or at the very least a phone number so that I can call in back up? I'm beginning to wonder who is pulling the strings here. Is O'Malley hunting us, or are we hunting him? Either way, we should all be dead, and he should now be on the next ferry to Ireland.'

Captain Warburton cut in. 'Jim, I've been working Intelligence for a number of years now, just as you have, and I can guarantee you that Julie is the key that will open many doors. Their entire operation will be brought to its knees. She has the names and addresses of at least 5 sleeper cells here in England, together with a list of all their targets, and that's just for starters. I've been her only contact outside of the Province for the last two years, so I of all people know just how valuable she is to us. She can place their whiter than white leaders in compromising places with people that they shouldn't have been with, *and*, at the scene of many an atrocity. Some of the shootings and bombings these high profile leaders even took part in.

Once this information gets out; funds from America, specifically from NORAID, will dry up completely, especially when they realize that they are funding terrorism and not Freedom Fighters. Those myopic idiots across the Atlantic still think that we are the Black and Tans. The other alternative of course is that we use the info as a bargaining chip in order to get them round the negotiating table. I'm not too sure that Maggi wants this, but she is under a lot of pressure, and it's coming from all directions and from both sides of the Atlantic.'

Julie shook her head. 'I've told you before, that's the last thing that the IRA want Allison, they are all making far too much money out of all this – they need the place to be lawless. Most of the top brass couldn't give a shit about the unification of Ireland anymore; the longer it lasts, the richer they become, and everyone is scared shitless of going against them. Look at what happened to my dad when he spoke up against them.'

'OK,' said Killeen, raising his voice a little too loudly. 'I can accept all that, but what I can't accept is – why we are alone. Why are we still here, when one single bullet into my head from O'Malley would have solved all of his problems; the car would have crashed, and we would all be dead?'

'And one single bullet from me would have solved all of our problems.' Captain Warburton interrupted, her face sporting a big grin. 'Why the fuck did you freeze Jim, and why did you move your thick head just as I was about to shoot? I could have emptied the entire magazine into the bastard's grinning face; there was no way that I was going to miss at that range. I could have got the driver as well, and that would have been the end of everyone's problem.'

'The boy didn't do too good Allison, sorry about that,' Killeen replied sheepishly. 'Mind you, looking on the bright side, we wouldn't have been travelling to Cumbria in luxury if he had crashed the car; we would still be in my estate with no windows.'

No one spoke for quite some time, as the silver Mercedes sped on ever northwards – past Manchester – past Preston, and past Lancaster, before turning off the motorway for the 40 or so mile drive to the Old Manor House by the lake.

'Pretty countryside here.' said Julie, as she spotted a yellow clump of daffodils in a well kept cottage garden. 'It reminds me very much of Kerry. Sean and I used to take a few trips down to Kerry in order to collect the odd consignment of goodies, as he used to call them, when they were smuggled in from America: lovely place except for the time when Allison almost got my head blown off.'

'That was Galway, not Kerry, and it wasn't my fault Julie. I do wish that you would stop blaming me.' Warburton sounded hurt.

'You are forgiven,' Julie laughed out loud as she spoke. 'But anyway, Kerry is much too full of tourists, mostly Americans searching for their Irish roots. Some of the stretches of road around the Ring of Kerry are completely impassable because of the coaches and caravans. I suppose that if you improve the road system, you'll destroy much of the charm and the attraction.'

'Exactly the same problem here Julie,' replied Killeen. 'Everybody and their dog want to visit the lakes in spring and summer. I much prefer winter. Julie and I used to walk for miles, just the two of us and her flee bitten old labrador. I always miss the old devil when I go back.'

'Which one – Julie or the dog?' Lieutenant Julie spoke in a matter of fact, unassuming way, yet with a hint of sadness in her voice, and a disappointed look on her face which she tried unsuccessfully to disguise.

Killeen smiled. He really should have said something much sooner instead of flirting with her. 'Not only has she got the same name as you, she even looks a bit like you,' he said. 'She does however have one major advantage. No one has ever tried to kill me when she has been around.' The three of them laughed. Julie's laugh was tinged with more than a little sadness.

CHAPTER 20

WHAT NOW?

'Nothing – Not a bloody word. He hasn't contacted either base or MI6,' Wardle said to Paddy, as he climbed back into the car. 'There was no way that he was going to make the Keele Service station. I can't see why we even bothered stopping. It's fair to assume that he'll go straight to Cumbria.'

'What now Ken?'

Wardle shrugged his shoulders as he spoke. 'You know him better than I do Pads, what do you think will be his plan?'

'Jim doesn't always make plans, more often than not he thinks on the hoof – operates on instinct. I still think we should go along with our last decision; let's go and pick some daffodils and sample a few gallons of Cumbrian Guinness while we wait for him to make up his mind. Those few pints last night have given me a thirst.'

'OK Paddy, as much as it grieves me, we will see what Molly has got mapped out for us. It should be pretty good and bloody complicated if I know Molly.'

'That *BOY* is too smart for his own good.' Paddy said with a smile.

As the journey took them further north, the conversation drifted away from their current assignment, and more onto past operations.

'I've often wondered what happened after we left Africa that time Ken?'

'Which time was that?' Wardle said with a shrug of his shoulders. 'We were never out of the bloody place until the powers that be decided that O'Malley was more important.'

'You know the one. When you first joined us, and you had to take out that General. What was wrong with the bloke? The people seemed to like him.'

'Maybe the people did like him Paddy, but the Americans were afraid of him getting into bed with the Russians.'

'Poof then?'

'Not really,' Wardle burst out laughing. 'They didn't want the Russians getting access to the port and establishing a naval base. That would have given them too much power in the region, and the Yanks wanted it for themselves.'

'How far was the shot that you made? I didn't see it myself as I was covering your arses – Bob reckoned it was well over half a mile.'

'No, it was just a bit less than that.'

'Head shot?'

'No Paddy. It was too risky to take a head shot at that range; he was bobbing up and down like a bleeding yoyo while he was speaking. I went for the chest.'

'How can you be sure that you would kill him when he was so far away then? Supposing the bullet had gone straight through him and missed all his vital organs?'

'I switched to a special bullet Pads when I decided to go for the chest shot. On impact, it fragments, and rips the internal organs to pieces. There would have been no exit wound, but his insides would have been in a bit of a mess.'

'That's illegal under the rules of warfare isn't it Ken?'

'Yea – sure is Paddy.'

'One thing I can remember about that job though Ken, is that we had to scarper pretty quickly. The whole country was after us. I still have nightmares about that fucking shark as we swum out to that US sub. It just kept swimming up to me, then turning away at the last second. It didn't seem interested in the rest of you lot, just me. Damn near shit myself. Why do you think it picked on me?'

'Could it be because it was pretty pissed off with you? Can't you remember? The first time it came up to you, you punched it on its nose. It was probably only being friendly, and you had to whack it. I can remember you treating a friendly goat the same way.'

'Friendly my arse.'

'Friendly with your arse – if I remember rightly.' Wardle was now laughing out loud.

'Fucking goat.'

The car moved on for another few minutes, when suddenly, and without warning, Wardle burst out laughing uncontrollably. Tears started streaming down his face. He was having difficulty keeping the car in a straight line, so much so, that Paddy had to hold the steering wheel steady.

'If you mention that fucking goat one more time – I'm going to punch your fucking lights out Wardle!'

'It's not the goat Paddy. I was just remembering that time in Singapore. The sight or you running down that street – completely bullock naked, one hand clutching your clothes, the other one holding your dick, and half a dozen china men chasing you with machetes. You still had a hard on.'

'Bollocks Wardle – you bastard!'

The section had been on a job sorting out a little insurgency trouble in the north of Malaya close to the Thai border. They had been brought back by Wessex helicopter to the Jungle Warfare School at Ulu Tiram, some 30 or so miles into Malaya, north of Singapore, and completed the journey by army truck back into Singapore. The Singapore puppet state run paper, the Straits Times, had reported later that week that 20 communist insurgents had died of starvation.

The DC10 flight out of Changi Royal Air force base back to Cyprus, stopping to refuel at Gan, had been delayed, and so a night out in Bugis Street was the obvious answer.

During the 1960's, 70's, and 80's, Singapore's Bugis Street was probably one of the most famous landmarks and attractions in all of the Far East. During the day time, the rather large square was pretty nondescript; however, as darkness started to descend, its most famous attractions came out to play. Bugis Street was the playground of the Kai Tais, unbelievably beautiful "women". These were transvestites – not women and not men. Physically they had been born men, yet in their minds, they were women trapped inside a man's body. They did not look like men; some of them were so beautiful that it was common to describe the Kai Tais as the beautiful ones, and the real women as the ugly ones. Many a man mistakenly went back with them for sex. Many men didn't mind, nor did they care.

After a period of taking female hormones, breasts start to develop, and waists begin to slim. Some of them even had the *operation*. This involved the creation of a false vagina out of the bits left over from the removal of the penis and the scrotum. These particular Kai Tais were in great demand for sex, many of them becoming extremely rich, and many of them marrying extremely rich men.

The team knew all about Kai Tais with the exception of Molly, and were greatly amused as he became more and more excited at the attention one particular raven haired beauty was paying him. Molly didn't notice or know about the Adams apple, this was a dead give-away. Oriental women very rarely have one, many Oriental men do. Molly's would be lover did.

Well tanked up with Tiger beer, the whole section had gone on to watch a private sex show involving two women, and an unusually large, inflatable dildo. Paddy had got a little carried away, grabbed one of the women, and taken her into the next room – some 20 or so Singapore dollars changing hands.

As the rest of the team waited for Paddy to finish his dirty deed, they heard the unmistakable creaking of bed springs being stretched to their limit. The whole team climbed onto the bed on which the two girls had been performing, and peered over the flimsy dividing panel between the two rooms. There was Paddy, lying on his back, eyes closed, and a big smile on his face as the woman bounced up and down on top of him. All the team burst out laughing. Paddy opened his eyes, saw them, and screamed such a mouthful of profanities that they all fell backwards onto the bed. The bed collapsed; the ceiling collapsed; and the whole lot landed onto a mahjong table on the ground floor below in front of all these very surprised china men, covering them in plaster and dust.

The 6 men ran outside laughing so hard that they completely forgot about Paddy.

That was why Paddy was running down the road, clothes in one hand, dick in the other, completely bullock naked, and chased by a bunch of angry china men with machetes – and still sporting a hard on.

'Bastards – all of you.' Paddy spit out the words. 'Not content with ruining what was turning into a bloody good shag, you left me to get sliced and diced by those little yellow bastards and their machetes. All I could think of was them cutting my dick off. I could hardly keep in front of them. Have you ever tried running with a hard on? Some shag that was, cost me 20 dollars and I never finished; *AND*, to add insult to injury, I caught a fucking dose off her, and had to have a fucking great needle rammed in my arse.'

Wardle was still laughing as he drove on.

'I was just wondering Paddy, why do these daft things always happen to you? It must be your hormones. What about that time outside Portadown during the Orange day Marches? Can you remember? Something about a randy dog – or was it several randy dogs?'

Paddy exploded. 'Muscles promised me that he wouldn't tell anyone. If he was still alive, I would fucking kill him.'

The team were well camouflaged and lying concealed in pretty secure positions, when a man with a dog walked by. This wasn't an ordinary dog – it was a bitch in season. The bitch sniffed around Paddy for a few seconds, then peed against his back. Paddy was forced to remain motionless so that the man wouldn't see him. Following behind the man with the bitch, came an almost endless procession of dogs which were in turn, following the irresistibly perfumed hormonal scent, as male dogs do. Every single one of them either peed on Paddy or tried to shag him. Paddy had to remain perfectly still so as not to be seen as each dog took its turn. Muscles was hysterical, and couldn't stop laughing for days. Paddy had threatened to kill him if he ever told anyone. One way or another, word had leaked out, and the entire Regiment was aware of the story. No one ever let on to Paddy for obvious reasons.

'Fucking dogs,' Paddy almost shouted. 'Any way Ken, why didn't you use a silencer for that shot at the African General? No one would have known where the shot had come from, and we could have got away much easier, instead of swimming with that fucking great shark.'

'Accuracy more than anything Pads, plus of course, a silencer wouldn't have worked. I would have had to use subsonic bullets. Remember that the bang you hear when you shoot is really two bangs, so close together that you only ever hear one. The first one is the explosion of the powder, and the second one is the crack of the bullet as it leaves the rifle and breaks the sound barrier. A silencer only muffles the sound of the powder exploding. To keep it almost completely silent, I would have had to use a bullet that travels slower than the speed of sound. At that slow speed, it probably wouldn't have even reached him let alone killed him. The bullet I used moved at least four times the speed of sound. The general was dead, and didn't know it, at least two seconds before anyone near to him even heard the shot.'

‘I think I would rather go that way Ken, not knowing what’s going to happen seems OK to me.’

‘I remember that you once told me that you want to drink and shag yourself to death, or have you changed your mind since that goat and those dogs shagged you?’

‘Bollocks to you Wardle, and if you tell anyone about those fucking dogs, I swear I will kill you!’

‘I would never dream of telling anyone Pads, your secret is safe with me – plus about 20 randy dogs.’

‘Bollocks.’

‘Anyway Pads,’ Wardle asked. ‘How come you never turned Pro? I’ve seen your record and seen you box on a couple of occasions, not that I could ever call it a boxing match, neither of them lasted more than 2 minutes. Did you ever lose?’

‘No Ken, only that fucking Gippo ever hurt me; none of my fights ever went past 2 rounds, and that was only because the guys spent the first round backing off or running away.’

‘Could you have taken Cooper out, he was the British champion for God knows how many years?’ Wardle glanced at Paddy as he spoke.

‘I don’t think Henry would have been much of a problem Ken, I went to a couple of his fights against London and Richardson.’ Paddy looked skywards as he spoke. ‘He really was pretty small for a heavyweight. I’m 6 inches taller and almost 4 stone heavier. He could punch a bit I know, Cassius Clay found that out, but a natural 17 stone boxer has a hell of a lot more power, and few of my opponents ever got up when I connected.’

‘Come on then Pads,’ Wardle frowned as he spoke. ‘Why did you stop boxing? Everybody wants to know the answer to that question; most of the people who know anything about boxing reckon that you could have gone all the way to the top. You could have made a fortune instead of doing this stupid job and trying to get yourself killed.’

‘It was the A.B.A. semi’s that caused me to stop Ken. I knocked this guy out of the ring, and he landed on his head. He was unconscious for 3 days in hospital. I thought that he was going to die. I told them I was ill when the final came around, so the other guy got the title. I never fought again, well not in the ring anyway. I believe I’ve had an odd skirmish or two when the Guinness has been involved.

Both men smiled before roaring with laughter.

'It's quite strange when you think about it Ken. I never really worried about killing people where the job was involved, but when I visited that guy in hospital after I had knocked him out, his wife and 2 kids were by the bed. I almost burst into tears thinking about what I had just done. I felt pretty much the same when I broke O'Malleys kid's neck.

Normally, when we were in the field, it seemed like just a job that had to be done – I never considered that all those people we killed had wives, kids, mums and dads.'

'It isn't something to dwell on Pads. I've been guilty of it myself in the past, if you don't let it go, it will eat away inside you.

O'Malley was pretty handy in the ring Paddy,' Wardle was testing, and needed to take Paddy away from his self pitying thoughts. 'I fought him a couple of times myself when I was a bit younger and still in the Marines. He could punch a bit, but was never fast enough to catch me with a clean one.'

'Did you beat him Ken?'

'Honors even kid, one each, both decided on points. If the fights had gone on for a couple of more rounds, I would have knocked him out. He was a little too muscle bound, and would have tired once the lactic acid kicked in.'

'He wouldn't have even heard the referee count him out if he had ever climbed in the ring with me Ken – few men ever did, and I never used more than 50% of my power. He would have got the full package.'

Wardle knew that Paddy was serious, and was not exaggerating.

He also knew that Cooper would have struggled to get passed the first round if he had ever climbed in the ring with Paddy.

CHAPTER 21

THE TRAP IS SET

Killeen drove on steadily through the picturesque Lakeland countryside, pointing out to his two attentive female passengers some of the more touristy places, all the time, giving a running commentary. He purposely avoided any further mention of *his* Julie. It was pretty obvious to him that Lieutenant Julie had been taking his flirting much too seriously. He stopped the Mercedes quite abruptly alongside a typical English red telephone box, and made a two minute phone call. As he climbed back into the car, he nodded to the girls. It was a long slow nod, the meaning being quite apparent. Everything was OK – everything was in place.

He drove on for another 15 miles, not directly towards the Old Manor, taking more of a crescent shaped route until he pulled in at a quaint little "Olde Worldie" coffee shop, in an equally quaint little Cumbrian village.

The look on the faces of the women was one of abject disappointment – horror almost.

'Surely you *are joking*.' Julie said in disbelief.

'This is it girls, would I joke with you?' His face broke into a big grin. 'Your chariot is required elsewhere. Don't drink too much of that coffee now, I don't want you peeing all over my new Mercedes when I pick you up.'

The women groaned, 'After what we've been through, you expect us to spend the rest of the day drinking fucking coffee? Stuff that Jim. If I was a higher rank, I would have you before a courts martial for even thinking it.' Warburton sounded quite serious.

'Sorry Jim, but I would back her up,' quipped Lieutenant Julie. 'I really need to get seriously pissed after what we've been through today. Six dead bodies in less than 24 hours is quite enough for one day thank you.'

'Seven Julie, not six, and don't forget the possible demise of a certain pig farmer, and one or two of his pigs to keep him company.' added Warburton, in a half serious and half laughing voice.

Killeen burst out laughing, which continued for a good half minute before composing himself. 'Oh, and by the way; if you walk about 50 yards round that corner, you will find one of the best little pubs in all of Cumbria. Tell the landlady that you are friends of Jimbo and Julie, and I promise you that you'll have one hell of a time. I recommend the giant Yorkshire pudding, filled with two disgustingly fat Cumberland sausages, and a bucket load of onion gravy – then you can get really pissed. I wish that I had time to join you both.'

The two women were now safe. Dressed in civilian clothes, as they had been for the entire journey, they looked like any one of the thousands of tourists that had started to pour into the Lake District at this time of year; many of them to be at one with Wordsworth. Spring was daffodil time.

As he drove the Mercedes away from the girls, he had one last guilty glance at Lieutenant Julie's ample breasts. He was spoken for, but Molly? Yes, she would indeed be perfect for Molly. The ladies loved Molly wherever he went, but for some strange reason, he always shied away from any form of long term emotional attachment. Killeen wondered why?

Molly was waiting in the village pub as Killeen walked in. He had chosen the pub for a specific reason. Molly was confused. Why this one? What was wrong with the pub in the next village? After all, that was where the Old Manor by the lake was. Molly stuck a hand in the air in the direction of the doorway to signal where he was, and instantly froze, before reaching inside his jacket for his pistol. Molly was intuitive, he could read body language at a glance. One look at Killeen, and he instinctively knew that something was wrong – he had seen him stiffen. His face had changed from friendly to almost fight or flight in an instant.

Killeen took a couple of strides towards the man sitting in the corner chatting to the barmaid.

Molly was up, instantly grabbing his hand and shaking it violently. He knew all about Julie and John, her ex husband. He also knew what Killeen was capable of. This was not the time, and this was not the place; they had some serious planning to do, and some serious work ahead.

John hadn't noticed what had gone off, he was too engrossed with his pretty little barmaid. This was a job for Paddy. Paddy knew how to hurt people without causing any lasting damage. Paddy would sort out this little problem. Molly knew that Killeen was too involved. He may cross the line.

Molly himself had crossed the line, and now there was no going back. His instinct now was to kill – with some reluctance, he resisted.

James Killeen was still rigid with anger, both fists tightly clenched, and his knuckles turning white as he sat down next to Molly.

'Thanks Mol,' Killeen spoke through gritted teeth, his eyes narrowed and focused on the object of his anger. 'That bastard has been bothering her again. He won't leave her alone since the divorce. Reckons he should have half the value of her cottage. He is the one who run off with a 16 year old kid who was still at school. Julie made me promise that I wouldn't hurt him: no fucking chance. I might just kill the bastard.'

Molly's voice was calm and reassuring, 'No problem there Jim; that's why we feed and clothe the *Apeman* so do not get involved, that way you will be keeping your promise to Julie. I will sort it out, and you can honestly say that you knew nothing about it. Anyway, why do you look like a scarecrow? Why are you covered in mud, twigs, leaves, and something that smells suspiciously like dog shit?'

'Just the little problem I told you about over the phone with O'Riordan's crew. I used one of Paddy's old tricks to get close. There was no other way as I was dressed in civvy's. I've brought along a pretty little W.R.A.C. for you as a present, and a nice lesbian one for Paddy. He has already had a run in with her.'

'Let me guess – was it something about screwing against a wall?' Molly said laughingly.

'You got it in one.'

'Why do they always fall for it?'

'It's the way he tells em,' as Frank Carson would say.' Killeen's face broke into a grin as his tension and anger began to subside.

Frank Carson was an extremely amusing Irish comedian whose catchphrase was always "It's the way I tell em". Killeen used the phrase on many occasions.

Both men laughed out loud. John looked over at them. There was something vaguely familiar about the taller, older man. He couldn't quite place him though. He returned to his conversation with the barmaid.

'We had better go over this pretty quick Jim, O'Malley has been spotted about 20 miles south of Preston, and appears to be heading this way. How did he find out about the Manor? Who's tipping him off?'

'I can't answer that question Molly – I've been going over it all day. I can understand him picking us up in the first place, as the W.R.A.C. lieutenant was carrying a tracker in her handbag. I can't really suspect her though as she found it herself, plus she was the one who shot O'Riordan and helped to catch his brother at the docks. We have used three different cars, none of which they could have ever suspected, so I'm totally confused. There has to be a leak pretty high up. How high, I don't know. The only good news so far is that we are not totally alone if they've been spotted on the motorway; the question is, who else is involved? As far as I can work out, only Ken, Paddy, and yourself have any idea of what's happening.'

'There's the Brigadier and his adjutant,' offered Molly. 'They know.'

'What, Brigadier Wardle? Don't tell me that he's still in charge there; he should have retired years ago. Well, not really, it just seems that he has been there forever. He was the first one to greet me when I was first posted to the Old Manor a million or so years ago. Great bloke; he helped me a lot when Julie and I broke up; in fact, he was the one who suggested that I join the Regiment.'

'He's got a lot to answer for then.' A big smile appeared on both men's faces. Molly then took out his hand drawn map, and laid it out on the table in front of Killeen. He then carefully, and methodically, explained his plan. 'The red crosses are where I would expect O'Malley to place his men, and of course, he will be positioned just here, 1000 yards from the front door of the manor, looking straight down the driveway.'

Killeen carefully studied the map, his face breaking into a frown before speaking. 'I'm sorry Mol, but I've walked the grounds a thousand times. He would *HAVE* to place a back up shooter at the end of the drive hidden behind the dry stone wall. As for the other two men; *they HAVE* to be flanking, somewhere in the bushes either side of the drive. Only a madman would place them where you say; these two men would never be able to escape, they would be like sitting ducks in the event of a contact.'

'Exactly Jim – only a madman. That is why we have never even got close to O'Malley before. He is completely insane. He does not conform to normal rules – there is no rational thinking – you have to trust me on this one.'

Molly paused, and took a deep breath before continuing. 'He will place a man half way down the drive in this small shrubbery with his weapon set on automatic fire. His thinking will be that once he has taken out the girl himself, matey here, cuts loose with the automatic and takes out everyone else while he gets away. Anyone coming out of the drive will be taken out by the man at the bottom end of the lake. By this time, O'Malley and his driver will be well on their way. He will purposely leave the two men behind to be sacrificed as a distraction. He no longer gives a shit about his own men since he went rogue.

Don't you see it Jim? *YOU* would always look to the safety of your own men as your first priority in any plan that you come up with. Are they concealed? Can they cover each other in the event of an engagement? Can they escape? – O'Malley's mind doesn't think like that. As he deploys, he will be fully aware that he will probably lose certain men. He will probably want to in order to slow everyone down. This is why we never got close to him. The only one that he's never prepared to sacrifice, *is himself*. That is why he always positions himself 1000 yards away from his target. It isn't that he shoots better from that range, it's because nobody else can hit him at that range. He is completely invulnerable. As for the third member of his team. O'Malley will use him as cover for himself, positioned on either his right or his left flank. I cannot predict which side though – there are no advantages for either position. As you know, the ground rises as you move away from the lake, and gives a 180 degree arc of fire, but is almost perfectly level horizontally.'

'Why would he want cover for himself if he thinks that he's invulnerable at 1000 yards Mol?' Killeen didn't sound too convinced. 'Surely that extra man would be better deployed covering any escape from the Manor House?'

'Because he is now entering into the final, and most destructive phase of madness Jim. He has hidden, disguised, and suppressed it for so long, that it is now running out of control. He is suffering from advanced paranoia. He can see enemies everywhere. He trusts no one. He will even be watching the man who he has chosen to cover him. I wouldn't be surprised if he isn't already at an advanced stage of schizophrenia, where the insane killer he has been suppressing has taken over, and now completely dominates whatever rationality he has held on to for all these years.'

'Fucking hell Molly, I shouldn't have let you read all that psychology crap when we were between jobs, you're starting to sound a bit nuts yourself.'

'It takes a *Nutter* to get into the mind of a *Nutter*.' As Molly said that, he rolled his eyes – swayed his head – stuck out his tongue and groaned. It made Killeen smile. It all looked so real.

It was real. Molly had not been joking, only play acting. To think like a madman, he had entered into the realms of madness. He had been fighting it for a long time. He no longer wanted to fight it – he simply had to disguise it. It was a release. It felt good. It was where he had wanted to be for quite a long time – ever since that enlightening moment in the desert. He knew though that he didn't have that much time before the madness completely took over his mind. Then he would close the book! There would be no doctors!

Molly was now at one with O'Malley. Molly had become O'Malley.

Killeen closed his eyes for a few seconds, and visualized the grounds of the Old Manor. It was almost like looking at a picture for him. How many times had he walked around, or simply just sat by the lake with Julie? Often, Julie had taken a few slices of stale bread to feed the ducks, who had to compete with the swans for the food. The swans usually won, attacking the ducks whenever they got too close. Once this little matter was concluded, they would again sit by the lake and feed the ducks, only this time – she would be his wife. There was just the little matter of the prick in the corner to take care of – that could wait! Not for long though – Paddy would see to that.

Killeen stood up purposefully. There were no doubts this time. There would be no freezing, and no trembles. This was the real deal. This was the Captain James Killeen of old. This was James Killeen, the killing machine. There was only going to be one outcome. This was to be for Muscles and Mac.

'I will take O'Malley Mol, and you and Paddy deploy as shown. Under no circumstances must you expose even one inch of your head or body until I have taken care of the madman. From his position, he will be able to kill anything within that 180 degree arc of fire – Let's go.'

It was now all beginning to fit into place.

Killeen was suddenly aware that to have brought in any more people than the D1 team, what was left of them that is, would have aroused too much suspicion. O'Malley would have smelt a rat, and scarpered long ago. That was why there were no helicopters or fast jets. That was why the four of them were on their own. There was a leak somewhere on high, that was for sure, and if a back up team had been deployed, word would have got out.

Lieutenant Julie wasn't only the package – she was also the bait.

Someone, somewhere, was being very, very, clever. They had successfully lured the 'A' team away from their Southern Irish bolt hole, and delivered them on a plate to the D1 team. Lieutenant Julie must be one hell of a prize for British intelligence, and one hell of a problem for the IRA.

This was going to be the only chance he would get to avenge Muscles and Mac. He had to get it right, if not, how many more British troops were going to die at O'Malley's hands? He was still concerned at the amount of leaks that were coming from somewhere – but from where?

If Sean Fitzpatrick had warned Julie about Mad Mitch, why did he place a tracker in her handbag? That somehow didn't ring true. Could it be that O'Malley was playing a game of double bluff? Was he using her to hunt down the D1 team? Was it all simply about revenge for the death of his son, after all, that is what had sent him over the edge in the first place.

What if... 'Oh bollocks to all this intrigue', as Paddy would have said. It doesn't matter now. All that matters is that he and his team stay alive, and the 'A' team don't.

Forget the whys and the wherefores – concentrate on the hows and the nows – as his father always used to say.

He had to retain his focus if O'Malley was half as good as Wardle had said. He thought about the binoculars that Wardle had handed to him; maybe, just maybe, they would prove to be the edge that he needed in taking O'Malley down.

CHAPTER 22

THE WRONG PACKAGE

Paddy moved into position halfway down the driveway of the Old Manor and concealed himself. He settled into a small depression in the ground, his camouflaged clothes covered in mud, sticking to which was an assortment of twigs and leaves, both dead and alive; a mosaic, with various shades of browns, yellows and greens. Even his hands and face were covered in leaves. He may not have been invisible – he was just impossible to see.

This was where Molly had indicated that the back-up shooter would be positioned.

'Don't argue Paddy,' Killeen had told him. 'We have got to trust Molly on this one. It's something about using a Nutter to catch a Nutter.'

'Are you calling me a Nutter *BOY*? I'll put you over my knee if you do.' Paddy growled menacingly.

Molly grinned.

Paddy did not have to wait for long. He heard a rustle of leaves and the snap of a breaking twig. He remained perfectly still – ready to pounce.

The camouflaged figure crept ever closer, almost stepping on Paddy's leg before settling into a crouch, shuffling in order to make himself comfortable.

The moment that he placed his rifle on the ground, Paddy made his move. Two steps, and his giant hands engulfed the head of Michael O'Riley. The left hand covered the mouth and most of the face. The right hand pulled the head up and to the right. There was a sharp cracking sound, not unlike the snapping of the twig that O'Riley had stood on moments before.

This was Michael O'Riley's first and last introduction to Paddy's calling card.

Michael O'Riley would not be killing any more British soldiers or making any more bombs!

Paddy redeployed.

Molly was in position at the top of the lake. He had needed to make a difficult decision. There was only one sensible placement for a shooter. That was on a slightly elevated grassy knoll, on the only patch of dry land. The rest of the area was swampy and boggy. This meant that he was now lying in several inches of mud and ooze. Even though it was spring time, the water hadn't had time to warm up, and he was beginning to shiver almost uncontrollable. Molly had neither his rifle nor his pistol to hand. Both were buried in the mud, and completely inoperable – Molly clutched his knife.

Mad Mitch Murphy crept into view; positioned himself on the dry ground, and laid his rifle in front of him – Molly dare not move. He would be in full view of the high ground across the lake from the Manor House. He dare not take out Murphy, O'Malley would spot him for sure.

He now knew why the torture chamber at Hereford was so demanding. Only one in a thousand men could survive for long under these conditions, and still operate effectively. He, like the rest of the Regiment, was that one in a thousand men.

Captain James Killeen now had Sergeant Major Michael Patrick O'Malley firmly in his sights and at his mercy. He was no more than 7 or 8 yards away.

Something worried him. This had all been much too easy. He glanced across the lake at the Old Manor House. Molly's map had been spot on; this was indeed the only position that O'Malley could shoot from; straight across the lake, and between the two rows of trees that flanked the driveway. He could clearly see the front door, and the range was about the 1000 yards that Wardle said he always chose. He was still worried, and did not want to break cover. Three men had been spotted making their way into the grounds, so where was the fourth one. Was he covering O'Malley as Molly had suggested?

It hadn't been quite so easy finding O'Malley!

Killeen had remained totally motionless in the cover of a dense shrub surrounded by thick grass, and slightly overlooking the expected firing point, as marked on Molly's map. He thought that he saw a slight movement, and switched to the color neutral binoculars that Wardle had provided. Everything was now in black and white, and after some 3 or 4 minutes he spotted O'Malley's rifle barrel. He could also make out the camouflaged body lying in front of it. The body moved a little and adjusted its leg position.

'No chances,' Killeen said to himself. 'You didn't give Muscles and Mac a chance. No warning for you, you bastard, just instant death. That's all you deserve you bastard.' He was only around 70 yards away – the 7-62 mm bullet would rip him to pieces.

He picked up his rifle, not an M14, but his own personal Israeli made weapon of choice. He looked down the telescopic scope, slipped off the safety catch, and prepared to fire. The bullet was already chambered.

'What the fuck,' he said quietly to himself. He could see nothing, not a damn thing, except for a beautifully patterned mosaic of grass, meadow flowers, and daffodils. Without Wardle's color neutral binoculars, he might as well have been blind.

Cursing gently, he picked up the color neutral binoculars again, and this time he had no trouble spotting both the rifle and the body, knowing exactly where to focus his gaze. Again the body moved slightly.

'Not quite as bloody perfect as you said, Kenneth Wardle old chap,' Killeen again whispered quietly to himself. 'He has moved twice already. Can remain perfectly still for hours my arse.'

He now knew that he had to get closer; not to take the shot, but in order to see the camouflaged target through the telescopic sights of his rifle. All he could see through them now was a beautiful picture postcard Cumbrian spring landscape.

There was one major problem with edging closer. Where was the fourth man?

'Left or right Molly?' He had asked.

'Don't know that one Jim.' Had come the reply.

'Fuck it – if he is covering this side, I am dead,' he thought. 'It's 50-50 so I have got to go for it.'

Slowly; almost inch by inch, Killeen crawled towards his target – hands and knees where there was cover – belly, where there was none, until he eventually reached the right area. He kept motionless for a couple of minutes with his head down, praying that he hadn't been spotted. No one had shot at him, so his 50-50 gamble had paid off.

Raising his head slightly, he slowly and methodically scanned the area immediately in front of him, looking for the rifle barrel and the prone, camouflaged figure. – Suddenly, it was there – closer than he thought – no more than 7 or 8 yards away. Finally, O'Malley was his for the taking – this was for Muscles and Mac.

He gently lowered his rifle to the ground, and took out his pistol, cocking it at the same time as he raised himself off the ground. He took four giant and purposeful strides forward.

'*Do not touch your rifle or you are dead O'MALLEY,*' he said, almost shouting. 'Now stand up, put your hands in the air, and turn around. Any sudden moves and I will pull the trigger you mad Irish bastard.'

He could have killed him there and then, however, he was desperate to let O'Malley know who it was that was going to kill him, and why. Killing him, without his knowing who was responsible, had never really been an option. He felt elated that he hadn't taken the shot with his rifle.

The figure did exactly as Killeen had said, and stood up. As it turned around, Killeen froze. – Instead of Michael Patrick O'Malley staring at him, he was confronted by the grinning face of Sean Fitzpatrick.

At that precise moment, there came the realization that he really was no match for O'Malley. He never had been. Wardle had been right about him all along. He was dealing with something the like of which he had never encountered before.

Who was the hunter, and who was the hunted?

The question now was – 'Where exactly is O'Malley?' Of one thing Killeen was pretty sure; he was close, and almost certainly already had him in his sights.

'Good Evening Captain Killeen,' came the rich, deep, Irish voice from behind him. 'I hope you will forgive me for not saluting you, but I am holding a pistol that is pointing at your head. Would you kindly drop your weapon and turn around – *Sir*?'

Killeen dropped his pistol to the ground, and slowly turned around – there was no one there. 'Fucking hell – Wardle was right – he is invisible.' He almost said out loud.

Then he noticed a hand reaching out of the bush in front of him. In the hand was a silenced pistol. Slowly, almost imperceptibly, the bush came to life. The branches and leaves moved first, and, as they dropped to the ground, the distinctive grinning face and shape of Michael Patrick O'Malley emerged.

That bloody kid with the AK47 flashed in front of Killeen's eyes, and he blinked hard. This was exactly as he had seen it in his dreams so many times.

This time though, Paddy was over half a mile away. He was on his own.

'Haven't you worked it out yet James?' O'Malley said mockingly. 'You have been guarding THE WRONG PACKAGE. – THE RIGHT PACKAGE is over there, the intelligence headquarters, and you were such a lovely fellow that you lead us right to it. We have been trying to find it for months. Did you enjoy driving my car?'

'Oh fuck.' Killeen suddenly understood. For months, O'Malley had out thought and out maneuvered him in Ireland, and now on his own turf, he was again second best, only this time the stakes were even higher. The entire British intelligence network was suddenly at O'Malley's mercy.

'What about the girl?' Killeen asked, feeling a strange sense of elation under the circumstances. Maybe the shear inevitability of his impending death had dissipated all of his pent up tension, maybe even his PTSD, both of which had been brought about by the deaths of Muscles and Mac.

Maybe he still had one last throw of the dice. His mind flashed back to Molly's parting message "A Madman to catch a Madman".

Would Molly's mad genius trump O'Malley's mad cunning?

'What about her?' O'Malley replied, in the same mocking tone as before. 'I have known about her ever since she took up with Sean again. I knew all about her before she even left England, while I was still in her Majesty's service – my sources are impeccable. We only ever let her have whatever information we wanted her to have. I knew that she would prove useful one day.'

'And me?' Killeen's voice was calm, officer like in its authority.

'I could have killed you anytime that I wanted to James. I had you in my sights the day I shot Muscles and Mac. I could have had you in the pub, in the lift, on the motorway, but what would be the point? I needed you to lead me here. Why do you think I left Ireland?'

'Now, however, I am going to collect my early pension. The kid that Paddy killed in the desert was the Sheik's son. I didn't have much of a problem convincing him that it was you that killed him. Now I am going to collect a few million pound reward money. The job offer was my little insurance policy in case you didn't take this bait. – I suppose you could say that *YOU* were really *THE RIGHT PACKAGE*. Where do you want it James, head or heart? I am giving you a choice, which is more than that bastard Paddy gave my boy. He wasn't even 15 – he hadn't even started shaving. Paddy will soon be taken care of, and so will Ken. Ken Wardle may have beaten me on the ranges, but when it came down to the real thing – the real killing – he never had the bottle. Ken Wardle was always scared of pulling the trigger in case an innocent bystander got hurt. He could never accept the concept of collateral damage. Wardle was a liability in the field. A rifle with a conscience doesn't work in our profession; you know that James.'

Captain James Killeen also knew something about Kenneth 'Sniffer' Wardle that O'Malley was yet to discover.

O'Malley was wrong.

O'Malley could not have been more wrong.

Killeen took a step backwards in the hope of O'Malley taking the bait.

O'Malley stepped forward and placed the pistol close to Killeen's head.

Killeen closed his eyes – he saw Julie – his Julie – his loving Julie.

He saw O'Malley's boy lying on the ground with his head twisted at a funny angle.

He saw the kid in the desert. That bloody kid with the AK47 pointing at him; and standing behind him; he saw O'Malley's grinning face.

The nightmare had become the reality.

His eyes still closed, Killeen heard a kind of popping sound – a dull thud – it was difficult to describe, and seemed to be accompanied by a shock wave. O'Malley's head exploded, covering Killeen in fragments of skull, brains, skin and blood.

Exactly one and a half seconds later, *TWO* 7-62mm, high velocity, soft nosed bullets, simultaneously ripped apart the chest of Sean Fitzpatrick, sending him spinning backwards, and several feet into the air.

Then came the two bangs – only two bangs in total. It had taken O'Malley two seconds to take two aimed shots at 1000 yards, when he had killed Muscles and Mac. It took Ken "Sniffer" Wardle one and a half seconds.

That one step forward, away from the obstructing bush, that Killeen had forced O'Malley to take, was all that Wardle had needed.

Kenneth "Sniffer" Wardle never missed, either on the firing range, and more importantly, in the field.

Molly's mad genius had trumped O'Malley's mad cunning.
The Brigadier's prophesy had come true.

On hearing the shots, Molly sprang into action.

Mad Mitch Murphy did not die easily. He did not die quickly. He died slowly, and he died in pain. His agonizing screams were heard at the Manor. Molly made sure that Mitch experienced the excruciating pain that many of his victims had suffered.

Before he died, he told Molly about Bob Kineer, the sixth active member of the D1 team, who they had captured while he was working undercover in the north of Ireland. He told him of the anonymous tip off that O'Malley had received from someone in London. He told him of the two days of torture that Bob had endured. 'Not a word,' Murphy had said. 'He never said a bloody word; it was as if he didn't feel pain.'

Murphy felt pain. Murphy felt real pain!

Molly had taken on the wild 1000 yard stare; he would have to hide it from the others.

Killeen looked down at the body of Sean Fitzpatrick. It was lying a good 4 yards from where he had been hit due to the force of the impact. He noticed the two bullet holes, no more than two inches apart – both spouting blood, and both of them dead centre of the chest.

He heard the screaming coming from the bottom end of the lake. It was a blood curdling scream: someone was going through agony. He knew that Molly was at that end of the lake, and Molly was usually so clinical – so efficient.

He picked up his Israeli made rifle and his pistol, brushed away the soil, and, adjusting the safety catches back to the safe position, started walking the 800 yards to the lake, before veering to the left in order to meet up with Molly. He found Molly knee deep in water, washing away the blood from his knife and body.

'What the hell was all that about Mol?'

'Molly stopped what he was doing. His eyes looked crazed. He studied Killeen for a few seconds before replying. 'He killed Bob last week Jim: tortured him for two days before he died. I only found out that he was missing when the Brigadier told me. I just had to find out what he knew before I killed him.'

'Bloody nice work Mol, keep it quiet though. Let's just say that he volunteered the information before he died.'

'That would be the truth anyway. A little poser for you Jim? – If someone cut your dick off, and made you eat it, do you think that it would hurt as you bit into it?'

'Bloody stupid question Mol. Why do you ask?' Killeen looked puzzled, yet he had a gut feeling of what Molly was about to tell him.

'Mitch reckoned that it did.'

'Fucking hell Molly. Now you are really starting to worry me. Not a word to anyone – *not to anyone*, or I will cut your fucking dick off and make you eat it. UNDERSTAND?'

'Understood Captain.'

The two of them walked the hundred yards to the end of the driveway of the Old Manor House, to be met by Wardle, the Brigadier, and a grinning sergeant Paddy Jackson.

'WELL?' said Paddy, almost shouting.

'Well what?' Killeen replied.

'Did you shit yourself?'

'Bollocks to you Paddy. Nice shooting though Ken. Two aimed shots in one and a half seconds; the first one to the head. Not bad at all. O'Malley thought that you would bottle it – he said so: that's why he felt safe exposing himself.'

'I only fired once Jim, Paddy made the second hit.' Wardle said, flashing Killeen a wink.

'I told you I could shoot the bollocks off a gnat.' Paddy said in triumph.

'You couldn't hit a fucking barn door Paddy, and you know it.' Wardle and Killeen spoke in unison.

As the five men walked towards the Old Manor house, still laughing, Killeen was wondering. 'Only two bangs, yet three bullets; one in O'Malley's head, and two in Fitzpatrick's chest. Wardle and Paddy must have fired at exactly the same time as each other, both hitting Fitzpatrick at the same time. That would explain why he shot so high in the air and so far back.'

Maybe Paddy was right.

Maybe he could shoot the bollocks off a gnat.

Providing of course, that he hadn't just drunk 20 pints of Guinness and a bottle of Jamesons' 12 year old finest.

CHAPTER 23

THE QUESTION

'You promised me that you wouldn't hurt John. Why did you lie to me Jim, you know that I hate violence?'

'I didn't lie to you Julie. I was here with you when they took him to hospital.'

'And who do you suppose was that eight foot ape that the whole village is talking about; the one that picked a fight with him and threw him through a window head first?'

Jim Killeen simply shrugged his shoulders. 'Molly told me that it was John that started it all; punched him for no reason at all; Paddy simply stepped in to calm things down.'

The previous evening, both Paddy and Molly had taken a little tour of the local village pubs, ending up at the one where Molly and Killeen had spotted John. Having waited for over an hour, they had just about decided to leave when John walked in, arm in arm with the same barmaid he had been chatting to the previous afternoon.

It was Molly who accidentally spilled the beer over John, and it was Molly who allowed John the first punch; pretending to go down unconscious. Paddy stepped in, allowing John the satisfaction of again throwing and landing the first punch – before going to work.

The police showed little interest as the ambulance took John away. 'I've never seen anything like it in all my life.' The land lady of the pub told the police sergeant. 'John just picked a fight with two strangers who were minding their own business, and started punching them for no reason; he knocked one of them out. The other feller looked like an ape, and must have been eight foot tall. They were lovely blokes, both of them. The big feller tried to calm things down, and John just hit him; he deserved everything he got. Lovely blokes, the younger one gave me fifty quid to pay for the damage.'

'Thank you Jim,' Julie said, leaning across the table and kissing him. 'And the answer is yes, before you even ask for the one hundredth time; I would love to marry you.'

Captain James Killeen's jaw dropped. His hands started to tremble, and tears filled his eyes. The 6 foot 4 inch, slim, muscular, killing machine, was suddenly reduced to a quivering jelly, unable to speak or move – unable to do anything other than tremble.

Julie looked over to the pub window, and saw Paddy's slightly misaligned nose pressed against the glass, and waved, raising her thumb as she did so. Paddy waved back, and into the pub walked the full crew – Paddy – Ken – Molly – the Brigadier, and W.R.A.C. Captain Alison Warburton. Each one of them was grinning from head to toe, and each of them was carrying a bottle of Champagne or wine.

'Happy birthday Jim, and congratulations to you both.' Said the beaming Brigadier, shaking Killeen's hand warmly before kissing Julie on the cheek. Ken, Molly, and Captain Warburton followed; then Paddy walked forward, and looking straight at Killeen, their faces only inches apart, said.

'Well?'

'Well what?'

'Did you shit yourself?'

'On this occasion Paddy, I think I might well have done.'

The evening turned into a wonderful alcoholic free for all. All 5 bottles of champagne and wine soon disappeared, before Paddy, returning to his beloved Guinness asked. 'Where is the other Julie, my favorite rack?'

'Paddy!' Warburton said threateningly.

'She has to work late at the Manor tonight,' replied the Brigadier. 'MI5 are sending their senior team to interview and de-brief her in the morning; it's a big day for her. She has got one hell of a future ahead of her in the army. I will be recommending her promotion to Captain with immediate effect.'

'And you have more power than God sir, I believe you told me.'

'Quite correct Molly; that I do.' The Brigadier replied with a grin.

'I think it's time for God's boss to get the next round in then.' Paddy couldn't resist saying. 'Anyway, why didn't Jesus turn the water into Guinness instead of poxy wine?' He continued, at the same time looking at Wardle.

'He probably couldn't find enough Irishmen to piss in it and put the flavor in Paddy.' Wardle replied.

It had been a stressful couple of days for everyone. The operation had been successful. There had been minimal loss of life. Two W.R.A.C. lieutenants, two Special Branch officers, and quite possibly an unfortunate pig farmer. In return, they had eliminated the most lethal killing machine that THE TROUBLES had yet thrown up, or would ever throw up, and in doing so had saved countless young soldiers' and civilian lives.

D1 team had also paid a high price. The death of Muscles and Mac had hit them hard, and now Bob Kineer had also fallen victim to the 'A' team.

Little did they know, but Molly was no longer the Molly of old. Wardle had noticed the eyes as he had joined them shortly after dispatching Murphy. He had been seeing eyes like those for the last twenty years.

They were O'Malley's eyes.

He knew the signs.

He had heard the screams.

Sniffer Wardle's nose never let him down.

CHAPTER 24

FROM THE GRAVE

O'Malley may have been dead, but he wasn't yet out of the game. He may have changed his plans somewhat: a little tweaking here, a slight modification there, but overall, everything was still on track. There had been a few hiccups along the way. Lieutenant Julie should not have discovered the tracker. In her defense maybe she had been compromised. Perhaps she didn't have a choice.

The pig farmer had upset their rhythm somewhat, and Mad Mitch had gone berserk.

The switch to the silver Mercedes by Killeen had all been down to *HIS* genius. He knew that O'Riordan's crew would be no match for Killeen, no matter how many of them there were. They were just a bunch of enthusiastic amateurs. The tracker in the Mercedes had simply led him straight to the Old Manor.

This was, and always had been the RIGHT PACKAGE. Hadn't he always planned it that way?

Why did his one time friend Ken Wardle, have to spoil it all by killing him? He thought that Wardle would have bottled the shot. He always did in the field. Wardle was only a Range shooter.

Hadn't he saved his life? Not once – but twice. Is that all the gratitude he was due?

He was now going to miss his greatest triumph.

Sometimes, the means justifies the end.

Killeen also owed him his life: Not once, but many times over. Killeen may have been good, but without Sniffer Wardle by his side, he wasn't even in the same ball game. So many times he had watched him through his rifle sights. On occasions, he had been close enough to listen in to his conversations. He was invisible: Sniffer Wardle was the only man that could ever find him. How the hell did he do it? He said that he could smell him – that he smelled of death. He took this as a compliment.

Wardle was good – good on the ranges, but not so good in the field. He had a conscience. That is no good when killing is your job. *HE* was better where it counted. Who in the world could take two aimed shots in two seconds at a distance of 1000 yards? Ask Muscles and Mac – they know. Wardle could never have made those shots – ask him? Wardle knows who is "***the true marksman***" when it really counts.

Medals are simply vanity – the ability to kill, without conscience, is sanity. Who would you rather follow into battle?

Maybe Wardle can smell death – *I DELIVER DEATH – EVEN IN DEATH.*

CHAPTER 25

THE MORNING AFTER

Jim Killeen had a restless night's sleep. He should have slept soundly after all that drink.

'But we are engaged to be married,' he had told Julie. 'You are going to be my wife, and I want to sleep in bed with you. I don't want to be parted from you ever again, especially not tonight.'

'On the settee for you tonight Mr. Killeen,' she had replied. 'Fiancee or not, you have had much too much to drink, and you will need at least half a dozen pee's during the night. I need to sleep; some of us have got to work for a living.'

That had been a sensible decision and Killeen knew it. The little cottage only had one toilet, and that was downstairs. It was a picturesque little cottage, bought as a wedding present for Julie when she had married John.

Julie's father neither liked nor trusted John, and had sensibly put the cottage in his own name. He knew that the marriage would not last. John could be a charmer, but he had wandering hands and eyes; Julie however, was so much in love with his charms, that she could see no wrong in him. John had been more than a little upset once he had discovered that he would not be receiving his half share of the cottage after the divorce, and having run out of money, was again pursuing his claim. This was the reason as to why he had started to make life difficult for Julie again.

It was also the reason why he was now eating his meals in hospital through a straw.

Killeen interspersed sleeping with dreaming and thinking. Everyone thought that the little matter with O'Malley and the 'A' team had been brought to a conclusion; he wasn't quite so sure. All those years working intelligence had left him with a suspicious mind. The jigsaw had been virtually completed, yet, there were still a few pieces to fit into place. He had to speak to Lieutenant Julie again. Some of the things that she had told him seemed to contradict each other.

He finally fell into a deep sleep in the early hours of the morning, and his subconscious mind took him far away, just as the sun was rising on the eastern side of the river Bann in Northern Ireland.

He was back in Portadown. The body of O'Malley's kid with the broken neck had been found the previous morning by a man out walking his dog. He was a Catholic kid, the son of a Marine Commando in the British forces. 'What the hell was a good Irish Catholic doing in the British military?' The Catholics had asked. Still, he was one of their own, a Catholic boy, and the Protestants of Portadown would have to pay. They would have to pay in blood.

The Town of Portadown had become a hotbed of religious intolerance; the Protestant Loyalist on one side, and the Catholic Republicans on the other. Up unto THE TROUBLES starting, both Protestants and Catholics lived a relatively peaceful co-existence side by side. This had now changed. The Catholic minority had been forced to move, and now lived in the north west of the town, the rest of the town being Protestant only.

A Peace Line, pretty much like a World War One 'no- man's land', had been built along the Corcrain road. It was easy to tell who lived where. The kerb stones by the side of the road on the Loyalist side were painted red, white, and blue – the color of the British Union Jack flag; and on the Republican side, they were painted green and white, or green, orange and white – the color of the Irish flag, or tricolor. The third color of the tricolor, orange, was usually missing due to its association with the Protestant Orange movement.

Today was flashpoint time. It was the 12th of July – Orange day – the Glorious 12th. The Protestant Orange Order was on their annual Orange day march called the Drumcree Parade, and the traditional rage and hatred of the Catholics against them was at boiling point, exacerbated by the death of the Catholic kid.

No one outside of Northern Ireland could understand this hatred. Both sides had the same God, and the battle of the Boyne had been in 1690, almost 300 years ago. If only King Henry the Eighth of England had kept his wedding vows, none of this would have mattered – there would not be any Protestant religion.

Occasionally, these religious problems spilled over into mainland Britain. Bombs and bullets were not the weapons of choice. Catholic football fans of Glasgow Celtic, and Protestant fans of Glasgow Rangers, preferred to punch the living daylights out of each other whenever the two football teams met. To a lesser extent, the sporting religious rivalry surfaced in Edinburgh between the Hibs and the Hearts fans, but it was much more subdued. Scotland still had its "Orange lodges", as did America and Canada, and the 12th of July was still celebrated by the Orange marches. Onlookers never ceased to be amazed that anyone would want to celebrate a relatively minor battle, by twentieth century standards, that had been fought almost 300 years ago.

Not having shown up the previous day, the supposed lone gunman or bomber, still posed a threat of igniting the powder keg that was Portadown. Just one well aimed shot, or one destructive bomb, and the whole country could explode. Civil war was always a possibility if the Protestants took up arms. Britain would then have a real war on its hands, which would certainly spread to both Southern Ireland and mainland Britain. This would then bring Southern Ireland's army into play; the memory of the Black and Tans, and their atrocities, still firmly engrained in the minds of every young Catholic hot head.

After a relatively quiet few hours, things suddenly took a serious turn, as the march entered its final stages.

'Oh fucking hell Jim; why the fuck have they turned down there?' Paddy had said, with a disbelieving shake of his head. 'That's the Catholic sector. Now we are completely blind. Do they all want to be shot or blown to fucking pieces?'

The Protestant Orange Order often did this. They knew that marching down the Catholic streets would only provoke the Catholics into even more hatred and violence. Their mantra was that it was their right to walk anywhere that they wished along the Queen's highway. The Catholics saw it as supremacist, sectarian, triumphalist.

The remotely controlled car bomb went off with a terrific explosion as the marchers drew alongside.

The Catholics had anticipated the move.

Jim Killeen awoke with a start. 'Jesus Christ,' he exclaimed out loud. 'That was some dream.' He had physically felt the explosion. That is what had awakened him. Was Paddy right about his PTSD? He was now beginning to feel that these vivid night time dreams, and day time operational flashbacks, were becoming reality. Now that he had decided to leave the SAS, maybe they would go away.

He looked around and smiled as he realized where he was. Memories of the previous night's celebrations came flooding back. The memory of Paddy telling the laughing landlord that only a fool would run out of Guinness on a night like this; and the memory of the landlord telling Paddy that only an even bigger fool would drink a whole barrel in one night.

'Bloody pee impregnated bog oil.' Wardle had said. 'Ask Paddy how it gets its flavor Julie, you seem to like it. If you do though, I promise you that you will never drink it again.'

Killeen reluctantly climbed off the settee, and moved his head painfully from side to side in order to relieve the stiffness caused by a night sleeping on a settee that was at least a foot shorter than his body. He walked into the little kitchen, remembering to lower his head as he did so. Many had been the times when he had almost knocked himself senseless on the low beams of the cottage.

He put on the kettle, and walked into the little bathroom, pausing as he stared long and hard at his reflection in the bathroom mirror. He realized that he was no longer the boyish figure of old. There were now lines around his eyes, across his forehead, and the odd grey hair was beginning to put in an appearance. He had never noticed any of these unsettling features before; it was only since the deaths of Muscles and Mac that the ageing process had started to accelerate. He seemed to have aged ten years in a matter of days.

There were to be no more flashpoints; no more life threatening situations. He was going to be married, and he owed that to Julie.

Killeen made his way upstairs with a cup of tea for Julie. Julie, his Fiancée, soon to be his wife. It sounded good. The bed was empty.

'Conscientious little devil,' he said out loud. 'Take the day off tomorrow, we have a lot of catching up to do, they are never going to sack you on the day after your engagement party.' He had told her, as they had walked home from the pub, both of them holding hands, and occasionally holding each other up.

Julie had left the cottage a little after eight thirty that morning, closing the door as quietly as possible so as not to awaken her future husband. She walked the quarter mile or so to work with a smile on her face that even a slight head ache could not erase.

She would have her morning cup of tea at work. She had not wanted to wake up Jim, who looked as though he really needed to get some sleep. He seemed to have aged more than a little over the last few months. The job was becoming too stressful for him. Lines were forming around his eyes, and shadows were beginning to appear beneath them. He had always looked so boyish, almost like a teenager, even when well into his twenties, but now, well now he was beginning to look like a man in his thirties. It had only been four months since they had last been together, and yet the changes in his looks were apparent to anyone who hadn't seen them evolve on a daily basis.

Still, Julie could not have been happier; she was going to marry the man that she loved, the man she had always loved ever since the very first day that she had met him at the party. He was the man who had waited patiently for her for all these years – the man who had helped her to survive the pain and anguish of a broken marriage.

There was so much to do – the wedding – the honeymoon – the children. Sure, that would be in the future, but both of them wanted children, and had discussed it over one of the many drinks the previous evening. Paddy had overheard the conversation, and naturally enough, offered to lend his assistance in case Jim had any problems on that score.

She was still smiling as she turned into the drive of the Old Manor by the lake, and walked happily between the two rows of mature trees, and past the little shrubbery where Michael O'Riley had been introduced to Paddy's calling card.

Life just could not get any better. Daffodils carpeted the landscape in a welcoming sea of vibrant yellow, and meadow flowers filled the air with an assortment of perfumes. Even the birds appeared to be noisier than normal as they gathered their nest building supplies. She was the luckiest and the happiest woman in the world. Only one person in the entire world was happier than Julie; that was the tall, slim, professional soldier, who had been reduced to a childlike state for much of the evening and night. He was going to leave the Regiment and revert back to the Intelligence Corps. Brigadier Wardle had backed his decision following a long talk with his brother Ken, and had guaranteed him a long term posting to the Old Manor House.

Brigadier Wardle had more power than God. Both Molly and the Brigadier himself had told her so.

As she walked down the drive, a dark blue van with blacked out windows passed her, going slowly in the opposite direction. That was as much as anyone ever saw of the cleaners.

They had just finished cleaning.

CHAPTER 26

FOR SEAN

W.R.A.C. Lieutenant Julie Bromley – Real name – Mary Fitzpatrick – Twin sister to Sean Fitzpatrick; checked her watch as she stepped off the ferry in Northern Ireland the next morning, before travelling on to Belfast.

It was five minutes past nine.

She smiled a smile of deep satisfaction, and said out loud, '*THAT WAS FOR SEAN.*'

Five minutes earlier, a small Cumbrian village had been rocked by a huge explosion.

The roof of the Old Manor House by the lake had collapsed, and had been reduced to a burning pile of rubble, killing everyone inside, including the top brass of the UK anti terrorism unit up from London.

Most of the silver Mercedes had been atomized; all that was left was a twisted pile of metal.

It had taken a madman to devise – plan – and deliver.

EVEN IN DEATH.

THE WRONG PACKAGE HAD BEEN THE RIGHT ONE AFTER ALL, AND IT HAD JUST BEEN DELIVERED.

CHAPTER 27

PADDY'S FAVOURITE RACK

Paddy put a giant arm around his friend Jim Killeen's shoulder, as they lowered Julie's charred remains into the open grave. Both Julie's and Jim's parents were present, as were Ken Wardle's. This was their second funeral of the day. The first one had been for the Brigadier. Major Wardle was never going to add that coveted VC to his family collection. Special Forces rarely received the Victoria Cross, anyway, they were not relevant to his collection if they were from a Nancy boy sailor, and not a cavalry officer.

Both of Major Waddle's younger sons were present; Ken Wardle's face devoid of all emotion. He was hurting. A pain brought on by acute guilt. He, Ken 'Sniffer' Wardle, and his brother the Brigadier, had devised, and been working on the plan for weeks. Why had his famed nose let him down on this occasion? At what point had O'Malley smelled the rat? How could a slip of a girl have fooled him so easily?

He thought that by keeping *only* D1 unit involved, he could effectively lure, and ultimately eliminate the 'A' team. Any more men would have led to greater opportunity for O'Malley to see through the deception. His father, the Major had suggested it, and had been working tirelessly on the plan with both of his sons and the now dead adjutant.

Major Wardle was an intuitive planner. He was the cornerstone, the necessary link, the glue that bound together the armed forces and the intelligence services. He was the one who smoothed over the ruffled feathers of Government ministers when things didn't go according to plan. He was also the one who now had to face the wrath of those same Government ministers. How was he going to explain to them how his plan had so spectacularly backfired, and resulted in the deaths of the entire Northern Ireland Intelligence section.

It wasn't even a fair exchange; the 'A' team, for the cream of British Intelligence! – British military intelligence was back to square one. They were now virtually blind; all their secret information lay below the smoldering ruins of the Old Manor House.

Both Major Wardle and his son Ken could not help wondering. 'Had they lured O'Malley, or had they been ambushed, and lured BY O'Malley into a deadly and successful trap?'

Maybe they had both been played. Played like a couple of old fiddles – *Old fools* – Played by a pretty young lieutenant.

Molly was not at the grave. He was armed and out of sight. It was his turn to keep watch over Paddy and the others. He observed proceedings through a one thousand yard stare. His anger was consuming him. 'I will find you my darling,' he said to himself. 'No matter what it takes, or where you hide; I will find you, and I will kill you.' He knew that he didn't have much time. His psychosis had accelerated with both the pleasure and the release that he had felt as he had slowly raked the point of his knife up and down Mad Mitch Murphy's ribs – pausing, and twisting gently, as he moved from rib to rib. The adrenaline had surged through his body with the force of a tidal wave, as he had manically watched him chew on his own dick.

Murphy's pain had morphed into his own orgasmic pleasure; both had no limits, and both were inextricably intertwined.

Killeen had hardly spoken a word for over one week since the funeral. Ken Wardle was concerned. He knew what Jim Killeen was capable of. The pressure was starting to build up. The time bomb had been armed, and the clock was ticking. Hereford had told Wardle to keep a lid on it until the grief had started to subside. He knew from years of experience of working with men like Killeen that the grief would not go away: soon it would turn to rage. This was the danger point. Julie had been his driving force, the one true motivation in his life, but he was now at a cross roads – he could turn. No one knew which way?

Wardle knew that Killeen was no hot head. He was clever, controlled, and cool under pressure. He also knew that the flashpoint was never far away – it laid dormant in most Special Forces men. He was also concerned with his mental state before Julie's death. There were definite signs of PTSD creeping in.

Which way would he jump? That was what worried Wardle the most. Men like Killeen and his team lived one mistake away from death; that came along the territory, but at what price to their mental health – their sanity?

In circumstances like these, people reacted differently. Most men grieved and brooded; some men lost themselves in drink and self pity. Men like Killeen – Paddy – O'Malley, and to some degree himself, reacted differently. They had been trained to kill without thought or remorse. One small sector of the brain retained this information, and was only accessed and activated when the Military wanted it activated.

The army could not afford to allow this sector of Killeen's brain to run out of control; it had to be caged. The cage door had been left open in the case of O'Malley. Wardle's job now was to ensure that Killeen's cage door remained firmly closed.

Until the army needed it opening again – of course.

It was now two weeks after the explosion at the Manor, and Killeen, Paddy, Wardle, and Molly were sat in the village pub sharing a few drinks, when the letter was delivered to Paddy by hand.

'I'm not going to fucking well open that for at least 2 more weeks,' he said. 'I will bet you any money that the bastards want me back off leave; well, I am not fucking going anywhere. I am staying here as long as the Guinness holds out.'

Paddy was not about to leave Jim Killeen at any price: he knew that Killeen needed him.

'I reckon I had better order a dozen more barrels then Paddy just to see you through to the weekend.' Laughed Steve, the tall, slightly overweight, and genial landlord.

'Make it 20 barrels Steve, I've got the last 4 months money burning a hole in my pocket, and this warm weather makes me thirsty.' Paddy's consumption of Guinness had accelerated sharply since the death of Julie. In his own way, he felt guilty at having been in strict competition with Molly over Lieutenant Julie's affections, neither man having been too successful. Perhaps this had obscured the obvious – there must have been signs, but those magnificent tits had diverted both their attention.

'Don't you think that you had better open it Pads,' smiled Killeen, who was starting to come round and talk a little at last. 'If you don't like it, you can always ignore it and wait for the MP's to come and arrest you.'

'They had better send a coach load then Jim,' Paddy raised a clenched fist. 'My record is 5 MP's in as many minutes, and I was pretty pissed at the time.'

'Pass it here you bog oil slurping *APE*, I'll open it for you.' Molly attempted to snatch the letter out of Paddy's giant hand. 'It could be important; it *WAS* delivered by military courier.'

'Here you are then *BOY*,' Paddy said, as he passed the unopened envelope to Molly. 'If it IS bad news, you can shove the lot up your arse, because if you don't – I will.'

The men were still laughing as the expression on Molly's face changed. It turned a ghostly white, and changed from smiling, to a look of horror. He passed the envelope to Killeen, who uttered only two words. 'OH FUCK.'

There was an animal scream, as furniture and bodies went flying through the air. A heavy oak table crashed through the bay window of the pub, almost decapitating the courier who had delivered the envelope – an envelope containing a picture of Paddy's father, mother, and two sisters; propped up on four chairs, with their hands tied behind their backs, and their throats cut. At the bottom of the photograph, written in felt tip pen was the simple message.

REGARDS – YOUR FAVOURITE RACK

It took several minutes, and four strong men to eventually subdue Paddy. Even the assistance of Steve, the landlord was needed. He was quite a big man, and sat on Paddy's chest as the others held him down. Wardle looked at the photograph, and its little message. 'Oh fucking hell.' Was all he said; looking after Killeen was bad enough, but looking after Paddy was something different – something very, very, different.

A regiment of Military Police would not be enough for that task.

CHAPTER 28

THE CONSEQUENCES

The loss of the Old Manor House by the lake was to be catastrophic for the British war on terrorism.

Most of the senior IRA anti terrorism personnel had been present as the roof of the old building had collapsed in on them, crashing through the tinder dry one hundred year old wooden first floor, and instantly igniting. The only survivor had been the receptionist who had greeted Molly on his first meeting with the Brigadier; she had been around the back of the building watering her precious flowers, as she did every morning. Years of Intelligence material on the IRA had been gathered and stored within the walls of the building. None of it survived the inferno. All the eggs had been in the one basket, and were now well and truly scrambled.

Knowledge of many IRA sleeper cells on the mainland was now non-existent.

Bombing of the British mainland now began in earnest, all with relative impunity. Birmingham – Warrington – Guildford – numerous London locations – Harrods – British Gas. Many of these atrocities resulted in massive loss of life and limb; most of them being innocent young drinkers in pubs, or ordinary people simply going about their everyday business – their only crime was being in the wrong place at the wrong time.

Politicians died; even Margaret Thatcher, the British Prime Minister, was almost blown up when the Grand Hotel in Brighton was bombed as she was staying there during the Conservative party's annual conference. Advance knowledge of this atrocity had been contained in the destroyed records, and its details had failed to be acted on – with fatal consequences.

Defiance radiated from Thatcher's eyes during the next day's conference. This was one enemy that the IRA underestimated at their cost. This was no ordinary British Prime Minister. This was Churchill taken to the next level.

If Bobby Sands and his fellow IRA hunger strikers didn't feel hungry, Margaret Thatcher was not going to cook for them.

Sands and his co-hunger strikers died of starvation in prison.

They could have been force fed – Thatcher forbid it.

The IRA Operatives who at one time had been under constant surveillance, were now completely under the radar, unknown, and invisible; slipping in and out of Britain, or across the Irish border almost at will. Details of known bomb makers and bombers had been lost, and more and more consignments of arms and explosives now entered the country.

Michael Flannery renewed his financial recruitment campaign from the NORAID offices in Manhattan, New York, using a system of pub collections, testimonial dinners, and fund raising events. Senators and Congressmen attended, many of them unaware of how the money raised was about to be spent – many of them were fully aware. Flannery had been in the Tipperary Brigade of the IRA in the 1920s, and was a fanatical believer in the unification of Ireland.

The scale of the influx of American arms continued to rise. The trawler Marita Ann, registered in Boston, was intercepted off the south west coast of Kerry containing 7 tons of arms. However, this seizure represented only a fraction of the arms coming into the country; the security forces were not often successful. There were now too many gaps in the information received by the intelligence services, and still there was the question of the mole. Someone was still passing information to the IRA. On far too many occasions, the military raided known IRA sympathizer's homes only to find that they had fled the previous day or during the night.

Charnock's – D2 SAS team were back in the province alongside two recently posted SAS units, but owing to the lack of quality Intelligence, none of them were making any headway. New recruits were joining the IRA in droves, hoping to emulate the heroic 'A' team. All too often, when it seemed that the military were gaining the upper hand, both gunmen and bombers simply slipped across the border into Southern Ireland; there, they had total safety and immunity from the security forces, allowing themselves time to regroup.

The security situation was sliding completely out of control; exacerbated by the Southern Irish authorities' point blank refusal to allow any British military incursions into the south.

This situation was impossible and intolerable to the British; something had to be done, but what? Southern Ireland was a sovereign state, and even though there was a limited amount of intelligence sharing, this had to be done discretely in order to avoid repercussions from the by now well armed, and in many ways, increasingly media savvy IRA leadership.

Margaret Thatcher, the British Prime Minister, made a secure phone call.

It was now time to take the gloves off.

CHAPTER 29

NO WAY – THEN AGAIN

Ken Wardle had travelled to MI5 headquarters in London to meet up with the two Army Generals.

All three men were dressed in civilian clothes, and met up at a little café for a coffee, in order to finalize their presentation, and to discuss tactics. They were on a very delicate mission with little hope of success; the only ace in their pack being the stubborn refusal of Margaret Thatcher, the British Prime Minister, to give any quarter what so ever to terrorists or to any form of terrorism.

Even President Reagan was wary of Maggi, and became more and more compliant towards her views against terrorism, and her anti communism rhetoric. Secretly, for fear of upsetting the enormous Irish contingent in the US, Reagan created a "black" operations force, with both links and attachments to their British equivalent. Before his death at the hands of the 'A' team, Bob Kineer, of Killeen's S1 unit, had been part of the "Black Ops" force.

'What do you think Ken,' asked General Kelly. 'Are we wasting our time here?'

'Not necessarily sir,' Wardle replied. 'We will be dealing with an ex Wing Commander who has actually seen active service in Korea. Father recommended that we speak to him personally, and by doing so, we would by-pass the interfering civil servants. It was father who fixed up the meeting; at times he can squeeze where water can't. The minister isn't your typical "Career Politician" sir. I don't think that he will be unsympathetic. I do think however that we have to emphasize the anonymous civilian angle; there is no way that he is likely to chance incurring the wrath of the PM. That would not ONLY be political suicide, – she would have his balls for breakfast – you know what the Iron Lady is like.'

Two of the British army's highest ranking generals laughed loudly, at the same time nodding knowingly. No one in any position of authority was safe from Maggi's handbag.

'Why don't we soften him up a little to begin with by requesting covert military incursions into southern Ireland. When he blows a gasket, we will suggest the alternative.' interjected General Platt.

'Very sneaky sir, that is precisely what father suggested when he first came up with the plan.' Wardle chuckled.

'He always was a sneaky old bugger himself when he was my adjutant,' laughed General Platt. 'He could never get over the fact that I was his superior, and five years younger than he was.'

'He did mention it sir.' Wardle grinned, and looked at both Generals in turn.

'It was his own bloody stupid fault Ken that he never rose above the rank of major, he just would not listen to reason. I tried to warn him on more than one occasion. He knew that messing about with that young Irish girl would spell the end of any promotion chances he may have had, and believe me Ken, he could have gone a bloody long way in the army. Did he ever let on?' General Platt asked before taking a drink of his coffee.

Wardle shook his head. 'No sir, but my two brothers and I knew all about it, we had done for years. I suppose that I only joined the Marines to piss him off. Clive, my younger brother, refused to join the army for the same season. He still saw her on occasions long after he married mother. We all kept quiet about it, but I think she knew. Women seem to have a way of knowing these things; female intuition they tell me. Both my brothers and I discussed it once or twice, but we decided to keep quiet about it and not let on to mum. What would have been the point? His career had already come to a dead stop, and neither of them were particularly close.'

General Platt smiled, and shook his head as he spoke. 'Still, seems a bloody bad show to me when a cavalry officer with a glittering future throws it all away for an Irish peasant girl. If he had wanted to play away from home, why didn't he choose one of the many debutant ladies that we all sniffed around when we were younger?'

Wardle laughed. 'He did sir – that is where he met mother. I have always thought that he viewed the marriage as a career move more than anything else.'

It was now General Platt's turn to laugh. 'There must have been something there Ken; three sons don't just happen, anyway, let's move on gentlemen, and go and see our Wing Commander before I put my foot in it anymore. Your father and I go back a long way Ken, and some of the antics that we got up to in our younger days are not for the ears of his son.'

The three men were still laughing as they left the little café, and headed for one of the most important meetings of their lives. There was much at stake, and the lives of countless individuals, both military and civilian, depended on them getting a result.

`NO – NO – NO… No way – No bloody way whatsoever. The British army must not ever cross the border into Southern Ireland, covert or otherwise. If one single soldier was captured, there would be hell to pay. The Prime Minister would have my guts for garters, and my balls for starters, if I gave permission without her authority; and she herself could never give permission as much as she would love to. It would be akin to an act of war. The damned Yanks would be all over us like a rash. Not one British military man or woman must ever cross the border on any form of military business; that also goes if they are dressed in civilian clothes as well.'

'**Now what did you really come to see me about**?' The former Wing Commander added with a smile. 'Never try to bullshit an experienced *bullshitter* gentlemen. I am now a politician, and bullshitting is my job.'

'Supposing that they weren't military men Minister – supposing that they were civilians, with no recognizable allegiance to any country or regime?'

'Keep talking general, you have my undivided attention.' The minister sat upright in his chair, and placed both arms on the desk in front of him, raising his head to look the general studiously in the eyes.

The general looked at Wardle and nodded.

Wardle spoke quietly, choosing his words carefully. 'Civilians sir – no military records – no identities – no dental records – not even birth certificates. Foreign mercenaries, paid for by anonymous American donors in order to counter the IRA. That would be their cover story, and you can take it from me Minister, there would never be any chance of them deviating from it.'

'Supply and equipment?' The minister leaned forward on his chair as he spoke, this time staring directly at Wardle.

'American equipment only sir.' Wardle answered, carefully avoiding the supply part of the question.

'You do realize that the Prime Minister could be a problem?' The minister's face broke into a big grin as he spoke.

'Really sir?' Both generals spoke in unison. 'I would have thought that this sort of operation would be right up her street: you are aware of the joint operations that we have with the American covert operatives?' General Kelly looked puzzled as he spoke.

'There is no such thing as joint operations with the Americans.' The Minister was very sharp and precise in his response. 'On this occasion however, I was referring to 'your' proposed operation with 'your' unknown civilian operators. Maggi could indeed prove troublesome. She will probably want to join the team.' All four men laughed. 'And she wouldn't need any fancy American equipment either – she would have her handbag.'

Prime Minister Margaret Thatcher's handbag, jokingly, had the reputation of being the most fearsome weapon on Planet Earth – after her tongue. Politicians and World Leaders' blanched and trembled at the mere sight of Maggie's weapon of mass destruction.

'And where would you find such foreign mercenaries gentlemen; they would have to be of at least Special Forces standard? I take it that you already have them in place, otherwise this meeting would not be taking place?'

'Yes minister, they are ready to move at a moment's notice,' replied Wardle. 'They also have unprecedented knowledge of the country and the terrain, and, a motivation that surpasses anything that you can ever imagine.'

The minister held up his hand to silence Wardle, he wanted to know no more. There was no need; Wardle had never intended revealing any further information; only a direct order from one of the two generals could have prized anything else out of him; even a government minister did not have that power.

This government minister already had a pretty good idea of the personnel involved; he was a military man through and through, and made it his own personal business to keep the interfering civil servants as far away as possible from the real world – the world in which he had once lived as a pilot, and the world in which the SAS occasionally broke the rules in order to achieve their objectives.

The minister got up to leave, and looking seriously at the three men in turn, he suddenly raised his voice in anger. 'I fucking hate the way these murdering bastards are able to hide from justice by simply slipping across the border. I can guarantee you that it wouldn't have happened in my day; sometimes I think that the Black and Tans had the right idea. I promise you one thing gentlemen, I will do everything in my power to make this happen. I will arrange a private meeting with the PM as soon as possible. This should be right up her street. If it is a positive, we will meet up again immediately. I will be in touch.'

The three men looked at each other as the minister left the room. Each man wore a satisfied smile. This was one politician they knew they could trust. A military man never stopped being a "Military Man"; even when he was a government minister. Bullshitting may well have been his job, but deep down, he was still a military man at heart – a military man who had seen combat in all its brutality, and realized that sometimes, the accepted rules of warfare had to be ignored.

His boss may never have seen warfare at close range, but he was aware that she was well up to the task. She was a formidable warrior in her own right – as Argentina was about to discover in the very near future.

The call to Ken Wardle came sooner than expected from General Platt, and was almost delivered in code.

'It's on – tomorrow – same office – 1300 hours.' The phone then went dead.

The meeting with the former Wing Commander turned Minister was similarly brief. 'The PM has given her approval. It took no more than five seconds. It was almost as if she had planned the whole thing herself, and was eager to get started. You will report to me and no-one else. I will keep the PM briefed as necessary. Mr. Wardle will be my only contact with the military. I do not want to know anything else, and I will deny that any meeting ever took place. If the government is replaced at the next election gentlemen, then you are completely on your own. No payment to the civilians in question must be made to, or through, any UK bank; everything goes to, and through America. The PM has authorized me to make available whatever funds you require, without question, and without audit. That will be all.'

With that he left the room. There didn't seem to be much, yet there was everything. Wardle now had a free hand. No rules – no laws – no restrictions, and unlimited funding.

The dynamics in Ireland were about to change.

The Iron Lady had nodded her approval. The three men never had any doubts about the outcome.

Boadicea had returned from her 2000 year exile.

The D1 SAS team were back in business, only this time, they were no longer restrained or restricted by any form of military law. The strait jacket had been discarded. They were however consumed by anger and hatred, and the future for many of the previously "immune" IRA men, on their own version of active service, was now looking pretty bleak.

The hunt for Mary Fitzpatrick was on; not officially, and not strategically, nevertheless, they would accomplish whatever the army had planned for them, at the same time working to their own agenda.

Military rules no longer applied.

Normal rules of humanity no longer applied.

CHAPTER 30

NO RULES

Wardle met Killeen, Paddy, and Molly, a couple of days later at the cheap Norfolk hotel where they had been staying for the last week. The weather had been fine, and the three of them had spent their days fishing on the many lakes in the area. Only Molly knew anything about fishing; still, it was essential that Killeen and Paddy learned. This was to be their cover when in Ireland.

Throughout the spring and summer months, Ireland was a Mecca for thousands of fishermen from all over Europe, and a group of three English anglers driving round the countryside and visiting the various lakes and rivers would not arouse suspicion.

'I thought you told us that there would be no rules.' Said Molly, with a glint in his eye, as he at first pointed, and then wagged his index finger at Wardle.

'No holds barred you told us,' said Paddy. 'If you reckon that my only job is to drag people from the south so that they can stand trial in the north, I'm not fucking interested. I will fucking well go on my own and do my own thing. I have a little unfinished business with a certain rack.'

'Let him finish Pads,' Killeen shook his head and grimaced as he spoke. 'We all feel the same way as you do, but we have to have some guidelines. You have got to remember that we will be operating without cleaners. We'll either have to clean for ourselves, or be a little more careful what we leave behind. How long do you think that we can operate in full view of everyone, if we start leaving a trail of dead bodies? The British Government most certainly don't want to know us, so we've got to avoid them wanting to know about us. If we don't get it right, the Irish Government will soon become suspicious, and then we'll be really stuffed. Remember, we don't exist, so we can't call for military back up.'

'I suppose you're right.' Paddy reluctantly agreed. 'But when I find that fucking rack, I promise you one thing; *SHE WILL NOT BE STANDING*

TRIAL. THERE WON'T BE ANYTHING FUCKING LEFT OF HER TO STAND TRIAL.'

'I've got a pretty good reason to find her as well Pads, I was going to get married, remember?' Killeen could feel the tears welling up in his eyes.

'And I lost a brother,' Wardle said. 'Don't forget that Paddy, we all have good reason to hate her, but we can't go in like a bull at a gate. We don't even know where she is; she might not even be in the country now. If I thought that you three bastards were after me, I would probably be in Alice Springs with a tribe of Abbo's.'

Alice – Alice – who the fuck is Alice, do I know her?'

Wardle held his head in his hands at Paddy's comment, before the lot of them burst out laughing.

'Fucking rack, I want to strangle her.' Paddy grabbed Molly round the neck.

'I would rather shag her first, she has fantastic tits.'

The three men glared at Molly; Paddy tightened his grip. Molly reached forward and gently squeezed Paddy's balls. Paddy released his grip from around Molly's throat, and winking at Paddy, Molly let go of his balls.

'Only joking – not about the tits though.' Molly raised both his hands above his head in a gesture of submission. 'Where do you fit in with all of this lot Ken? I thought you were retiring in a couple of months.'

'So did I Molly. "Active for an indefinite period", I believe the general said. It looks like my pension pot is due to expand somewhat though; I'm being transferred to the Long Service List, and have been promoted to WO1.'

'Well get the drinks in you tight fisted bastard, let's celebrate.' Paddy said, laughing, as he grabbed Wardle around the waist, and effortlessly lifted him off the ground.

'You can't speak to a WO1 that way, you Irish bog oil gobbler.'

'Oh yes I can Sgt Major *Wanker*. I am a civilian now – remember, and if I don't exist, what are you going to do about it?' Paddy was returning back to form, Paddy always had to have the last word.

Wardle slowly raised two fingers to Paddy, as he loosed his grip, and allowed him to fall to the ground. Wardle continued speaking. 'I will be based in the north with access to a secure telephone line, performing like a regular warrant officer. Supplies and intelligence will all come through me and no one else. As far as the base commanding officer is concerned, I am supplying Special Forces based in the north, and basically, I am to be indulged without question.

I will be your only link with all things military. The two generals that I set it up with have given me the power to requisition whatever I wish; at that point, they both walked away and cut me loose. Unlike you lot however, I do exist, so I do have certain parameters that I have to work to.'

'What are the restrictions imposed on us then Ken, come on, come clean?'

'None really Molly, no obvious restrictions. How can there be any form of military control over a bunch of American mercenaries who were recruited in the States and are funded by the States. If you are ever captured you know the script. Dates and locations are all in place, so your stories can be corroborated. Once they have tortured, mutilated, disemboweled, cut off your balls, and then killed you – they will be none the wiser as to who you really are.'

Killeen looked away as he tried to suppress a laugh. He was unsuccessful, and immediately all four of them were laughing out loud at the absurdity and humor of Wardle's comment.

Wardle resumed his composure and continued. 'I think common sense should determine how you operate. People who frequently travel across the border in order to cause problems in the north, can easily go missing. The papers, or the television, are never going to report anything like that, but if known Republicans start turning up dead everywhere, it'll be like leaving a calling card. You will have the entire Southern Irish Army on the lookout for you.'

'And our remit?'

'Again, I can't really tell you that at the moment Molly. You are simply an undercover anti terrorist unit that does not exist, and you will be supplied with the most up to date information together with target details. It really isn't a lot different to what you've been doing for the last few months, except that you'll be sleeping in beds, doing a lot of fishing, and you will have no border restrictions to worry about. You can come and go as you please, and you will also not have a certain mad Irishman shooting at you.'

'We'll be taking our very own mad Irishman with us instead.' Molly moved away from Paddy as he spoke.

'You mean that we will be shitting in real bogs, drinking real Guinness, and getting paid for it Ken. It sounds more like a holiday from heaven to me.'

'That is exactly how you must conduct yourselves, you are on holiday Paddy, a fishing holiday. Oh I forgot to mention Jim. Tomorrow, you'll be taking possession of a brand new estate car in order to replace the one that you forgetfully left in a field somewhere in England. Damn careless of you to forget where you left it. The general agreed without questioning it. My brother always reckoned that once he reached brigadier, he had more power than God. If that's the case, the general has more power than God's boss.'

As they all laughed, Molly recalled his initial meeting with Brigadier Wardle at the Old Manor House by the lake. He remembered his God comment. He had never met a brigadier before – he had seemed like a nice bloke – his charred remains now buried under 6 feet of Cumbrian soil.

The three anglers, complete with mountains of fishing tackle, drove off the ferry at Dublin, and headed north through County Meith on their way to County Cavan. For the first few weeks, Cavan was to serve as a base, and give them time to familiarize themselves with the surrounding countryside. The county north of Cavan was Fermanagh, and located an easy drive due east through Monaghan, were the troubled Northern Ireland counties of Armagh and Tyrone. Armagh wasn't referred to as bandit country for nothing. It was mainly from these three counties, Fermanagh, Armagh, and Tyrone, that the IRA passed over the border into the south, disappearing into the counties of Donegal, Cavan, Monaghan and Louth.

It was in county Armagh that O'Malley had killed Muscles and Mac; the sight of every sign bringing back bitter memories, as the three fishermen drove on.

Jim Killeen's new estate car began to gradually work its way through these southern counties; all the time listening and observing, and everyday stopping at different phone boxes – always primed and eager to get back in the thick of the action – always awaiting instructions.

Their days were spent fishing the many rivers and lakes throughout the region that they were covering, and their evenings were enjoyably spent moving from pub to pub – always listening – always looking for familiar faces that may recognize them, and maybe blow their cover.

Both Killeen and Paddy were beginning to enjoy the sport; it was peaceful and relaxing, and most days would find one or the other asleep by their fishing rods. It almost seemed as if they were catching up on the years of sleep deprivation brought about by the job – a job where falling to sleep could result in death for the entire section.

Molly rarely slept, even during the night. The congenitally inherited insanity was beginning to take over his mind. He fought with all his might to remain lucid. He couldn't afford to lose all control; he still had one task to perform for his friends. Once accomplished – then he would move on.

At long last, after a period of weeks, the first orders came. The target was a very low profile bomb maker named Patrick Flynn. Flynn however was very high, if not right at the top of the security forces most wanted list. He was responsible for close on 50% of all bombs that were making their way into the north. He was also responsible for training a new band of ever more sophisticated bomb makers. The death of O'Riley, at the hands of Paddy, had had a serious impact on the number of bombs going off in the province. O'Riley had been an apprentice of Flynn during his early bomb making days, and had constructed the bomb that had been concealed in the Mercedes at the Old Manor House. Flynn was working overtime to fill the void left by O'Riley.

Observe, photograph associates, and deliver Flynn to a fixed point in the north, were the simple instructions. At last, they were in business.

Flynn lived in a remote Monaghan farmhouse, not more than 300 yards away from a rather picturesque little lake. Their cover as fishermen was perfect: Sniffer Wardle hadn't let them down.

After three days of fishing and observing, the team moved in on Flynn and his two associates, who were both unfortunate enough to be collecting their next consignment of booby trap bombs at that precise time. The operation was all too simple. No one was armed, and no one was expecting trouble. After all, they were in the south, and British security forces weren't allowed to cross the border.

Southern Ireland's security forces were not allowed to upset the IRA, and so Flynn had conducted his deadly business in his own secure fool's paradise, totally immune from all interference.

'What are we going to do with these two?' Asked Paddy, as he delivered a knock- out blow to each man in turn. 'They shouldn't have been here. We can't let them go, or our cover will be blown.'

'That's not a problem,' replied Molly. 'They can all three of them go the same way as the people at the Old Manor House went, this bastard probably made the bomb. Why don't we ask him when he wakes up?'

Molly asked him – and as the point of his knife slowly moved up and down his rib cage in direct contact with his rib bones, Flynn was only too willing to disclose everything that he knew about his IRA warlords. Names, addresses, contacts, all were readily supplied, but the one that both Paddy and Killeen sought the most was missing. None of the three men knew the whereabouts of Mary Fitzpatrick. They were only too aware of her, she had now achieved legendary status after her exploits at the Old Manor House right under the noses of the despised D1 SAS team – the team that had eliminated O'Malley's legendary 'A' team.

The true identity of Lieutenant Julie Bromley, W.R.A.C. had been confirmed weeks earlier by Charnock's D2 team, using similar tactics to the ones Molly now employed. Wardle had suspected her true identity within minutes of the explosion at the Old Manor House – only on this occasion, his famed nose had been fooled by a very clever actress.

A massive explosion that could be heard for miles around, rocked the Monaghan countryside, leaving behind the tiny traces of three charred and disintegrated bodies.

'That's for Julie.' Killeen said as they drove away, tears filling his eyes. There was going to be much more getting even before the surviving members of the disbanded D1 SAS team had finished.

No one was suspicious of the explosion. Blowing yourself up was an occupational hazard for all bomb makers.

Flynn's body was too badly burned for the police to notice where Molly had shoved his dick.

Killeen and Paddy had looked on in squeamish horror. Molly was beginning to resemble O'Malley in both maniacal looks and actions, and was now in his own chosen hell. A hell from which there could be no escape, and only one possible release.

Slowly; little by little, the Intelligence services began to get their act together, and overcome the damage caused by the loss of their most experienced personnel at the Manor. More and more information was starting to flow Wardle's way, and the three fishermen were kept busy. People began to disappear. Cars moving explosives into the north mysteriously exploded, as did ammunition and arms dumps in the south.

Jim and Paddy were worried. Molly was becoming more violent and sadistic with each job undertaken. Very few IRA men were being delivered to the security forces in the north. Molly wanted to torture them for information, then to kill them – slowly, and painfully. Sometimes there was no information to be gleaned from their captives. Molly continued to torture them.

His eyes had permanently taken on the 1000 yard stare. The stare never left him. He would no longer listen to either Paddy or Killeen. His over-riding obsession was his pursuit of Mary Fitzpatrick. This was to be the last act in his short life: his final "thank you" to his three friends – his personal vengeance for the deaths of Muscles, Mac and Bob.

Molly knew that he didn't have much more time left. His dreams were punctuated by ever more violence; violence that he himself was inflicting. It was becoming harder to control by day, and impossibly by night. Each job, no matter how routine, furnished him with an urge to kill – to kill slowly – to kill painfully.

The screams of agony excited him. The look of terror and pain in each of his victim's eyes seemed to satisfy his bloodlust, but only temporarily. It wasn't long before the desire to kill and torture again returned.

Molly knew that now there was to be no going back – no returning to society; his condition was hereditary, irreversible, and accelerating. A madman was dangerous – a psychopathic madman that had been trained to kill, and had no rules to restrict or restrain him, was something else. He still had one final act to perform – a favor for Jim, Paddy, and Ken – an act of vengeance – a labor of love.

What remained of his sanity and his genius was put to work devising the demise of Mary Fitzpatrick. Killing her was not the only objective. She had to know who was responsible. She had to experience the fear of knowing that she was about to die.

He decided to give her a sporting chance. It was to be him or her. The plan was hatched; the execution of the plan was to be a work of shear genius. He would not tell either Killeen or Paddy of his plan, they were not interested in his genius, they simply wanted her dead – eliminated with a passion far greater than the hatred that they had ever felt for O'Malley.

Ken Wardle had warned Killeen that the powers that be were becoming restless. The Irish Prime Minister had been in touch with his British counterpart, convinced that British Special Forces were operating in the south. He in turn had been threatened by the IRA with another wave of bombings in Dublin if it wasn't sorted.

It was now late autumn, almost winter time, and very few fishermen were still holidaying in Ireland. The three of them were becoming more and more exposed. Things had started to go wrong. Little things at first. Targets failed to appear, ammunition and arms had mysteriously been cleared days before the team arrived, and on one occasion, an unarmed Molly had been shot at while reconnoitering an old farm house in county Armagh.

The situation had looked desperate, as two gunmen, with armalite, M16 rifles, had him pinned down with no possible escape route. Now completely insane, he was still in possession of the most basic survival instinct, and knew that the only means of rescuing the situation would have to come from Killeen and Paddy.

Killeen and Paddy were on surveillance of a leading IRA paymaster, and fishing nearby when they heard the shots. Armed with only pistols, as their rifles were in the car some half a mile away, they slowly made their way to the old farmhouse and surveyed the situation.

'He's completely bollocksed if we don't get him out of there quick Jim,' Paddy had said. 'I bet that they have already called in reinforcements, and all we have got are these poxy things.' Paddy waved his pistol in Killeen's face.

'We've got to play the bluff card Pads, there's no other way that we can get close enough for a shot without being seen and shot ourselves. Do you reckon that you can still speak fluent Belfast gibberish?'

Paddy grinned. 'Sure I can be jeabers sir – so I can – just forkin watch.' With that, Paddy stood upright, and walked in full view towards the two gunmen, firing a couple of shots in the direction of Molly, and shouting in his best Belfast voice. 'Keep you heads down boys, there may be more of the forkin bastards nearby.' The two men took the bait, and as he approached them, two shots rang out, and two IRA gunmen died painlessly, each with a bullet in the head.

Killeen was becoming concerned. There were simply too many things going wrong – too many coincidences. It was if the IRA was always one step ahead of them, and were anticipating their every move. As he phoned Wardle from a Monaghan village pub, he felt a chill go through his body.

'Jim, we've got to get you out, pronto; you've been fingered. There's been a leak, fuck knows how, but MI5 have been monitoring phone calls trying to find out where all the leaked information is coming from, and they picked up a message regarding your team. The cat is out of the bag and the PM wants the entire operation wound up and brought to a dead stop before the Irish PM gets to know. Someone has informed on you to his defense secretary, and he is now asking Maggie some embarrassing questions.

I have spoken to dad, and he has agreed to make all the necessary arrangements. Drive to Dublin *NOW*: don't even stop for petrol if you can help it, half of fucking Ireland is looking for you. Use all the back roads and ditch the weapons just before you get to the ferry. Dad has arranged for Charnock's team to meet you at the docks and accompany you to England. From there, you'll be taken to somewhere safe. Try to get out of England if you can. All your identities have been blown, and there is more than a million quid on all your heads. I'll bet my pension on Paddy's rack being behind all this.'

'SORRY LADS, YOU'RE ON YOUR OWN, I'M STAYING.'

'You can't stay Molly,' Killeen said. 'You'll be on your own with no support; what the hell are you going to do, you haven't even got a car?'

'I am going to take a little trip to County Mayo for a spot of salmon fishing on the River Moy, and I am going to kill a certain Mary Fitzpatrick.'

'You can't be sure that she's there *BOY*. That poor bastard that you were filleting last week, would have said anything that you wanted him to just to make you stop. What the hell has got into you?'

'He's the third one that's said Mayo Paddy. "Ballina", to be more specific. No one else has said a dickybird – I *am* going.

One thing that the pair of you need to think about though is: "*What are the authorities going do with you when you get back*?"

They can't afford to let you stay alive. You know too much. You will be dead men walking as soon as you touch down in England; that's if you even get that far.'

'Bollocks; you are talking pure fucking bollocks Molly, after what we've done for the country. Britain doesn't treat its people that way. Maybe the Yanks do, but we don't.'

'No, I'm not talking bollocks Paddy. They've given us a free hand to do virtually whatever and whoever we want to over here. We are expendable, and we will be dispensed with. Remember, we do *NOT* exist; therefore, we will not be missed. I'm not going back until I am sure that you two are OK, that's not negotiable: in fact, I can never go back at all.'

Molly, for the very first time, proceeded to tell his two best ever friends about his mental problem.

'Fucking hell *BOY*, why didn't you tell us sooner?' Paddy was visibly upset. 'Jim and I thought that you were going fucking nuts.'

'He is Paddy – don't you listen?'

'Of course I listen Jim. I just refuse to accept that there's nothing anyone can do about it.'

'Believe me *APEMAN*, there really is nothing that can be done. I never intended winding up in a lunatic asylum, going out in a blaze of glory is more my style. Watch and see – just watch and see. It's you two that should be worried though. Think about it Jim, as far as I can see, your only option is to completely disappear off the face of the earth. The British Government simply can't take a chance on you living.'

Jim Killeen was deep in thought: deep down, he knew that Molly may well be right. They were expendable – they had outlived their usefulness. What possible use could they be to the British military? They were very dangerous liabilities, an embarrassment – a diplomatic incident waiting to happen. There was to be no going back to Ireland now either. He wondered exactly what they had got planned for the two of them on their return to England?

One thing he was sure of though, and it was a comforting thought, was that if Sniffer Wardle and his dad, the Major, had made the arrangements, both he and Paddy were safe. Sniffer Wardle's hooter had never let them down – it had never failed them.

CHAPTER 31

THE RIGHT PACKAGE

'Good morning Molly my dear, and how is the delightful little town of Ballina suiting you?'

Molly had not been sleeping, and pretended to wake with a start, slowly opening his eyes, and focusing on the pretty face of Mary Fitzpatrick.

'Good morning Lieutenant Julie Bromley, how very nice to see you, and how delightful is your little hideaway; the salmon fishing is quite superb, and the Ridge Pool really is as good as everything I have ever been told about it. I was beginning to worry that I would never see your smiling face again – that would have been a great shame.' Molly smiled; he had been dreaming of, and planning this moment, for quite a long time. His rather none too subtle questions over a few drinks in the local pubs over the past week, had, as he had planned, aroused suspicion.

Like all good fishermen, Molly knew that sooner or later, even the most wary of fish eventually rises to the bait, even if only out of irritation.

It was only a matter of time before Mary Fitzpatrick came looking for him; and now, in his final vestiges of lucidity, and as the last reserves of sanity drained away from him – he would give her a sporting chance – after all, even though their views differed, she was loyal to her cause, and deserved the respect of a fellow professional assassin.

'I believe that you have been looking for me Molly my dear, not very discretely I might add. Well, now that you have found me, that only leaves one – soon to be none.'

'What do you mean Mary? That only leaves one.' Molly looked puzzled.

'Just a certain Mr. Ken Wardle: then, I will have all the D1 team – the full set – just the way O'Malley, father, and I planned it all along.'

'What about Jim and Paddy? You can't get at them, they are somewhere safe back in England, maybe much farther away than that by now.' Molly faked a grin, at the same time suppressing an overwhelming urge to kill.

'Major Wardle has taken care of them for me; they are anything but safe; they are being well looked after though, and both their operations were a complete success. Neither of them will ever be a problem to us or to anyone else again. Major Wardle phoned me this morning to tell me the good news.'

'What – Ken's dad – that Major Wardle?'

'That's right Molly – Ken's Major Wardle – MY DAD.'

'How do you think that we always stayed one step ahead of you? He loved my twin brother Sean and I far more than he loved the rest of his family. The army and his overbearing military family would never allow him to marry mum, a poor Irish peasant girl. He always loved her and vowed to get even, now he has succeeded beyond his wildest dreams. First the Manor and the entire Northern Ireland intelligence section, and now the final remnants of the D1 team.

It was his plan all along that helped us to find the Intelligence headquarters Molly dear, the one place that his stupid son Ken couldn't tell him about simply because he didn't know himself; only Killeen and the Brigadier knew that, and neither of them ever disclosed its whereabouts. Both of his two stupid sons simply, and blindly, went along with the plan. Now close your eyes Molly dear, this is not going to hurt one little bit.'

Mary Fitzpatrick slowly raised the automatic pistol and pointed it at Molly's head.

'Before you pull the trigger Mary, I am going to give you a sporting chance. I would hate it if you died without you being aware of who killed you.'

'You seem to be forgetting who is holding the gun, Molly my dear.' She said with a smile – a none too convincing smile – suddenly she felt fear. There was something in the tone of Molly's voice that alarmed her.

'So sorry Mary, please forgive my deplorable manners, I seem to have forgotten to mention the five pounds of Semtex explosives that I have under my bed; a present from a certain Patrick Flynn, who I believe was a business associate of yours. I would guess that there is enough to take out half of this entire row of houses. Now Mary dear – do you think that you can put a bullet in my head before I can press this switch?' Molly then took his right hand from beneath the sheets, and revealed a small white plastic box, with his thumb on the flashing button.

'Now that you know who killed you Mary – doesn't it make you feel much better? The Major will be so disappointed – first Sean, killed by Ken, his own half brother – and now you.'

'I have to die you see Mary – I am now completely insane.'

'GOODBYE Mary my dear.'

Mary Fitzpatrick responded immediately – the split second that Molly said GOODBYE. She pulled the trigger of the pistol with all her might; fear, panic, and desperation fueling her strength.

There was a flash from the pistol, and as the bullet sped towards his genius endowed, yet scrambled brain, Molly, with an insane grin on his face, made his move – a move many months in its planning.

CHAPTER 32

A BROKEN MIND

Sometimes I become confused, dreams become reality, but reality doesn't seem real.

Memories are not what they used to be, they keep changing. Memories should always be the same.

They say that I have Post Traumatic Stress Disorder. Paddy used to say that.

Can you remember Paddy? – We used to be in the SAS together.

The doctors say that I am delusional. There are no records of me ever having been in the army.

I was, honestly, but I must not tell anyone, it's a secret.

I hope that Julie calls in to see me today – I haven't seen her since we got engaged.

I can't imagine living without Julie. I don't think I would want to.

I keep getting these head-aches. They tell me that I had an accident.

I've got a dressing on my forehead. Paddy has one in exactly the same place.

Paddy says that we were never in the SAS. I'm sure he's wrong.

Paddy has been acting very strange since they put that dressing on.

Why isn't Molly with us; Can you remember Molly? Paddy can't. The Major came to see me today. He is a nice man. He brought us here.

He told me that his son Ken is in the navy. 'A Nancy boy,' he said.

He told me that he phoned his daughter Mary today. He said that I had met her once.

I can't remember her. I will ask Paddy to see if he remembers her.

'Come with me Mr. Killeen – It's time to change your dressing – Paddy is waiting for you.'

Cont'd

POSTSCRIPT

Killeen and Paddy began to regain their memory a couple of years after their unsanctioned lobotomy. Both men died mysteriously in their sleep shortly afterwards – in the secure nursing home. Major Wardle was present. Margaret Thatcher was never consulted nor informed – Molly had been right.

The Wing Commander, turned Minister, died in a car bomb explosion. With him in the car were the two Generals. They were on their way to a meeting with Major Wardle. It was assumed that the IRA planted the bomb. The IRA denied all involvement.

Major Wardle, the MI5-6 mole/informer, was eliminated in the late 1980's by his son, the only known surviving member of the D1 SAS team.

HE died in 2014, and with him died any form of corroboration to his story.

Both he, and Margaret Thatcher, took their secrets with them to the grave. No government details are available.

This novel is the story that he wanted the world to know about.

Maybe it was all just a dream.

You will have to decide for yourself.

The names, and many of the locations, have been changed in order to remain within the constraints imposed by the Official Secrets Act – and to protect the innocent – as they say in Hollywood.

Billy Makin.

OTHER BOOKS BY THE AUTHOR

Jihada 1 – The Lost Scriptures.

Jihada 2 – A Bride for Allah.

Jihada 3 – In the Name of the Prophet.

Fishing and Testicles.

21709454R00122

Printed in Poland
by Amazon Fulfillment
Poland Sp. z o.o., Wrocław